Waking
the
World

Waking *the* World

CLASSIC TALES OF WOMEN
AND THE
HEROIC FEMININE

A. B. Chinen

A Jeremy P. Tarcher/Putnam Book

Published by G. P. Putnam's Sons

New York

Most Tarcher/Putnam books are available at special quantity discounts for bulk purchases for sales promotions, premiums, fundraising, and educational needs. Special books or book excerpts also can be created to fit specific needs.

For details, write or telephone Special Markets, The Putnam Publishing Group, 200 Madison Avenue, New York, NY 10016; (212) 951-8891.

A Jeremy P. Tarcher/Putnam Book
Published by G. P. Putnam's Sons
Publishers Since 1838
200 Madison Avenue
New York, NY 10016
http://www.putnam.com/putnam

Library of Congress Cataloging-in-Publication Data

Chinen, Allan B., date.
Waking the world : classic tales of women and the
heroic feminine / A. B. Chinen.
p.   cm.
"A Jeremy P. Tarcher/Putnam Book."
Includes bibliographical references and index.
ISBN 0-87477-818-2 (acid-free paper)
1. Fairy tales—History and criticism.   2. Women—
Folklore.   3. Fairy tales—Psychological aspects.
4. Femininity (Psychology)   I. Title.
PN3437.C48   1996   95-49165 CIP
398.2'082—dc20

Design by Judith Stagnitto Abbate

Printed in the United States of America
1   3   5   7   9   10   8   6   4   2

This book is printed on acid-free recycled paper. ∞

ACKNOWLEDGMENTS

This book would not have been possible without the generous support, personal wisdom, and critical insights of three dear friends and colleagues: Karen Signell, whose passionate knowledge and sage advice—in long, delightful conversations over Chinese food, on hikes, and while roller-skating— led me to deeper insights about the fairy tales and women's experience; Gloria Gregg, with her astonishing and original perspectives on psychology and life; and Anna Spielvogel, for her quiet encouragement. I would also like to thank my agents, Jim and Rosalie Heacock, and express my sadness over Jim's untimely death—I will sorely miss his warmth, humor, ready smile, and practical advice.

A special note of appreciation to Jeremy Tarcher, Lori Fuller, Lisa Chadwick, and Joyce Newill for their support with this book and the two previous ones; to my editor, Robin Cantor-Cooke, for her many helpful insights; and finally to Irene Prokop, for finalizing everything with such vitality and élan.

To my mother and grandmothers,
Winifred, Fumiko, and Shizuko

CONTENTS

Fairy tales and folk legends are beloved to young and old because they offer images that echo those of our own fantasies—the impossible situations we get ourselves into and the miraculous ways we'd like to use to find our way out. All of us experience suffering as uniquely our own, yet these wondrous tales make clear that we are each and all victims of the common human condition. Life challenges us to find creative solutions that can, with a little help from our friends, transform us from victims into something approaching the heroic.

Women are protagonists in the stories you will read in this book, yet it would be a misunderstanding to assume that it is necessarily women who play the leading roles in the subplots. For the subplot is the archetypal story, which is not a story of the war between men and women, but rather of the alienation—and eventual reconciliation—between the Masculine and the Feminine. (We capitalize these words so that you, the reader, will not forget that we are talking about archetypes, aspects of human nature that have been traditionally associated with one sex or the other but which are actually present in both sexes.) Women, in these classic tales, embody the qualities that are associated with "the Feminine." Often they appear as Queens or Princesses, signifying that they belong to the ruling class and consequently have a special position to uphold. Or in other tales they appear as Hapless Daughters of a Cruel Parent or Step-Parent with the loving parent absent from the picture. Or, if one is unusually wise, she is a Crone who knows from experience what a woman needs to do in order to realize who she is and where her power lies.

It is amazing to discover—whether the stories we read are

gathered from the people of windswept steppes of Siberia, the Tiwa Pueblo of the American west, from Italy or Iraq, from the African interior, or the islands of Japan—that there are common themes associated with women. These point to the archetype of the Feminine. Everywhere, the Feminine is situated in a secondary position. She is expected to be receptive to the demands of others; she is to stay in the background or behind a screen; she is to be faithful to her husband and, if she loses him, she is to move heaven and earth to find him again. Even this she does in her own Feminine way. More clever than forthright, she uses magic and deceit; she assumes disguises when necessary, and she is patient beyond belief. She must behave in this way in order to preserve herself, because traditionally the Feminine has less power than the Masculine. As the moon derives her light by reflecting the sun's, the Feminine functions as she does because of her relationship to the Masculine.

We hear today that our society is suffering from an overabundance of Masculine energy. There's too much action, too much violence, too much use and abuse of power, too much competition, too much personal ambition, some would say "too much testosterone." Many women feel victimized by the dominance of the Masculine. None of the attributes that have been traditionally associated with the Masculine is altogether missing from women—but in women as a rule they are better disguised. Psychiatrist Allan Chinen has researched thousands of tales about women in his efforts to find working models for many women, patients, and others, who complain about suffering from "the patriarchy," as they term the Masculine. The stories he tells us about women who have managed to overcome their "victimhood" strike deep into the heart, for they describe the travail of everyone who journeys on the rocky path to consciousness. The world, in which most people identify themselves with either the Masculine or the Feminine while demonizing the Other, is a world asleep— and those people who sleep are out of touch with their own inner reality. In order to address this sleeping world, we must enter into the sleep ourselves in order to find out how to wake ourselves up, because only the one who is fully awake can wake the world. The fairy-tale world we enter is the dreamworld in which nothing is as it appears, where Kings and Queens are outwitted by simple people, where men turn into fishes and women emerge from eggs and a handless maiden becomes whole when she plunges her hands into the water of life to retrieve her drowning child.

With the characters of the dramas narrated here, we plunge into the depths of the sea or struggle through the narrow passages of the underworld to break with the conventions of society that bind us to our false selves. In these mysterious dark places, we are told, we must not listen to the shades of the past who would pull us down and away from our resolve. This is a test of our commitment to put aside the past and open ourselves up to the possibility of becoming whole and free persons.

Transformation, a symbolic process that produces a change in consciousness, is a feature of nearly all of these tales. The change can be likened to falling asleep, or to being caught in the trap of a strange body, or imprisoned in a strange location. Sometimes people are magically turned into fishes or frogs, or parts of their bodies are cut off and reappear. Or the change in consciousness may be heralded when a tear awakens a lost husband from his drugged sleep. But transformation has an even deeper, archetypal meaning. It is required when we have lost contact with our essential nature, which is free and spontaneous, loving and caring. This loss can occur in childhood or adolescence or in the first bloom of sexuality. We are taught to blend in with the tradition of our elders and our ancestors, and not to change "the system." There is pressure to develop a false self that will fulfill the expectations of society, a pressure that would lull us to sleep. But there is another part of the psyche that demands just as urgently that we stand for being true to our essence, to love fully and without reservation, and to overcome the demons that would overpower the authentic self. This latter urge asks us to wake up.

Waking demands a struggle; it means squaring off and confronting the somnolent side. In the stories this tends to be done through indirection. Often the young feminine character seeks out the Old Wise Woman, who has learned how to deal not only with her own feminine nature but with the Masculine also. For his aggressiveness she has the magic antidote, cleverness. For his drive for immediate action, she has the twin remedies, patience and determination. For his desire to be the hero and win the prize, she knows how to call upon her sisters for help and she shares her successes with them. Since she cannot win through raw power, she turns the tables with humor, with wildness, and with outrageous behavior that shocks the Masculine into his senses.

What a wonderful guide this book is for both women and men who want to free the Feminine from her secondary role and to free the Masculine from trying to keep her in check! Instead of the Feminine and Masculine remaining locked in an eternal struggle, the tales show us how these opposite elements in our nature can perform a lively dance. If we pay attention to these stories, we will all stay awake—at least until dawn!

June Singer

PROLOGUE

In familiar fairy tales like "Sleeping Beauty," a girl or young woman sleeps under an evil spell until a brave hero awakens her. Not so with the fairy tales in this book. Gathered from around the world, these stories focus on adult women and reverse the plot of "youth stories"—it is now the king who sleeps, and the queen who must awaken him, liberating their land from a curse. In portraying strong women changing the world, the tales are deeply relevant to women today. Handed down over many generations, the stories offer astute advice and encouragement for women seeking deeper, more fulfilling lives.

The tales in this collection may be unfamiliar to readers. The stories were often forgotten in old library collections, just like buried treasures, and I located them only by reading through some 7,000 fairy tales and picking out dramas with adult women as protagonists. After retelling each story, I add comments to help interpret the symbolism. Feminists may wonder why women should read a man's interpretations here, since there is now a growing literature by women on fairy tales—from Rosemary Minard in *Womenfolk in Fairy Tales* or Angela Carter in *The Old Wives' Fairy Tale Book* to Ethel Johnston Phelps in *Tatterhood and Other Tales* and Clarissa Pinkola Estés's *Women Who Run with the Wolves*. What might a man add?

My suggestion: an outsider's viewpoint. I have not run with the wolves, but have flown overhead, looking at women's tales from many different cultures. From this bird's-eye view, features of the terrain become clear that are often not visible from the ground. These cross-cultural themes in women's tales offer deep insights into women's lives. In making my comments, my aim is simply to foster reflection and dialogue. Ultimately each individual must interpret the stories for herself or himself.

WEAVING WOMEN'S STORIES

When assembled together, women's tales quickly reveal several distinctive features. First, the stories do not fall into a linear pattern. This baffled me at first, because psychology usually describes development as a linear sequence. So I anticipated that the stories would do the same. But when I tried to arrange the tales in a neat line, beginning with younger protagonists and moving to older ones, no coherent pattern emerged. Shuffling the tales around did not solve the problem, nor did arranging the stories in a circle.[1]

What solved the problem were two metaphors from writers Carolyn Heilbrun, Mary Catherine Bateson, and Naomi Lowinsky: women weave their lives together, creating a tapestry of many concerns and activities, or women compose their lives, creating a symphony with many parts and voices. Women's tales parallel this structure. Like a tapestry or symphony, women's stories contain basic themes that are woven together in different ways so that every drama is unique.

A second feature of women's stories is that they typically include many leading characters, reflecting a traditional feminine interest in relationships. (Men's tales, by contrast, have fewer main characters.) Women's stories also portray their characters with great insight, and are surprisingly clear about men's developmental tasks. Yet the tales do not imply that women are supposed to take care of men. Quite the contrary—when women's tales refer to men's developmental tasks, it is to challenge men to wake up and start moving toward a deeper, more egalitarian relationship with women.

WOMEN'S STORYTELLING

Since women's stories focus on female protagonists, it is natural to assume that the tales originated with a woman storyteller, but until recently anthropologists and folklorists often did not collect tales from women. Fortunately, the situation has changed. Folklorists like Linda Degh, Susan Kalcik, Margaret Yocom, Karen Baldwin, Donna Eder, Penelope Eckert, and Kristin Langellier are now discovering that women tend to tell stories in a characteristic, cooperative way. For example, one woman may begin by describing a problem she had with a male boss who made sexual advances. Another woman may empathize with the storyteller, briefly noting a similar difficulty she encountered. A third woman may comment on how brave the first woman was in rejecting her boss's overtures. A fourth woman might then tell an anecdote of her own about sexual harassment, before asking the original storyteller to continue with her tale. In a sense, the storyteller is the whole group of women. The result is a tale full of different themes, multiple perspectives, and many characters—typical of women's fairy tales.

Women's turn-taking in storytelling is particularly clear with mothers and daughters, who often tell tales as duets. This helps explain a third feature of women's tales—the dramas often include several generations and stages of life. Typically, the stories start off with a young girl who then marries and must cope with the problems of married life. In embracing both youth and maturity, women's tales reflect an inclusive, holistic spirit, which men's tales lack, addressing only youth or the middle years or old age.

SUBVERSION

A fourth trait of women's tales is that they are subversive, rejecting misogynist conventions in subtle ways. When I came across these seditious themes, I worried that I was overinterpreting small details, but as I analyzed more and more tales, the subversive motifs became increasingly evident. Then I came across *Feminist Messages*, edited by Joan Newlon Radner, which describes how women convey hidden, dissident messages in their crafts, arts, and storytelling. In Ireland, for example, women traditionally sang mourning songs at men's funerals, but the women often included scathing criticisms of the deceased. The women were supposed to be wild with grief, so men were not allowed to criticize the women's songs. Women's fairy tales reflect this ingenious, defiant spirit because women usually tell their stories in informal, private gatherings—among friends and kin—where they can speak their minds freely. This makes women's tales like dreams—the stories bring up truths that conventional society represses or ignores.

Women's tales show women triumphing over great adversity and reclaiming their rightful place in the world, yet the stories do not represent wishful thinking. The tales are utopian—they show what women can be, rather than conventional roles. Annis Pratt, Irene Neher, Phyllis Ralph, Sigrid Weigel, and Carolyn Heilbrun, among others, have noted that women authors often had trouble imagining happy endings for women in their novels, because social conventions were so oppressive. Fairy tales, drawing directly from the unconscious, provide an antidote to this cultural constriction.

This leads to a fifth feature of women's stories. The tales are not merely psychological, containing insights about women's individual development. The stories are also visionary, and deal with broad social and cultural issues. They provide new paradigms for society, beyond patriarchal tradition. The tales apply to psyche and society. As feminists note, "the personal is the political," but the social dimension has often been overlooked in psychological interpretations of fairy tales.

The visionary function of women's tales revives an ancient tradition. Among numerous Native American tribes, women's dreams were treated as divine messages, offering guidance about tribal decisions. Even in classical Greece, with its strong patriarchal bias, women's visions were vital: the

Oracle of Delphi was a woman, and her prophetic images influenced the decisions of city-states from Athens to Sparta. Women's stories preserve this wellspring of wisdom about society.

A PERSONAL NOTE

Writing this book took me over eight years, not counting the time spent collecting the stories. For me the stories did exactly what they portray—they woke me up. To understand the dramas, I read literature from the women's movement, something I had, like many men, avoided. But I could not ignore the fact that women's stories from around the world begin with women being exiled, enslaved, humiliated, silenced, attacked, terrorized, and imprisoned. For the first time I could emotionally appreciate the reasons for women's anger. Yet the tales also show what comes after the anger— the tasks women face after they break free from oppressive social convention.

Although I will speak frequently of "the feminine psyche" and "the feminine," I do not want to imply that either is a fixed, eternal truth, that they apply to all women, or that they apply only to women. And I leave unanswered to what extent "the feminine" or "the feminine psyche" is biological or cultural.

HOW THE BOOK IS ORGANIZED

From the many women's tales I collected, I have chosen a dozen that seemed most representative of the whole group. Some tales are variants of familiar dramas such as "Beauty and the Beast," "Psyche and Amor," or "The Handless Woman," but I have deliberately chosen unfamiliar versions, using stories from different cultures to highlight the breadth and depth of women's tales. I have grouped the tales in this book into five sections, each addressing a major theme. The first deals with power as traditionally defined in most cultures, the second with a woman's inner wisdom, often ignored or repressed by society. Nature as a sanctuary and source of healing for women is the theme of the third section, while the fourth focuses on the ancient motif of sisterhood. The last section sums up the preceding themes and portrays reconciliation with men.

Ultimately, women's tales contain a challenge and a promise. Handed down from grandmother to granddaughter, the stories show women reclaiming their wisdom and strength, waking the world from a long, oppressive slumber.

Waking
the
World

PART I

Power

CHAPTER 1

"The Queen and the Murderer":

Oppression and Self-Liberation

(from Italy[1])

nce upon a time, a beautiful Princess lived in a palace with her father, the King. But he was a miser and kept her locked up in a tower to prevent her from marrying and keeping her dowry. One day, a murderer came to town and learned about the Princess. Curious, one night he climbed up the Princess's tower and peeked at her. She screamed for help. By the time the servants and guards arrived, the felon had run away, so nobody believed her story of an intruder. Her father refused to move her to another, more secure room, and told her to stop imagining things.

The second night, the murderer again climbed the tower, opened the window, and peeked at the Princess. She ran for help, but by the time the guards and servants arrived, he had vanished. "You are making up stories!" everyone told the Princess.

The next evening, the Princess chained the window so it opened only partway, and took a knife from the kitchen. Then she waited in her room. After dark, the thief climbed up the tower, stuck his hand under the window, and tried to open it. At that moment, the Princess drew her knife and cut off the man's hand.

The brigand screamed in pain and fled. As he ran away, he shouted, "I'll get you for this!" When the guards and servants arrived, the Princess showed them the villain's hand. Everyone had to admit that she had been right all along, and the King had to move her to another room.

Some time later, a young man came calling at the palace. He wore white gloves and rich clothes, and said he was a nobleman from a foreign land, looking for a wife. He added that he was so wealthy he needed no dowry. When the miserly King heard that, he summoned his daughter and commanded her to marry the nobleman.

The Princess felt uneasy. "Your Majesty," she whispered to her father, "I think he is the man whose hand I cut off!"

"Don't be ridiculous," the King exclaimed. "You must marry him!"

To escape her father, the Princess consented, and the wedding was soon celebrated. It was a simple affair, and the stingy King gave his daughter only a necklace made of walnut shells and a worn-out foxtail. Then the Princess left with her new husband, riding in a grand carriage. They journeyed for some time and went deeper and deeper into the woods. The Princess became fearful and asked where they were going.

"Take my glove off," her husband replied, holding up his right hand. She obeyed and discovered only a stump. She screamed, her worst fears confirmed.

"Yes," the man exclaimed, "you chopped off my hand and now you'll pay for it!" They arrived at a house hidden in the woods, overlooking the sea. The man explained that he was a murderer by trade, and that his house was filled with the treasures of his victims. Then he laughed wickedly, chained the Princess to a tree like a dog, and rode off.

The Princess tried mightily to wriggle out of the chains, but she could not. In the distance she saw a ship sailing by, and she waved at it desperately. The sailors, who were cotton merchants, saw her, landed, and freed her. She showed them the treasure in the villain's house, so they loaded the riches on their boat, took the Princess with them, and sailed off.

The murderer returned and saw his wife and treasure were gone. He spied the boat, jumped onto his own ship, and swiftly caught up with the merchants. As the brigand approached, the merchants hid the Princess in their bales of cotton. The murderer boarded the ship, seeking his wife, and ordered the merchants to throw the cotton into the sea.

The sailors pleaded with the murderer. "We are cotton dealers! You will bankrupt us!" "Run your sword through the bales," one merchant suggested, "so you know there is nothing hidden inside!" The murderer plunged his sword into each bale. He wounded the Princess, but she kept silent, and the cotton wiped her blood from the sword, so the murderer was none the wiser.

The brigand returned to his own boat and sped after another ship. The merchants quickly took the Princess out of her hiding place and dressed her wound. It was only a small injury, but she was so terrified of the murderer that she begged the sailors to throw her into the sea to drown. The merchants refused, and an old sailor offered to take her home to his wife. "We have no children of our own," he explained, "so you can be our daughter!"

The Princess went to live with the old sailor and his wife. Fearful of the murderer, she refused to go outside the house, and asked them to let no one see her. The Princess took to embroidering with the old woman, and finished a tablecloth. It was so beautiful the woman took it to sell to the King of their country, a young man.

The bachelor King was astonished when he saw the tablecloth. "Who made this?" he asked. "My daughter," the old woman replied proudly, but he refused to believe her. "How can the daughter of simple people sew so well?" he wondered.

A few days later, the Princess finished embroidering a folding screen, and the woman brought it to the King, who bought it immediately. But this time, he secretly followed her home, and when she opened the door to her house he jumped in behind her. The Princess fainted in terror, thinking the murderer had finally found her.

When the Princess awoke, the King asked the reason for

her great fear. The Princess would not explain, and he did not press her. Instead he visited her each day, and finally asked her to marry him. The Princess agreed, not mentioning her marriage to the murderer. She asked only one thing: "You must never let any man see me, except you and the old sailor, my father." The King agreed, so the two were married in a secret ceremony, and the new Queen remained secluded in the palace.

The King's subjects were unhappy that they could not see their new queen, and soon rumors began to circulate. "She is a witch!" some gossips claimed. "A hunchback!" others whispered. To ease the public discontent, the King decreed that his wife must appear before the people.

On the appointed day, the whole kingdom gathered to see the Queen. When she stepped out onto the balcony of the palace, everyone cheered, seeing how beautiful she was. But all the Queen noticed was a man dressed in black, standing in the middle of the crowd. He raised his right hand, took off his glove, and revealed a stump. The Queen fainted. She fell ill, and from that day would not leave her room. Doctors tried everything but nothing eased her ailment.

A few days later, a foreign nobleman came calling on the King. He was richly dressed and well-spoken, so the King invited him to a banquet. The foreigner brought many casks of fine wine as a gift, which the King gave freely to all the palace staff. The wine was drugged, and soon the monarch, his servants, and the guards fell fast asleep. Then the foreigner, who was none other than the murderer, went through the palace, room by room, seeking the Queen.

Finally, he came upon her. "I have come to kill you!" he snarled and took out his sword. "But first," he told her, "fetch me a basin of water. I must wash your blood from my hands after I kill you!"

The Queen ran to wake the King, but he would not awaken. In terror, she filled a bowl with water and returned to the murderer. "You forgot the soap," he snapped at her. So she hurried out, and shook her husband again. But the King snored on, as did everyone else. The hapless Queen picked up some soap and returned to the assassin. "What about a towel?" the murderer growled, as he sharpened his sword. "Have you forgotten your wifely duties?" The Queen ran back to her husband, but this time she took the pistol from his belt, hid it in a towel, and returned to the murderer.

"And now," the villain hissed, "prepare to die!" He lifted his sword, but at that moment she took out the pistol and fired at him. The sound awoke everyone and they came running to the Queen's chamber. The King arrived and found the murderer dead at his wife's feet. But there, standing tall and serene, stood the Queen. From then on, the Queen knew no fear, and she and the King lived the rest of their days in happiness and peace.

WOMEN AND OPPRESSION

This story is astonishing. The usual reaction when I tell it at workshops is stunned silence—followed by cheers for the Queen. "The Queen and the Murderer" is not unique—many stories from around the world are almost identical.[2] These tales shatter the romance of youth stories, such as "Cinderella," where a young prince rescues a helpless princess and they live happily ever after.

The story begins with the Princess imprisoned by her miserly father in a tower, and there are several psychological meanings to the situation. In real life, many fathers are emotionally stingy with their daughters, giving energy and affection to their work or sons, not their daughters. Other fathers shower their daughters with attention, but expect the women to remain devoted to them, feeling jealous if their daughters attend to other men. The fathers build psychological prisons around their daughters.

The Princess's father is a king, the head of state, and personifies social convention. In locking his own daughter up, the King dramatizes the oppression that women suffer in most cultures, and other tales repeat the theme. The stories are astonishingly feminist, yet they come from traditional sources, antedating the modern women's movement. The tales emerge from the unconscious and speak the unvarnished truth. Significantly, the Princess has no mother, sister, or women friends. Aside from the old sailor's wife, who appears later in the tale, the Princess is quite alone in a masculine world, and thus all the more vulnerable to oppression.

THE MURDERER

When the murderer comes to town, he peeps at the Princess in her tower. Similar male characters—mysterious, threatening, and dangerous—are common in other women's tales and haunt women's dreams at night.[3] Comparable male villains emerge in women's literature and art.[4] The murderer in the fairy tale is thus an archetypal figure and offers yet another symbol of women's oppression: he peeps at the Princess, violating her privacy and treating her as a sex object, and later persecutes and harasses her without end.

When the Princess tells her father about the intruder, the King refuses to believe or protect her, reflecting how bad a father he is. Here lies another meaning of the murderer: he may be interpreted as the King's "shadow." This is Carl Jung's evocative term for the unsavory aspects of an individual—for a person's faults, sins, and vices. In the King's case, his shadow involves stinginess, selfishness, and carelessness, all of which injure his daughter psychologically. The murderer dramatizes this emotional assault.[5]

Ignored but undaunted, the Princess fetches a knife from the kitchen, chains the window, and when the villain tries to lift it she chops off his hand. This action may seem rather extreme at first; however, the story notes that the man was a murderer, so he probably would not merely peek at the princess, but might rape or kill her. There is further meaning here. Cloistered in her tower and ignored by her father, the Princess has many reasons to be frustrated and angry, but cannot express these feelings freely—most societies condemn women for expressing anger. A vicious cycle results—prevented from expressing anger or asserting themselves, women become more frustrated and angry, but also fearful of those feelings. The brigand may be interpreted as this frightening repressed anger. He illustrates what Jung called an animus figure, a character who represents the female protagonist's "masculine" qualities, such as anger or aggression. Initially experienced as threatening, he might be called an "ominous animus." When the Princess finally kills him, she reclaims her rightful assertiveness.

MARRYING THE MURDERER

When the silver-tongued foreigner comes calling, the Princess warns her father that the man is actually the intruder, but the King ignores her. Here we see just how perceptive the Princess is. Her intuitions are accurate, but nobody recognizes this, even after she is proved right about the intruder. In real life, the same thing happens to women when their comments are ignored by men with power over their lives—whether at work, in school, or at home. As Mary Belenky, Lyn Mikel Brown, Carol Gilligan, and others have found, girls are silenced and ignored so often that they come to distrust their own judgments and gut feelings. The Princess does exactly that, when she marries the foreigner against her own good sense. This is a common mistake many young women make—they flee from a dysfunctional family into an equally dysfunctional marriage. The Princess presumably hoped that the charming gentleman would rescue her from her misery. The story makes clear that this fantasy does not work—the new husband turns out to be a beast, not a hero.

At the wedding, the King gives his daughter only a necklace made of walnut shells and an old foxtail, and the gifts are symbolic. The ancient Greeks and Romans displayed walnuts at wedding feasts as symbols of fertility and longevity. Here, though, the King gives only shells—empty, lifeless, and useless, just like his relationship with his daughter. His second gift conjures up a fox's cleverness and cunning, virtues the Princess possesses, but the foxtail is old and worn out, and the story soon shows how the Princess becomes worn down by the attacks on her. As objects from Mother Nature, the walnut necklace and foxtail also highlight the crucial figure missing in the story—a mother. In most fairy tales, a daughter receives a gift or token from her mother, and the gift later saves the daughter from a terrible danger, especially a cruel husband. The Princess lacks this connection to her mother and the motherline, so she is even more vulnerable to social oppression.

After the wedding, the Princess's husband reveals himself to be a murderer, and chains her to a tree. Other women's tales repeat the theme: for a woman, marriage means imprisonment, humiliation, exile, or death, however carefree or exalted her origin.[6] Literature written by women repeats the motif. Women writers from George Eliot and Charlotte Brontë to Joyce Carol Oates and Joan Didion consistently portray marriage as degradation and confinement for the wife, often resulting in her insanity or death.[7] Fairy tales and novels reflect social realities. Today, marriage for women is less a case of bondage than of double-binding. Women are expected to be assertive and to have careers, while they are also supposed to be nurturing, sympathetic, and motherly. Not surprisingly, married women express more dissatisfaction than single women, and single women live longer than married women. Marriage is stressful for women. Many cultures recognize this and explicitly equate weddings with funerals.[8]

FROM STRENGTH TO DESPAIR

After the murderer chains the Princess to a tree, she does not despair. She remains resourceful and signals a passing ship, whose crew rescues her. Notice that the Princess finds help when she is in the middle of the wilderness. The detail is a small one here, but reappears prominently in other women's tales. Helpful as they are, the merchants cannot protect the Princess. They are not swift enough to outsail the murderer, nor are they brave enough to resist him, despite their greater numbers. If the Princess hoped for gallant heroes to save her, she is again disillusioned. Her task, as the tale soon makes clear, is to rescue herself. That lesson can be a hard one for women raised on romantic stories.

When the murderer boards the merchants' ship, the Princess hides in a bale of cotton. The location is symbolic, since cotton is used for spinning and weaving, traditionally women's work. Metaphorically, the Princess retreats into stereotypes of the feminine. This is precisely what happens to many girls during adolescence. Girls are often outspoken, confident, and assertive, but as they move into the teenage years they are forced to play dumb and silence themselves.[9] The young women are muffled and stifled under bales of feminine stereotypes.

While searching for the Princess, the murderer shoves his sword through every bale and wounds her. The theme has many symbolic meanings.[10] The most obvious is a reference to sexual assault, and the wounded Princess dramatizes the plight of all raped women. More generally, she symbolizes all traumatized women, from the Hindu widow burned alive on her husband's funeral pyre to American women battered by husbands or African girls undergoing the horrifying ritual of clitoridectomy. The story adds a sobering insight about the violence. When the murderer wounds the Princess, she does not cry out, and his sword is wiped clean by the cotton. All evidence of her injury is hidden. Even in pain the Princess is silenced, and other women's tales repeat the theme.[11] These tales are all too accurate, because sexually abused girls often keep the violence secret, and battered women often do not report the violence, terrified of further beatings, despairing of finding any help, or blaming themselves for their suffering.

Exactly this despair soon overwhelms the Princess. After the murderer leaves, she asks the merchants to throw her into the sea. Terrified of the brigand, she sees death as her only solution. The murderer's violence has forced the resourceful Princess into becoming a stereotype—the helpless female. The Princess even becomes explicitly suicidal, and this mirrors a sobering fact: women attempt suicide much more frequently than men. Indeed, many highly talented and successful women—Sylvia Plath, Virginia Woolf, Anne Sexton—have killed themselves, partly because of the stark disparity between their abilities and the opportunities that society offered them.

There is another reason women take their own lives. As a woman explained, speaking for many others, "I would rather die than hurt somebody else." Because of deep protective feelings toward other people, many women are loath to attack others even in self-defense, and often turn on themselves instead. A woman's task, the fairy tale emphasizes, is to redirect her anger and frustration at the true cause: she must kill the murderer, symbolizing oppressive social customs and abusive relationships.

WITHDRAWAL AND SANCTUARY

At this point, an old sailor takes the despairing Princess home to his wife. The old couple become good parents to the Princess and she later calls him her father. Yet the Princess, terrified of the murderer, secludes herself, asking the old man and woman not to let anybody see her. The situation is tragic: The Princess began her story imprisoned in a tower by her father. Later she was chained to a tree by the murderer. Now finally free, she imprisons herself. In psychological terms, she has internalized the oppression of her father and the cruelty of the murderer. In real life women neglected by their parents often choose callous, distant, and uncaring partners, recapitulating their original trauma. Similarly, girls educated in schools which expect nothing of them grow up to expect nothing of themselves, imprisoning themselves within lowered expectations.

While staying with the old couple, the Princess begins to embroider, a traditional feminine activity, and this might be interpreted as one more stereotype forced on her. However, there are further meanings. The Princess embroiders with the old woman, and by working with her comes upon a powerful resource—feminine solidarity. In working with each other, women air their grievances about husbands and community events, find sympathy and solidarity with other women, and solicit help from more experienced women, the way American frontierswomen discussed community issues when sewing quilts or canning food, or like African tribal women helping one another plant their crops and pooling their savings to start their own businesses.

Sewing itself is profoundly significant. Traditionally a feminine craft, the activity is usually considered minor or trifling in most male-oriented cultures. Yet sewing represented a major technological innovation at the dawn of human civilization. Needle and thread were presumably invented by women, and these new tools made tight-fitting clothes possible, which allowed humanity to survive the Ice Ages.

The old woman goes out on errands, meaning the Princess must sew alone at times. Working in seclusion provides the Princess time to reflect on her life. Previously thrown from one disaster to another, she had no chance to make sense of what happened to her, or to hear her inner voice. In the calm of the old woman's home the Princess can now sort things out. Today, women often create such a sanctuary through psychotherapy or by writing in a journal. The fairy tale reveals, though, that this healing phase is only one stage on a longer journey. The Princess must eventually return to the world and deal with its problems. The same applies to psychotherapy and any other inner work.

THE YOUNG KING

The old woman sells the Princess's embroidery to the King of the country, bringing the young woman to his attention. In linking the two, the elder plays the traditional role of go-between, or matchmaker. By her action, she also forces the Princess out of her comfortable seclusion and compels her to resume her life journey. The old woman is thus guide and goad, the archetypal wise crone. Similar figures appear in women's dreams, offering advice, encouragement, and sometimes coercion.

For his part, the young King appears to be a decent man, in contrast to the Princess's niggardly father. In real life, his part might be played by a helpful male mentor, or a caring lover who supports a woman in her own development. A woman with such a man in her life might think her problems are over, but the story says otherwise.

When the King follows the old woman home, the Princess faints in terror, mistaking him for the murderer. The young monarch asks the Princess why she is so terrified, but she says nothing. Her silence is painfully realistic, the silence of battered women who fear retaliation from a violent lover and of women accustomed to being dismissed or ignored. Fortunately, the Princess is not completely paralyzed and eventually marries the King. She draws courage from hidden depths, and starts to move forward with her life.

However, she agrees to marry the King on one condition— she insists that no man see her other than the King and the old sailor—and after the marriage secludes herself in the palace. She began her story imprisoned in a palace by her stingy father, and now imprisons herself in another palace. Significantly, she is married to two men, the murderer and the kind young King. Terror of the former casts a shadow on the Queen, dramatizing how abusive past relationships can damage healthy new ones. For example, growing up with a destructive father often causes difficulties for a woman in any intimate relationship with a man. The story reveals how a woman can exorcise this negative effect.

The citizens of the kingdom resent their new Queen's seclusion, so the King breaks his promise to her and compels her to appear in public. In ignoring his wife's wishes, he turns out to be a little like her father. Both monarchs dismiss her fears and force her to do what they want. Although the young King is more decent and caring than the Princess's father, he is still a King, used to patriarchal authority, and probably has not experienced the terror and vulnerability his wife has known all her life, and so cannot understand her plight.

TERROR AND SICKNESS

When the Queen appears in public, she sees the one-handed murderer and promptly faints. Her unconscious and helpless state dramatizes her social situation, ignored and dismissed by everybody. Fainting spells are stereotypically associated with women, especially in Victorian literature, where women are portrayed as swooning upon hearing anything traumatic or sexual. Whether women did so in real life is another matter, although many, forced to wear the tight corsets fashionable at the time, almost suffocated. But there is logic to the fainting. As Irene Stiver notes, in cultures which ignore their feelings and needs, women must amplify their communications to be noticed. When a simple verbal expression would be ignored, fainting can communicate something of a woman's distress.

When she sees the murderer, the Queen becomes ill and her terror takes a new, more virulent form. Symbolically, the traumas now attack her body and health. In fact, women have more health problems than men do, and these difficulties used to be dismissed by doctors as unimportant or psychosomatic. The fairy tale reveals the true cause: unremitting cultural oppression, the fear of violent attack, and the frustration of being constantly devalued. It is actually a testament to her resilience and strength that she did not fall ill sooner.

The murderer again assumes the guise of a charming foreigner and the Queen's new husband takes a liking to him, entertaining him at the palace. The monarch thus falls for the murderer's ruse, just as the Queen's father did. The young King is more generous and nurturing to his wife than her father was, but he is still careless or blind.

''SLEEPING BEAUTY'' REVERSED

At the banquet, the murderer drugs the wine, so that the King and all the palace staff are soon sound asleep. The drugged sleep makes the King's mental state explicit. He could not see through the murderer's deceits and is therefore psychologically unconscious. Here the story reverses the plot of "Sleeping Beauty"—it is the men, not the women, who are unconscious, lulled by male prerogatives.

The murderer hunts the Queen down and demands that she fetch him water, soap, and a towel with which to wash after he kills her. At first the Queen runs to the King for help, but finds him unconscious, and so returns to the villain. Here she resembles many abused wives: after seeking help, not finding it, and then being beaten by their husbands for the attempt to escape, women often fall into a terrified daze. Not related to gender, this condition is a basic human response known as the hostage syndrome. When women or men are taken hostage by terrorists or as prisoners of war, they usually start helping their captors after a while, and do not attempt to flee when opportunities arise.

In ordering the Queen to fetch water, soap, and a towel, the murderer deliberately humiliates her and revels in his power over her. This sadistic element is prominent in rapists, who typically attack women less for sexual reasons than to feel powerful and dominant. Fortunately, the Queen is not witless. After twice trying to awaken her husband, she finally takes matters literally into her own hands. On her third trip out, she retrieves her husband's pistol, returns to the murderer, and shoots him when he tries to kill her. This is the climax of the story, and like the crux of a dream, it has many deep meanings. On a literal level, some women are driven to desperation by years of abuse by a husband or lover, and finally kill their assailants. Most women, of course, are not murderers—at any age. But the image of killing an evil attacker is deeply appealing to women who have suffered injustice and abuse. The theme has become more prominent in women's literature and movies within the last century, as Carol Pearson and Katherine Pope, Irene Neher, and Jennifer Waelti-Walters have noted.

CONFRONTING DEMONS

If we interpret the murderer as a symbol of the demonic side of society, which restricts, denigrates, and attacks women, killing the villain seems necessary. The Queen kills off oppressive social conventions and paves the way for a new society. In real life, many women arrive at this liberating moment when they embrace feminism. Women then articulate their anger and frustration and, with the support of other women, reject constricting feminine stereotypes. Many men and women find the passion beneath the feminist enterprise frightening, but here the story is instructive. If we just heard the end of the tale, where the Queen shoots the murderer, we might be shocked at the violence and wonder about what kind of person she is. When we know the whole story, though, the end no longer seems horrifying. It is simply poetic justice.

The murderer also represents the shadowy side of the Queen's father—the miserly old King. In shooting the murderer, the Queen symbolically confronts her father's shadow and destroys his power over her. In real life a grown daughter may need to face her father, demanding that he account for his actions toward her. As mentioned before, the murderer is also an animus figure, personifying the Queen's "masculine" energy, her anger and assertiveness. In fleeing the murderer, the Queen flees her own assertiveness, as many women do. By killing him, the Queen reclaims her aggressive energies. The theme reappears in a host of fairy tales—women must reclaim their assertiveness, and often begin doing so at midlife. The process occurs in many cultures: the Amazon tribes of Brazil, the Athabascans of North America, the Bemba and Kaliai of Africa, and on to Hindu India and Confucian China. Women who do not reclaim their animus energies by midlife often become depressed and unhappy as they age.[12]

Astonishing as it seems, "The Queen and the Murderer" is not merely a fairy tale, because its themes emerge in women's dreams. For instance, a client of mine in her late twenties, whom I shall call Julia, dreamed that she was a police officer, hunting down a dangerous robber. She finally cornered him in an alley, and when he tried to attack her, she shot him. The dream was a turning point for Julia and she began speaking up for what she wanted, pursuing a childhood dream to become a writer. As with the Queen killing the murderer, Julia's dream of shooting the criminal ushered in a new, more rewarding phase in her life.

In shooting the murderer, the Queen offers women an important lesson. Individuation—the process of becoming a unique individual and actualizing one's talent and potential—sometimes involves a measure of psychological disruption, which fairy tales dramatize as violence. This is particularly true in competitive cultures which value independence over relationship and rely upon power rather than negotiation or collaboration. Women tend to avoid hurting others, because continuity and relationship are so important to them,[13] but "The Queen and the Murderer" points out that sometimes forceful confrontation and self-assertion are necessary, even if another person will feel hurt.

THE INNER ENEMY AND WOMEN'S DEVELOPMENT

One detail about the murderer is subtle but significant. Although he is described as a villain and says that he is a murderer by profession, we never actually see him do anything criminal, except for peeping at the Princess and chaining her to the tree. At the end, of course, he threatens to kill her. Yet he then gives her three chances to escape, by sending her out for water, soap, and a towel. His actions recall some kind of ritual.

Ominous men, in fact, are sometimes involved in women's initiations among indigenous cultures. For instance, among the Nyoro of Uganda, only one man is allowed into women's initiation rituals, and his role is specific—he pretends to attack the initiate with a spear. He is a "ritual enemy." The novice does not know his attacks are part of the ritual, so she is terrified, and her fear helps break down her childhood assumptions, preparing her for a deeper understanding of feminine mysteries, taught by the women elders. (The novice's terror is momentary and the women elders quickly take over, sending the attacking male away.) The murderer in the fairy tale plays a role reminiscent of the ritual enemy. When the Princess is locked in the tower, the outlaw peeps at her until she finally asserts herself, chaining the window shut and chopping off his hand, compelling the King to let her out of the tower. So the murderer forces the Princess to move into a larger world, which is the goal of most initiations. Later the murderer pursues the Princess with single-minded determination, forcing her to keep developing. Such a ritual enemy, however, must be carefully distinguished from outer figures who often intend real harm to a woman. The ritual enemy is not destructive, but fosters a woman's growth. He serves the woman's deeper self.

RECLAIMING THE SHADOW AND LIBERATING SOCIETY

If in some ways the murderer is not as evil as he seems, psychologically speaking, the Queen must project her shadow on him. Here the story offers a warning. It can be tempting for women to castigate men for being violent, aggressive, and competitive, allowing women to claim the role of peacemaker and mediator. Several feminists have eloquently warned about this temptation: Shahla Chehrazi, a psychoanalyst; Madonna Kolbenschlag, a social critic; and Carol Pearson and Katherine Pope, two literary scholars. Women's task in maturity is to confront and acknowledge society's shadow—and their own, too. As Clarissa Pinkola Estés notes, women must face their inner predator, what Linda Leonard called the "beast within." (Men have the same task, of course.)

At the end, when the Queen takes her husband's pistol and shoots the murderer, the sound awakens the whole palace. Symbolically, when she asserts herself, she awakens all of society, drugged by social conventions. The same theme appears in recent literature by women, as Carol Pearson and Katherine Pope have noted. The result of the Queen's development—and that of women in general—is the transformation of society. The motif surfaces in women's dreams, too, as a client in her late thirties, whom I shall call Jan, illustrates.

Jan dreamed that she visited a Third World country, run by a cruel dictator and torn by a civil war, with many guerrillas fighting to overthrow the tyrant. Jan was an innocent tourist and had not known about the conflict, but she found to her surprise that she had a pistol in her purse. At that moment, the dictator of the country appeared without his usual guards, and Jan shot him dead, knowing that there was no other way to end the war. Like the Queen in the fairy tale, Jan asserted herself and emancipated a whole country.

CHAPTER 2

"The Warrior Wife":

Reclaiming Power

(a Tiwa Pueblo tale[1])

ong ago, a woman and her husband lived with their tribe. The woman's father was the chief, and her husband was a warrior named Blue Hawk. One day, Blue Hawk went on a war party with his best friend, Red Hawk. On the way, Red Hawk said, "You are leaving your wife alone. I bet she will sleep with another man tonight!"

Blue Hawk shook his head. "My wife is faithful to me and I trust her."

Red Hawk, who was not married, laughed. "I'll wager that I can go back and sleep with your wife tonight!"

Blue Hawk became indignant. "You are wrong!"

Red Hawk said, "I'll bet everything I own that I can sleep with your wife tonight." Reluctantly, Blue Hawk agreed to the wager, and both men pledged their horses, weapons, clothes—everything they possessed.

Red Hawk returned to the village and loitered around Blue Hawk's wife all day, smiling at her, but she ignored him. "She is true to Blue Hawk," Red Hawk thought, feeling desperate about losing his wager. Finally, he sought the help of an old woman, explained his bet with Blue Hawk, and promised to pay her handsomely for her help. "All you have to do," Red

Hawk said, "is find out what Blue Hawk's wife looks like without her clothes. If I know that, I can tell Blue Hawk I slept with her." The old woman agreed, and went to the wife's tepee.

The old woman limped by, looking as tired and forlorn as she could. Blue Hawk's wife took pity on her. "Grandmother, you look tired, come inside and rest."

"Thank you," the old woman replied, "I am far from home and have no place to stay tonight."

"Well, then," the wife offered, "you can stay here." When evening came, the wife gave the woman soft furs and blankets. The elder woman pretended to sleep, but watched closely as the wife undressed for bed. The wife brushed a long golden tuft of hair growing from her abdomen, plaited it together, and then wrapped it around herself five times. The old woman also saw that the wife had a birthmark on her back.

The next morning, the woman thanked the wife and then hurried to Red Hawk, telling him what she had seen. Red Hawk laughed with delight and rode out to meet Blue Hawk. "I won the wager," Red Hawk exulted. "Last night, I slept with your wife!"

Blue Hawk refused to believe this, until Red Hawk described a golden braid of hair and a birthmark. Blue Hawk fell silent.

"You gave your word," Red Hawk went on, "so give me your horse, your pack, and all your possessions." Blue Hawk said nothing, returned with Red Hawk to the village, and gave him everything he owned.

"What are you doing?" Blue Hawk's wife demanded. Blue Hawk remained silent, went outside, made a trunk out of animal skins, and put cooking gear, money, and food in it. Then he told his wife that he was going on a trip on the river, and wanted her to come along. He asked her to wear her finest clothes and then to step inside the trunk. When she did, he tied the trunk shut, set off for the river, and threw the casket into the water.

Blue Hawk returned alone to the village, and when his neighbors asked him where his wife was, he refused to answer. After a few days, the chief became concerned for his daughter, and asked Blue Hawk where she was. Blue Hawk remained silent, so the chief ordered a hole dug all the way to the underworld, and threw Blue Hawk into it.

Meanwhile, the wife floated in her trunk down the river. A man was fishing, saw the box, pulled it out of the water, opened the cover, and the wife stepped out. She asked him to exchange her clothes for his and he agreed, so she dressed as a man and went to a nearby village.

A war party was about to leave, and the wife joined them. As they set out, the young men started talking among themselves. "The stranger has the face of a woman!" one murmured. "And a woman's hands," another added. A third one said, "I'll be friendly to him and find out if he's really a woman."

That night, when the war party made camp, the wife set up her tent apart from the others. "I am a medicine man," she explained, "and I need to protect my power for our raid." She showed the men a sacred white eagle feather she possessed, and said that her medicine came from the sun. When everyone turned in for the night, one warrior went over to the wife and asked if he could sleep in her tent. She refused but he was persistent, so they lay down on opposite sides of the tent.

In the middle of the night, the youth reached out to touch the wife, but she remained on guard. "What are you doing?" she demanded. The youth waited and tried again a little later, but the wife still did not sleep. "I do not like you touching me!" she exclaimed, and the youth gave up. The next night when the party made camp, another youth asked to sleep in the wife's tent, and tried touching her, but she never went to sleep and foiled his attempts. Each night another warrior tried and failed. At last the raiding party neared enemy territory and they pitched their tents. The wife told the men to stay inside while she used her medicine power.

The wife took out her medicine bundle and spat magic, killing all the enemy warriors instantly. She gave a war cry, waking the young men in her party, and they scrambled out of their tents, thinking they were under attack.

"I have killed the enemy!" the wife declared. "I will ride

out to collect their scalps and weapons." She leaped on her horse, rode to the enemy camp, and returned with her trophies. The men were amazed. "Well," they thought, "he is surely a man, to kill all the enemy by himself!" The war party returned to their village, and the young men sang praises of the wife's valor. The chief of the tribe wanted to honor her with a feast, but she declined.

"I am on my way back to my own tribe, and I wish to return quickly," she said. The chief offered an escort, but she asked only for a horse to take with her, and he gave her a fine one. The wife set off for home, and on the way, still disguised as a man, she met a group from her tribe. "What's new?" she asked and they told her the story about Red Hawk's wager with Blue Hawk, and that Red Hawk had seen the golden hair and birthmark on Blue Hawk's wife. They added that Blue Hawk had killed his unfaithful wife, so her father, the chief, threw him into a pit. When the wife heard the story, she understood everything.

The wife returned to her village, and showed everyone the scalps and weapons she had won. Then she took off her warrior's clothes, and revealed herself as Blue Hawk's wife. "Blue Hawk shut me up in a trunk and sent me away, because he thought I was unfaithful to him, but he was tricked by Red Hawk," the wife declared. She explained how Red Hawk and the old woman had conspired together. Then she ordered Blue Hawk released and he was fished out of the pit, looking pale and thin. When he saw his wife, they ran to each other and embraced.

The wife turned to the villagers and declared, "Now we must punish Red Hawk and the old woman!" She asked her tribesmen to bring the two forward, and as punishment, Red Hawk and the old woman were tied to wild horses and dragged in the dirt until they died. Then the villagers put on a feast to celebrate the wife's return, honoring her for her great courage. And so she lived with her husband in happiness for the rest of their years.

WOMEN PROTAGONISTS

This Native American tale is similar to others from around the world.[2] The story begins by focusing on Blue Hawk and Red Hawk, and the emphasis on the men is paradoxical, since the story is really about the wife—she is the only person who changes dramatically. It turns out that women's stories often start out by focusing on men, and only later introduce the woman protagonist. The incongruity is symbolic. In most cultures, women are expected to center their lives around men, and from adolescence, girls are forced to do so. Women's tales such as "The Warrior Wife" suggest that women's task in maturity is to attend to themselves.

The drama starts with a wager over whether Red Hawk could sleep with Blue Hawk's wife. In making the bet, the two men treat Blue Hawk's wife as a sex object, and this reflects the devaluation of women in many cultures. The story accentuates the point by not naming the wife at all—only the men have proper names. Later, when Red Hawk claims to have slept with Blue Hawk's wife, Blue Hawk does not ask her what happened. He ignores her side of the story completely, as many societies do with women in general.

THE NEGATIVE MOTHER

When Red Hawk fails to seduce the wife, he turns to an old woman for help, and she spies on her for him. Such a negative crone is a common figure in youth tales, where she takes the form of a wicked stepmother, like in "Cinderella," or an evil witch, like in "Hansel and Gretel." These wicked women are negative mother figures, symbolizing all the unsavory, nasty, destructive elements in mothers that daughters often must contend with. In the present tale, the crone may also be interpreted as the feminine side of Red Hawk, personifying his distorted ability to relate to other people, something not surprising in a young warrior trained to kill rather than to love. The crone also functions as an outer character—a meddling woman who interferes in other people's business. As such, she reminds us that women can be harmed or oppressed by other women, not just by men—a realization that is often sobering and painful, as Luise Eichenbaum and Susie Orbach note in *Between Women*.

The wife's tale offers an explanation of why the old woman is destructive: Red Hawk promises her a generous payment. The old woman may act out of greed, but she may also be desperately poor and needy. Old women are often in difficult straits, particularly in societies that provide no place of honor for old women, and instead obsess about young ones.

SIGNS OF GREATNESS

When the wife undresses and goes to bed, the old woman observes two distinguishing features—a birthmark on her back, and a long braid of golden hair on her abdomen. A birthmark is common enough in real life, and often appears in fairy tales as the means by which a person's identity is recognized. The golden braid is unusual. It is on the abdomen, the site of the womb, hinting that it may refer to a uniquely feminine power—childbearing. The abdominal position also suggests a parallel to the umbilical cord, everyone's original link to a mother. The braid thus alludes to the motherline—to traditions and wisdom passed from mother to child, and especially to daughters. The culture of the Tiwa Pueblo Indians was matrilineal, tracing descent through the mother's side, not the father's. So the story's reference to the motherline is not surprising; what is surprising is that the motherline is so weak. One reason may lie in the dramatic changes that Western contact precipitated in Native American cultures.[3] As white colonialists invaded native territories, forcing many tribes to adopt a warrior culture, women's status declined precipitously. Male warriors and their battle equipment became paramount, and in some tribes women were soon counted as less important than good war horses. Although it alludes to the motherline, the story does not mention any children. This is typical of women's tales and surprising, since childrearing plays a large part in women's lives across cultures. One reason for the absence of children in the tales is that mothers normally think about their children a great deal and do not need more reminders about them. Instead mothers need encouragement to attend to their own development, which women's tales provide.

There is another symbolic meaning behind the wife's golden braid. In Native American lore, the abdomen is a source of mystical power, and some traditions describe filaments of energy emanating from a person's abdomen. Other cultures, like those of India and Japan, echo the theme. This suggests that the braid symbolizes a numinous source of power, and the golden color—unusual for Native Americans—underscores the point.

DEATH AND REBIRTH

After Blue Hawk gives all his possessions to Red Hawk, he makes a leather trunk, asks his wife to lie in it, and seals her in it and throws it in the river. Blue Hawk does not seem to be trying to kill his wife since he makes the container watertight and puts money, food, and cooking gear inside, presumably for her to use when she arrives at her destination. Nevertheless, being shut up in the casket makes a good symbol for death. She even dresses in her finest clothes, just as a corpse would be laid out in a coffin.

The wife's symbolic death is something many women experience at midlife. Women who follow conventional roles in youth as wife and mother often find their lives collapsing in the middle years. A woman may discover that her husband is having an affair, or she may find herself at loose ends after her children leave home. Menopause also signifies a literal death—of the capacity to bear children. Or a woman may have devoted much of her energy to a career, until she hits the infamous glass ceiling, and encountering it often destroys a woman's faith in the system, murdering her hopes and dreams. These death-like experiences are painful, as the wife's story dramatizes: it is easy to imagine her confusion, fear, anger, and feelings of betrayal as she lies in the trunk and floats down the river.

The wife floats along until she is rescued. The theme recalls the story of Moses, who was also abandoned on a river and fortuitously rescued. In folktales, it is usually a baby boy who is forsaken, and he becomes a great hero. The wife's story reverses gender, emphasizing that greatness and leadership are not the sole province of males.

ROLE REVERSALS AND VIGILANCE

When the wife is set free by a fisherman, she exchanges clothing with him and enters the village disguised as a man. The cross-dressing theme appears in women's tales around the world,[4] and the motif is deeply symbolic. On a practical level, because of the risk of attack or rape, it is dangerous for a woman to travel alone. Moreover, in disguising herself as a man, the wife frees herself from constricting feminine roles and gains male privileges. Such a masquerade is not mere fantasy—two modern women writers, George Sand and Willa Cather, sometimes masqueraded as men in order to gain greater personal freedom. Many women performance artists and rap singers follow suit today.[5]

On a psychological level, when the wife dresses like a man, she symbolically reclaims her masculine energies, her assertiveness, strength, and leadership. This is difficult for women in competitive cultures because they are punished for being assertive, yet such assertiveness is necessary for survival. The terrific stress on women is clear in the story when the wife joins the war party and the young male warriors try to uncover her disguise by sleeping in her tent and touching her. She foils the men by staying up every night and we can imagine how exhausted she must be, riding all day and staying up all night. Her situation dramatizes the exhaustion many women feel, pursuing a career in a competitive workplace while raising a family at home. By day the women must be tirelessly active at work, and by night they are expected to be nurturing mothers, spotless housekeepers, and alluring wives.

The wife identifies herself to the other warriors as a medicine man, a shaman, and she shows them a white eagle feather as proof of her power. Eagle feathers were hard to obtain, and highly prized in Native American tradition. Her possession of one parallels the golden braid on her abdomen: she has the marks of great personal mana or power. As proof, the wife uses her magic to kill the enemy warriors from a distance.

Women with supernatural powers are usually condemned as witches. Because they are supposed to be accommodating and nurturing "by nature," forceful, assertive women threaten traditional gender roles and are called "unnatural." The story rejects this stereotype by praising the wife, not condemning her. "Masculine" traits such as courage and leadership are simply human. Historic women warriors like Joan of Arc offer dramatic proof of the point. When France was invaded by the English, the King of France vacillated between suing for peace or fighting back, and the French kept losing battles. Then Joan of Arc came forth, wearing a man's outfit and armor, just like the wife in the Tiwa tale, and led the French troops to victory over the English. Today, reclaiming assertiveness does not mean women must become warriors; it means, more generally, becoming a leader, whether in government, institutions, or communities.

DEPRESSION AND AGGRESSION

When the wife emerges from the trunk, she is symbolically reborn and becomes a warrior who kills other people. Why are liberation and rebirth linked with deadly aggression here?

Psychologically a woman must often take bold action, breaking out of confining social roles or leaving restrictive relationships, symbolically killing off these limitations. Only then does she find new life, and this is true particularly in competitive cultures focused on power, where one individual's gain means another's loss. The theme is dramatic in the ancient myth of Inanna's descent into the underworld. She was killed there and the condition for her resurrection was finding a replacement: she had to kill somebody in order to be reborn.

The wife's imprisonment in the leather trunk and Inanna's descent into the underworld make a good symbol for depression. These two tales suggest that reclaiming aggression will often resolve such a depression. The case of "Esther" illustrates how this occurs in real life. Esther grew up with an alcoholic father who regularly beat her and her siblings. Esther had few recollections of the violence, although she was plagued by chronic depression and headaches. She hesitated to assert herself, even going along with her husband's suggestions about what to wear each day. Then Esther was mugged and the violent encounter brought back a flood of memories about her father's drunken violence. She came to therapy, and for a year we struggled together with her traumatic recollections, deep depression, nightmares, suicidal thoughts, and agonizing headaches. But she also dealt with her anger at the injustices she had suffered, and learned to assert herself, standing up to her husband. Her nightmares gradually changed. Instead of being attacked and beaten by her father, she dreamed of attacking and murdering other people. She reclaimed her aggressiveness and as therapy progressed became more outspoken with her husband, family, and friends. Her nightmares, headaches, and depression subsided, and she confronted her father, quit her low-paying secretarial job, and returned to school to complete her degree. Symbolically, Esther became a warrior wife, freed herself from her depression, and was reborn into a new, authentic life.

In the tale, the warrior wife does not have much trouble reclaiming her aggressive energies. She simply puts on a man's clothes and goes to war. There are probably two reasons for this, and the first involves her father. When Blue

Hawk returned from the river without his wife, her father demanded to know where she was. Blue Hawk refused to answer, so the chief threw him into a pit. Clearly, the chief cared about his daughter, noticed she was gone, and tried to do something about it. Other stories confirm that a supportive father greatly helps a woman in exercising her strengths. Second, the story comes from the Tiwa people, where women traditionally had important roles, so the wife would have cultural support for her assertiveness and leadership.

RETURN AND RECONCILIATION

After her victory, the wife is honored by the tribe she helped, but insists on returning to her own people. She does not stay to bask in her newfound glory and power, the way young male heroes usually do. The same theme appears in other women's tales: when women adopt warrior ways, it is to survive or to defend their people—not to win power or glory.

When the wife returns to her tribe, she reveals herself as Blue Hawk's wife and tells everybody about her war victories, showing the scalps of the enemy warriors she had killed. The episode is important because many women underplay their achievements, and even highly successful women minimize their success. In their autobiographies, for example, Golda Meir and Eleanor Roosevelt attribute their accomplishments to luck rather than to hard work, courage, and resourcefulness. The pattern is even stronger among women friends, who often do not report their successes for fear of making their friends feel bad. The warrior wife abandons this artificial modesty. She demands credit for her accomplishments and receives it from society.

The wife denounces Red Hawk and the old woman, and asks that Blue Hawk be released. The villagers obey her, so the wife clearly has become a person of some authority in her tribe. Having reclaimed her assertiveness, the wife now assumes a position of leadership among her people. She does not return to a traditional wifely role, but speaks up and decides tribal activities. Her individual development leads to a public, community role.

In freeing Blue Hawk from the pit, the wife introduces a theme found in many midlife tales from around the world—a courageous wife must rescue a helpless husband, reversing the usual drama of youth tales, where the helpless princess is rescued by the hero. The reversal emphasizes the complementary tasks men and women face at midlife in heroic cultures: women must reclaim their courageous, assertive energies, while men must come to terms with their vulnerability, dependence, and the importance of relationships. Only when both women and men do this inner work does a deep, authentic relationship become possible.

JUSTICE

After Blue Hawk is released, his wife orders Red Hawk and the crone killed by being dragged behind wild horses. The historical situation explains the severity of the sentence. (The presence of horses and the absence of guns in the story help date it.) Executions were not unusual in Native American cultures, or among American colonialists in Massachusetts who were burning women as witches around this time.

The old woman and Red Hawk can be taken as inner, psychological figures. As a symbol for a negative mother, the elder woman's death represents the final resolution of maternal issues with which a woman may have struggled for many years. For his part, as an interior character, Red Hawk would represent a part of the wife's psyche. He is a negative animus figure, personifying an immature form of assertiveness centered on raw aggression, self-aggrandizement, brute force, and fighting. The wife adopts this simplistic warrior mentality when she first rides off and kills "the enemy," without asking why they deserve to die. When she returns to her own people, however, she has matured and is much more reflective. Although she demands the death of the crone and Red Hawk, she does not kill them herself. She asks for the tribe to act, and this transforms the issue from personal vengeance to one of community justice. Even more significantly, she forgives her husband and orders him released. She can balance justice and love, aggression and forgiveness.

The execution of Red Hawk and the woman can also be interpreted as the end of the old cultural order. Red Hawk personifies the warrior mentality behind many patriarchal cultures, while the old woman dramatizes the denigration of women. Both must be destroyed to foster a new society in which authentic relationships between men and women become possible.

The tale does not explain why the wife forgives Blue Hawk. Presumably, she realized that he was deceived. As in other women's tales, it is the man who is unconscious and asleep, and the woman who must awaken him and tell him what is going on. Moreover, their reconciliation is not a simple, romantic fairy-tale ending. For one thing, the wife rescued the husband, so their new relationship will presumably be more egalitarian! She is also now an acknowledged leader in her community. So her reconciliation with Blue Hawk represents a deeper, mutual relationship between woman and man, feminine and masculine, than occurs in traditional romance.

CELEBRATING THE AMAZON

To summarize "The Warrior Wife," I turn to a remarkable series of paintings by Anna Fengel.[6] Entitled *Amazons with Their Serpents and Dragons*, her sequence of images recapitulates the major themes of the fairy tale.

Fengel's five visionary paintings, done between 1976 and 1982, begin with one called "Lancelot," depicting a young man who looks too delicate to be a warrior. The second work, "Prince of Hell," shows a man fighting like a raging demon. He has serpents and dragons coming out of his head, each battling another. These first two paintings parallel the opening scene of "The Warrior Wife" in focusing on two men, the way most societies put men first and women second. In addition, Lancelot is delicate and gentle, and seems too ethereal to be a real warrior. He is like Blue Hawk, who is too meek to reject Red Hawk's wager and his claim about sleeping with Blue Hawk's wife. Fengel's second male, in "The Prince of Hell," highlights the dark side of the warrior, and Red Hawk plays this role in the story in being brash, boastful, competitive, and destructive and seeing women only as objects.

Fengel's third painting portrays a melancholic woman, who looks Native American. Surrounded by mist, depressed and withdrawn, the woman recalls the warrior wife, imprisoned in the trunk and thrown upon the river. The painting and story dramatize a death-rebirth process many women experience, descending into a dark world of grief and reemerging energized and strengthened. Fengel portrays the renaissance in her fourth painting, "She Wants to Become a Knight," which depicts a young woman who is resolute and fit. Dragons surround her, but not in a threatening way: they are her helpers. The largest dragon is blue and hovers above the women's head, while light pours in around her. The dragons graphically symbolize the woman's assertiveness, which she has reclaimed. The depressive theme thus vanishes.

Dragons are magical beings, and the fact that they assist and protect the woman in "She Wants to Become a Knight" suggests that she has supernatural approval. This parallels the warrior wife, who had a white eagle's feather and great magic powers, allowing her to kill the enemy from a distance. Both the painting and the folktale break with convention here, refusing to condemn a powerful woman as a witch.

Fengel's last painting portrays a mature woman with serpents and dragons for hair. The woman radiates light and a cosmic dragon arches over her. Psychologically, she has fully integrated her "Amazon" energy, and her radiance dramatizes her self-actualization. This is equivalent to the warrior wife claiming credit for her accomplishments.

Missing from Fengel's paintings is the last stage—a woman's return to society, reconciliation with men in a new, egalitarian relationship, and assumption of a leadership role.

This is the importance of "The Warrior Wife" and other women's tales. They reveal the complete story, and emphasize that women's development results not just in personal, psychological change, but in a transformation of society, too—nothing less than waking the world.

CHAPTER 3

"Maria Morevna":

The Limits of Power

(from Russia[1])

nce a prince named Ivan lived with his three sisters, Princesses Olga, Maria, and Anna. Before the parents died, they asked Ivan to make sure his sisters married quickly, and Ivan promised he would. One day, as Ivan and his sisters walked in their garden, a storm gathered, lightning struck the castle, and a falcon flew inside. The bird turned into a handsome knight and asked to marry Princess Olga. Ivan replied, "If my sister desires it, so be it." She agreed, married the knight, and went to live with him in his castle.

A year later, as Ivan walked in the garden with Maria and Anna, another storm gathered and lightning again hit the castle. This time an eagle flew inside and it changed into a gallant knight who asked for the hand of Princess Maria. "If she desires it, so be it," Ivan answered. Maria agreed, married the knight, and moved to his faraway castle.

One year later, Ivan walked in the garden with his youngest sister, Anna, when a storm blew against the castle, lightning hit the walls, and a raven flew in. The bird changed into a dashing knight and proposed marriage to Princess Anna. "If my sister desires it, so be it," Ivan answered. She agreed, the two were married, and Anna departed with her new husband.

A year went by and Ivan grew tired of living alone, so he went to visit his sisters. He walked and walked and came to a field littered with dead soldiers. A terrible battle had just ended.

"Who won such a great victory?" Ivan asked a soldier.

"It is our Tsarina, the beautiful Maria Morevna," the trooper answered.

Ivan walked up to the queen's tent. She sat outside with her generals, and Ivan bowed to her. "Greetings, Majesty," the Prince said.

"God be with you," Maria Morevna replied. "Who are you and where do you journey?" she asked. "Do you travel of your own free will, or by necessity?"

"I am Prince Ivan," he answered, "and I journey by choice."

The two talked for a time and the Tsarina took a liking to Ivan. They soon fell in love and married. Ivan went to live with Maria Morevna in her great castle, and the two were as happy as could be. One day, the Queen was called to war. She assembled her troops, and gave her kingdom and household into Ivan's care. Before she left, she told him, "Go where you wish in the castle, except never open this closet." She showed him a door that was secured with many locks, and then departed with her army.

Ivan was curious and wondered, "What could be in the closet?" The Queen was scarcely gone before he opened the forbidden door. He was horrified to find an old man inside, fastened to the wall with twelve chains.

"Who are you?" Ivan asked.

"I am Koschey the Deathless," the old man replied feebly. "Please, in God's name, give me some water. I have been locked in this closet for ten years without food or drink." Ivan took pity upon the poor man and fetched him a barrel of water. Koschey drank it in one gulp. "I still thirst! Have mercy and bring me more!" the old man cried out. Ivan brought another keg, and Koschey downed it instantly, so the Prince gave him a third barrel.

"Ah! My strength has returned," Koschey declared as he swallowed the contents of the last cask. He broke all his chains and laughed wickedly. "Thanks to you, foolish prince," he cackled, "I am free. And now you will never see Maria Morevna again, because I will seize her and lock her up in my castle!" With that, Koschey magically flew out the window. Fearing for his wife, Ivan set out looking for her, walking as fast as he could. He came upon her army milling about in confusion, and the soldiers explained that the Queen had been kidnapped by Koschey the Deathless.

"I must find Maria Morevna," Ivan said, "and undo my foolish mistake!" So he walked on and on until he came to a majestic castle. A falcon perched on a nearby oak tree flew to the ground and turned into a handsome knight.

"Hail, Prince Ivan, my brother-in-law!" the knight said. Hearing those words, Princess Olga came running out of the castle to greet Ivan and he stayed with them for three days. Then he prepared to leave.

"I cannot remain longer," Ivan explained. "I seek my wife, Maria Morevna, who has been kidnapped by the evil sorcerer Koschey the Deathless."

"That is a hard task," the knight responded. "But if you must go, leave us your silver spoon, so that every time we look at it, we will remember you." Ivan gave it to them and departed. He walked for three days until he came to a castle even larger than the falcon's. On an oak tree, a mighty eagle perched, and when it saw Ivan, the bird flew down and turned into a gallant cavalier.

"Hail, Prince Ivan, dear brother-in-law!" the eagle declared. Hearing his words, Princess Maria ran outside and embraced her brother. Ivan stayed with them for three days, then made ready to leave. "I cannot linger," Ivan explained. "I am searching for my wife, Maria Morevna, who has been imprisoned by the evil Koschey."

"That will be dangerous," the eagle-knight warned. "But if you must go, leave us your silver fork, so that every time we look at it, we will remember you." Ivan gave them his fork, embraced his sister and brother-in-law, and continued on his way. He walked for three more days until he came to a castle even mightier than the eagle's. On an oak tree perched a raven, and when it saw Ivan, it flew down and changed into a dashing knight.

"Hail, Prince Ivan, dear brother-in-law!" the knight declared. Hearing Ivan's name, Princess Anna came running out and embraced her brother. "Stay with us," she asked Ivan, and he remained with them for three days. Then he took his leave. "I am searching for my wife, Maria Morevna, who has been captured by Koschey the sorcerer," Ivan explained.

"Alas," the knight murmured, "that will be difficult." He thought for a moment, and said, "Leave us your silver snuffbox, so that every time we look at it, we will remember you." Ivan gave it to them and departed.

On and on Ivan walked, until he came to a grim castle, dark and foreboding. A woman looked out from a window, and it was none other than Maria Morevna. When Ivan saw his wife, he broke into the castle, rushed to her side, and they embraced.

"Alas, dear Ivan," Maria Morevna lamented, "why did you disobey me and look into the closet! You have undone us both! Koschey the Deathless has reclaimed his powers and imprisoned me. Today he is away hunting, otherwise he would surely kill you."

"Dear wife," Prince Ivan exclaimed, "forgive me for my foolishness! But let us not waste time with regrets now. We must flee from this evil place." Maria Morevna and Ivan quickly gathered a few provisions and escaped from the castle.

Far away, Koschey was riding his horse and it stumbled. "Why do you falter, faithful steed?" the sorcerer asked. "Is there some misfortune brewing?"

"Maria Morevna and Prince Ivan have escaped from your castle," the magic animal answered.

"Can you catch them?" Koschey demanded.

"As surely as the sun will rise tomorrow," the animal replied, and galloped off. In no time at all, they caught up with Maria Morevna and Ivan. Koschey seized the Queen and turned to Ivan. "I should kill you," the sorcerer threatened, "but because you gave me water, I will forgive you this time. I warn you, if you try to rescue Maria Morevna again, your life is forfeit!" Then Koschey rode off with the Queen.

Ivan sat in the forest and wept all night. The next day, he made his way back to Koschey's castle, broke into the stronghold again, and went to Maria Morevna. "You must flee," the Queen warned Ivan, "or Koschey will kill you!"

"I do not care," Ivan declared, "as long as we are together. If I have to die, at least I will be with you a few hours." Maria Morevna and Ivan then hurried out of the castle, but far away, where Koschey was hunting, his horse stumbled.

"Why do you falter, faithful steed?" the sorcerer asked. "Is there some misfortune brewing?"

"Prince Ivan has returned to your castle," the horse answered. "He and Maria Morevna are escaping."

"Can you catch them?" Koschey asked.

"As surely as the sun will set tomorrow," the animal replied, and galloped off. In the blink of an eye, they caught up with Maria Morevna and Ivan. Koschey seized the Queen once more. "I will forgive you this second time," the sorcerer told Ivan, "in remembrance of the second drink of water you gave me. But try to rescue Maria Morevna a third time, and I will cut you into little pieces." Koschey dragged the Queen back to his castle.

Prince Ivan wept all night, and then arose the next morning to return to Koschey's castle. When he broke into the fortress, Maria Morevna came running. "You must flee, dear Ivan," the Queen warned. "Koschey will surely kill you this time."

"I do not care," Ivan exclaimed. "I love you too much." So Maria Morevna and Ivan fled the castle together.

Far away, Koschey's horse stumbled beneath him. "Why do you falter?" the sorcerer asked. "Is there some misfortune brewing?"

"Maria Morevna and Prince Ivan have escaped a third time," the horse replied.

"Can you catch them?" Koschey asked.

"As surely as darkness comes with night," the animal replied, and galloped off. In a moment, they caught up with

Maria Morevna and Ivan. Koschey seized the Queen, then cried, "Now, foolish Prince, prepare to die." Koschey raised his sword, struck the Prince dead, and then cut Ivan's body into little pieces. He threw the pieces into a barrel, sealed the vat, cast it into the ocean, and finally dragged Maria Morevna back to his castle.

In the homes of his three sisters, Ivan's silver spoon, fork, and snuffbox turned black. The falcon, the eagle, and the raven noticed the change and cried out, "Alas! Something terrible has happened to Ivan!" The three birds flew together and divined Ivan's evil fate. The eagle raced to the ocean to retrieve the barrel with the pieces of Ivan's body. The falcon flew off for the water of life, while the raven fetched the water of death. When the three birds met again, they reassembled Ivan's body. The raven bathed it with the water of death so that all the pieces joined together, and the falcon poured the water of life on the corpse. In an instant, Ivan opened his eyes.

"Ah, what a terrible dream I had," he said. "I dreamed that Koschey the Deathless killed me."

"It was no dream," the three birds replied. "He murdered you, and cut you into little pieces, but we brought you back to life. Now you must rest with us and your three sisters."

"No," Ivan declared, "my place is with my wife, Maria Morevna. She is still imprisoned by the evil Koschey, and I must go to her." The falcon, the eagle, and the raven tried to dissuade Ivan, but he would not change his mind. He made his way back to Koschey's castle and found Maria Morevna inside.

"You have returned from the dead!" Maria Morevna exclaimed.

"My brothers-in-law revived me," Ivan replied, explaining how the falcon, eagle, and raven had resurrected him. Ivan went on, "I see now we cannot escape Koschey because his magic horse always catches us. But I have a plan. You must ask Koschey where he found his horse, so I can obtain one like his. Then we can escape safely." Maria Morevna agreed and Ivan left the castle to hide nearby. When Koschey returned from his hunt, Maria Morevna spoke sweetly to him and asked about his adventures and victories. Soon enough, Koschey boasted about his magic horse.

"No other man has a horse like mine," Koschey declared, "because Baba Yaga, the great witch, gave her to me. She lives beyond thrice-nine lands, in the thrice-tenth kingdom, across a river of fire. She has a mare that can gallop around the earth in a few hours, and all the mare's colts are magic, too. My horse is one of those animals, and the witch gave her to me because I herded her mares for three days."

"But how did you reach Baba Yaga, across the river of fire?" Maria Morevna asked.

"It is simple," the sorcerer explained. "I have a magic hand-kerchief, and when I wave it three times to the right, it creates a bridge high enough to cross any flames. When I wave it three times to the left, the bridge vanishes." He showed Maria Morevna the enchanted cloth, and left his castle.

The Queen stole the handkerchief and, when Ivan returned to the castle, gave it to him and told him what she had discovered. Ivan immediately set out, seeking Baba Yaga. He walked and walked, until he was ravenous with hunger. Then he came upon a bird from beyond the sea, sitting on her nest. "I am starving," Ivan told the bird, "and I must eat one of your chicks lest I die."

"Noble Prince," the sea bird pleaded, "spare my chicks and some day you will be rewarded."

Ivan sighed and went on. He walked and walked, until he came upon a beehive in a forest. "I must eat some of your honey," Ivan told the bees, "or I will perish." The queen bee flew out and pleaded, "Spare the honey for my bees, Prince Ivan, and one day I will be of use to you."

Ivan relented and went on his way. He walked and walked until he came upon a lioness with her cubs in the wilderness. Ivan drew his sword. "I must eat one of your cubs, or I will die of hunger," the Prince said.

"Spare my cubs," the lioness begged, "and you will not regret it!" Ivan could not bring himself to kill a cub, and went on his way.

At last Ivan arrived at a river of fire. He took out Koschey's magic handkerchief and waved it three times to the right. A bridge appeared high above the flames, and Ivan crossed safely. Then he waved the handkerchief three times to the left, and the bridge vanished. Ivan soon came upon the house of Baba Yaga and saw that it was surrounded by twelve wooden stakes. On eleven of them were human skulls, but one was empty. Baba Yaga came out of the house, and Ivan greeted her. "Good day, dear grandmother," he said.

"Good day, Prince Ivan," Baba Yaga replied. "What brings you here, so far from home? Do you come of your own free will, or from some compulsion?"

"I seek a magic horse from you," Ivan replied. "And to earn such a horse, I am willing to work as your herdsman."

"That is easier said than done," Baba Yaga said. "Still, if you want to try, all you have to do is herd my mares for three days and not lose any one of them. If you succeed, I will give you one of the horses. If you fail, I will kill you and stick your head on the post there." She pointed to the empty stake. "But do not hold that against me," she concluded.

Ivan nodded in agreement, and Baba Yaga gave him a hearty meal. Then she sent him with her mares to the meadows. As soon as the animals reached the fields, they ran off in all directions. Ivan tried to catch them, but they were too many and too swift. Exhausted, he sat on a rock, wept with despair, and then fell asleep. Just as the sun began to set, the bird from beyond the sea flew to him.

"Ivan, Ivan," the bird cried out, rousing the Prince. "Return at once to Baba Yaga. I have gathered many birds and we have driven the mares home." Ivan hurried back to Baba Yaga's house, where he overheard her yelling at the mares. "I told you not to come home tonight!" she shrieked. "I cannot kill Ivan today!"

"We could not stay away!" the horses explained. "Birds appeared from everywhere and pecked at our eyes until we returned here."

Baba Yaga frowned and thought a moment. "Well, tomor-

row do not stay in the meadow. Run and hide in the forest.
Ivan cannot find you there."

The next morning, when Ivan herded the mares to the
fields, they bolted into the forest and vanished. Ivan tried
chasing them, to no avail. He sat down, wept with exhaustion, and fell asleep. As the sun began to set, a lioness appeared from the forest.

"Ivan, Ivan," the lioness called to the Prince,. "return
quickly to Baba Yaga. I have gathered the beasts of the forest
and we have driven the mares home for you."

Ivan rushed back and overheard Baba Yaga berating her
horses. "I told you to stay away, and what do you do but come
home!"

"We dared not stay out," the mares exclaimed. "Lions and
wild beasts attacked us and we barely escaped alive!"

Baba Yaga frowned. "Tomorrow, run into the ocean and
stay there. Ivan cannot fetch you from the sea! Then I can
chop his head off!"

The next morning, Ivan herded the mares to the fields, but
they immediately ran off into the ocean. He tried to retrieve
them, but failed, so he sat on the beach, weeping with fatigue,
and fell asleep. When the sun began to set, the queen bee
flew up to him.

"Ivan, Ivan!" the bee called out. "Return to Baba Yaga
quickly. The mares are already home." Then the bee added a
warning. "When you return, do not let Baba Yaga see you.
Hide in the stables, behind the manger. There you will find a
sickly colt sitting on a pile of manure. At midnight, take the
colt with you and flee. Otherwise, Baba Yaga will kill you!"

Ivan thanked the queen bee, and went back to Baba Yaga's
house. He hid in the stables and overheard the old woman
rebuking her mares. "I told you to stay in the ocean until
tomorrow. What are you doing back here?"

"Bees flew at us and stung us until we came back here,"
the horses answered. Baba Yaga gnashed her teeth. "Now I
have to find some other excuse to kill the wretched Prince!"

When the witch left the stables, Ivan went to the manger
and found the sickly colt there, just as the bee had described.
He waited until midnight, and then mounted the colt and

rode off. When he reached the river of fire, he drew out his enchanted handkerchief, waved it three times to the right, created the magic bridge, and crossed safely. Then he paused and waved the handkerchief to the left only two times. The bridge remained, but greatly weakened. Ivan rode to a pasture, and let his colt loose to graze. As soon as the horse ate a few mouthfuls of grass, it grew into a large and immensely strong steed.

When Baba Yaga awoke the next morning, she discovered her colt missing and Ivan gone. In a rage, she rushed to her magic mortar, and climbed in. It lifted her up and carried her swiftly after Ivan. She came to the river of fire, saw the bridge that Ivan had left behind, and started crossing it. But the bridge collapsed, throwing Baba Yaga into the river of fire, where she burned to death.

Far away, Ivan galloped onward to Koschey's castle. When Maria Morevna saw him, she cried, "You have returned with a horse from Baba Yaga!"

"Yes, but we must leave Koschey's castle at once!" Ivan replied.

"Koschey will catch us again," the Queen protested, "and he will kill you!"

"No," Ivan said. "My horse is more powerful than his. We will be safe." Maria Morevna climbed behind him and they fled.

Far away Koschey the Deathless was hunting, and his horse stumbled. "Why do you falter, faithful steed?" the sorcerer asked. "Is there some misfortune brewing?"

"Maria Morevna and Prince Ivan have escaped once again," the horse answered.

"The Prince has come back to life?" Koschey inquired. "Well, it will be easy to catch them, just like before!" the sorcerer declared.

"It may not be possible," the horse answered. "Ivan rides a horse from Baba Yaga, and she is more powerful than I."

"Silence!" the sorcerer commanded. "I will not let Maria Morevna escape! Go after Ivan! This time I will make sure the miserable Prince stays dead!"

Koschey and his horse galloped like the wind, and after a

long time they reached Maria Morevna and Ivan. Koschey turned to the Prince and cried out, "Prepare to die!" The sorcerer dismounted, and drew his sword.

At that moment, Ivan's steed reared up and struck Koschey. The sorcerer fell down unconscious, and Ivan struck the villain with a mace, killing him. Then the Prince burned the wizard's body, and scattered the ashes to the wind, so that no trace of his evil remained. Finally Ivan mounted his horse, and Maria Morevna took Koschey's. They rode together, side by side, and the first thing they did was go to Ivan's sisters, Princesses Olga, Maria, and Anna. Ivan and Maria Morevna thanked the falcon, the eagle, and the raven for rescuing Ivan, and at each castle they made merry and feasted for many days. Finally, Maria Morevna and Ivan returned to their own kingdom. And there they lived in happiness and peace for the rest of their lives.

WOMEN OF STRENGTH

The story begins by introducing Prince Ivan, then focuses on his many adventures. So the tale might seem to be about him and male psychology—except for an important detail. The story is called "Maria Morevna," not "Prince Ivan." Moreover, different versions of the story give various names to the Prince, such as "Alexey," but all versions call the Queen "Maria Morevna." She is the unvarying element, indicating that she is the real focus. Several details in the story confirm her central role.

First, only Maria Morevna has a complete name. Everyone else is given only a first name, like Ivan, Olga, or Koschey, or no name at all, like the falcon, eagle, and raven. The story thus says, in symbolic fashion, that only Maria Morevna is a unique individual. She is the leading character. Second, the story always refers to Maria Morevna by her full name, rejecting patriarchal tradition, in which women are typically addressed by their first names only, like children, while men are addressed more formally. Third, Maria Morevna has the highest-ranking title in the tale—queen or tsarina. Ivan is only a prince, even after his marriage to Maria Morevna. Finally, for most of the story, Ivan walks whenever he goes anywhere, whereas Maria Morevna rides a horse. The story literally puts her above him.

In dwelling on Ivan's adventures, although the Queen is the main protagonist, "Maria Morevna" recalls "The Warrior Wife," which initially focused on Blue Hawk and Red Hawk, and only later shifted to the real protagonist—the wife. Both tales are similar to a dream: a woman or man may dream about many different characters, and she or he may play only a small overt role. But the dream is really about the dreamer.

Maria Morevna is a powerful, independent, and victorious warrior queen. Unlike the Princess in "The Queen and the Murderer," Maria Morevna never gave up her youthful courage and strength. Her story is profoundly relevant to women today who have benefited from the feminist movement and have begun to take up positions of influence in society. Maria Morevna's drama reveals the pitfalls women face on the path to authority and leadership.

THE FATHER'S DAUGHTER

The story introduces its first insight about women and power in a small but perceptive point: the "Morevna" in "Maria Morevna" contains the suffix -evna, which means "daughter of," usually referring to the father (Tsarevna, for instance, means "daughter of the tsar").[2] One version of the tale explicitly notes that she inherited her throne from her father. This reflects historical fact in most cultures: ruling women like Isabella of Castile and Elizabeth I of England usually inherited their positions from powerful fathers. (The women often had to fight to keep their power because of opposition to the idea that women could rule a country.)

There is also a psychological meaning here: women of accomplishment today usually enjoyed a close relationship in childhood with successful fathers.[3] Often called "father's daughters," these women had fathers who encouraged them in worldly endeavors, took pride in their achievements, and offered a model of assertiveness, confidence, and independence. If Maria Morevna starts out as a father's daughter, though, she quickly becomes her own woman. The father's daughter is a stage of development, not a final personality type, and reflects adaptation to a particular kind of society—namely, a heroic, masculine-oriented one.

IVAN

In the tale, Prince Ivan is a complex and intriguing figure. We can interpret him to be an inner character, an animus figure, personifying Maria Morevna's masculine side. Yet Ivan does not fit traditional masculine stereotypes. He is kind, nurturing, and accommodating. When the falcon, eagle, and raven come wooing his sisters, for instance, Ivan's only condition is that his sisters desire the marriages. He does not demand a dowry, or try to arrange marriages that might be politically useful to him, instead he respects his sisters' wishes and honors their feelings. He favors relationship over power, emotion rather than wealth. Moreover, after he and Maria Morevna marry, Ivan goes to live with her, which is unusual because in patriarchal cultures the bride normally forsakes her family and friends to live with her husband's. Ivan is presumably the ruler of his own country, having inherited the throne from his father. Yet he leaves his ancestral land for Maria Morevna's. Again he chooses love over authority. Ivan's move to Maria Morevna's homeland also recalls the practices of ancient matrifocal, matrilineal cultures, where husbands customarily left their families and moved in with their wives' clans.

Later in the drama, Ivan keeps returning to the Tsarina

despite Koschey's threats to kill him—even after the sorcerer does kill him! Ivan is devoted to Maria Morevna and says he cannot live without her. He dramatizes love and relationship. Here we come to a deeper symbolism behind Ivan. The Tsarina is willing and able to kill—she first appears in the story right after a battle, amidst many dead soldiers, and later leads her army off to war. Ivan, on the other hand, avoids killing—he spares the bird's chicks, the queen bee's honey, and the lioness's cubs. Psychologically speaking, Ivan brings up the qualities that Maria Morevna has neglected in herself. Immersed in her role as ruler, Maria Morevna has had to develop her aggressiveness, independence, cunning, and willingness to fight when necessary. Ivan reminds Maria Morevna of communion and intimacy rather than competition and power. Here the tale neatly reverses traditional gender roles, offering another example of how subversive—and liberating—women's tales are.

Ivan exemplifies a gentle animus, and contrasts sharply with the "ominous animus" in "The Queen and the Murderer." Yet the function of the gentle animus is the same—to bring up issues that a woman ignores or neglects in her life. For many women who have taken the path of power and achievement in youth, the task at midlife is to come to terms with family, relationship, and intimacy.[4] The process is not always easy, as "Maria Morevna" quickly reveals.

KOSCHEY THE DEATHLESS

Sometime after marrying Ivan, Maria Morevna goes off to war and leaves him in charge of the household. Once more they switch traditional gender roles. Maria Morevna tells Ivan not to look into a certain closet, and so, as usually happens in fairy tales, the forbidden door is soon opened. The plot is familiar in myth and legend, but it is usually the woman who breaks the taboo. So Maria Morevna and Ivan continue their role reversals.

In the closet Ivan finds Koschey the Deathless, who breaks out of his chains and kidnaps Maria Morevna. Koschey essentially forces Maria Morevna into a stereotypical feminine role—waiting for a male hero to save her. The theme, familiar in folklore and literature,[5] dramatizes the backlash women encounter when they break out of conventional roles. When women become more outspoken and assertive, the men around them—husbands, fathers, and co-workers—often feel threatened by the change, and oppose it, consciously or unconsciously. Koschey stands out on a broad societal level, too: in many cultures, witch hunts start when women begin to assume more outspoken, active, nontraditional roles.[6]

Koschey has further meanings as a shadow figure, representing Maria Morevna's own dark side as a queen. When Ivan first meets her he is astonished by all the dead soldiers on the battlefield. The grisly scene suggests that the Tsarina, as a warrior queen, has a cruel or bloodthirsty streak in her. Here her name is relevant. *Evna* in "Morevna" means "daughter of," as mentioned before, while the *mor* is related to the Russian word for "death." So Maria Morevna may mean Maria, daughter of death. In fact, rulers often must be deadly. Koschey personifies the violence and cruelty that usually accompany power. He represents the shadow of anyone taking the path of leadership and authority.

THE SHADOW OF THE FATHER

One version of Maria Morevna's tale explains that Koschey was imprisoned by her father. Koschey's name reinforces the paternal theme. In Russian, *koschey* means "skeletal" or "corpselike," and thus points to death, too. But *morevna* refers to "daughter of death," so Koschey may represent the shadow of Maria Morevna's father. The story is psychologically astute here. Successful women often admire and model themselves on powerful fathers, not recognizing the fathers' dark sides.[7] Joan illustrates the point.

Joan was a successful executive, a graduate of a prestigious business school, advancing rapidly in her company by her early thirties. At that time, however, she became depressed and an old problem with binge eating reappeared after a long absence. In therapy, the reason for her depression and eating disorder soon became clear. Joan harbored almost boundless ambitions for herself, which were for the most part unconscious. Given her abilities, her dreams were realistic in the long run, but she felt impatient—even driven—to succeed immediately. She constantly berated herself for not advancing fast enough, nor performing as well as she wanted to. As the inevitable obstacles, delays, and disappointments multiplied in her career, she became depressed and turned to eating as a way of soothing herself. Although not significantly overweight, she obsessed if her weight went up a pound or so. The source of Joan's compulsive ambition lay with her father, who was a highly successful businessman. He had started out as a poor immigrant and made a large fortune, but he, too, had almost boundless ambitions and, because of them, felt frustrated and depressed with his life despite his great achievements. Past retirement age, he placed all his hopes in his daughter. This unconscious expectation fueled Joan's drivenness. Metaphorically, Joan was captured by a Koschey from her father's psyche.

Joan's predicament introduces another meaning to Koschey, which hinges on a significant detail in the story: when Ivan first encounters the sorcerer in the closet, Koschey begs for water and drinks enormous amounts of it. Deprived of food and drink for a long time, Koschey dramatizes bodily instincts and needs which have been ignored or suppressed and personifies a problem that plagues many accomplished women. Bulimia is often the result, where a woman follows a harsh diet, only to binge and purge periodically. Metaphorically she locks up her hunger and physical instincts in a secret closet, but like Koschey, the instincts burst forth now and then, and take her captive.

Maria Morevna presumably knew the sorcerer's dangerous power. Despite being chained, he remained a constant threat to her. So on some level she must have felt anxious and insecure. This holds true for many successful women. Despite their worldly achievements, they feel as if they are under constant threat,[8] part of which is a realistic fear of a backlash from men—and women—who resent successful women. Another fear, though, comes from feeling like a fraud: "If people really knew me, they would not like me," a woman might tell herself, or "I don't deserve this success—it's only luck." They fear that a Koschey might leap out, exposing and ruining them.

SECLUSION

After being kidnapped by Koschey, Maria Morevna is imprisoned, apparently alone, in Koschey's castle. Her enforced inactivity is compensatory. Up until now, the Queen has been ceaselessly active, ruling her kingdom and going off to many wars. When imprisoned by Koschey, she is forced into introspection, and can thereby discover new aspects of herself. (Here Maria Morevna resembles the princess in "The Queen and the Murderer," who secluded herself in the old woman's house.) In real life, such a period of seclusion may be forced upon a woman by illness or depression.

In many indigenous cultures, menstruation provides the opportunity: women retire to a secluded hut and spend several days by themselves or with a few other women, freed from normal social responsibilities. For women accustomed to activity and mastery, such a retreat may seem like imprisonment, yet the seclusion offers them a chance for renewal and reflection.

As a dark, demonic character, Koschey is an underworld figure. Maria Morevna's imprisonment by him is equivalent to a journey into the lower world, to the realm of death and suffering. Her descent recalls Inanna's journey into the underworld and dramatizes an experience common among women who take the path of power and achievement. Somewhere in their middle years, these highly successful women often fall into depression. Those who postpone marriage and family begin to yearn for both, and fear they will find neither. Many successful women also begin to deal with long-repressed vulnerability—feelings of childhood neediness they ignored, as Gloria Steinem so poignantly notes in *Revolution from Within*. Indeed, in the Tsarina's story, only after she is imprisoned do symbols of feminine vitality begin to emerge, shifting away from warrior themes and masculine models of power.

FEMININE VITALITY

When Ivan is killed by Koschey, he is resurrected by the magic falcon, eagle, and raven. The three birds are male, but they aid Ivan because they are married to his sisters. So help comes to the Prince through his connection to the feminine. This link recalls ancient matrilineal societies which traced kinship through sisters and wives, rather than fathers and husbands. In a subtle way the tale introduces the life-giving power of the feminine.

Feminine symbols become more prominent when Ivan seeks out Baba Yaga. She is the equivalent of a great goddess, with the power of life and death. On his way to her, Ivan encounters three animals: a seabird, a bee, and a lioness. All three are mothers, emphasizing a uniquely feminine capacity—the ability to create new life. The three creatures are also specifically linked with ancient goddesses. Sculptures of bird-like women, for example, appear in the earliest European agricultural settlements, as Marija Gimbutas notes. Many of these bird-women sit on thrones, suggesting that they are divine. Bees are also linked with goddesses. The Greek goddess Demeter was known as the Mother Bee, for example, and the Pythia, the woman who served as the Oracle of Delphi, was known as the Delphic Bee. Lionesses, in turn, are associated with ancient goddesses like Sekmet from Egypt or Atargatis from Mesopotamia.

When Ivan threatens to eat the bird's eggs, the bee's honey, and the lioness's cubs, the animals persuade him not to. The creatures do not offer themselves as substitutes to save their children, but protect their offspring—and themselves. They reject the traditional stereotype of the self-sacrificing mother, who gives up her life for her children. Here the tale offers an important insight. Western tradition separates nurturing and power. If women became mothers, they were expected to give up their ambitions and nurture their children. If women pursued power and careers, they were considered unsuitable as mothers and wives, because they were not nurturing. "Maria Morevna" rejects this old dichotomy with the mother animals, who are both nurturing and powerful. While female birds spend much of their time incubating their eggs or feeding their chicks, they retain the power to fly, which is a potent symbol for freedom. The queen bee devotes all her time to laying eggs, and is the mother of the whole hive. But bees also can sting, and so symbolize a potent aggressive energy. The lioness, in turn, is famous in folklore for tenderness and protectiveness toward her cubs. Lionesses, of course, can be ferocious, and regularly kill large animals. So the three animals in the story specifically symbolize power and nurturing, assertiveness and tenderness. Integrating the two sides is Maria Morevna's task—and that of women today.

The seabird, queen bee, and lioness form a symbolic sequence with the male falcon, eagle, and raven. The falcon and eagle are predatory birds, usually associated with warriors and kings, and the eagle is a traditional image of patriarchal power. The first two birds thus symbolize the kind of power that Maria Morevna starts with—masculine, warrior energy. The raven then enters. Not predatory, but rather a carrion eater, it is linked to death, and foreshadows Maria Morevna's descent into the underworld, with her imprisonment by Koschey. During this descent, she is forced to give up all her masculine power and only then do the symbols of feminine vitality emerge—the mother bird, queen bee, and lioness.

HERDING HORSES

When Ivan meets Baba Yaga, he asks for one of her magic horses and the story notes that all the animals are mares, accentuating the feminine focus. In exchange for a magic horse, Baba Yaga tells Ivan to herd the animals for three days. If he loses any one of them, she warns, he forfeits his head. It is no trifling matter to deal with her! At the same time, she feeds Ivan. In being both deadly and nurturing, she resembles ancient great goddesses, who held the keys to birth and death. Approaching such a numinous, feminine archetype requires great care and caution, which helps explain why Ivan acts as Maria Morevna's go-between with Baba Yaga. The Tsarina has had little contact up till now with the archetypal feminine. She has been a father's daughter, wielding power in a traditionally masculine way, and needs help in dealing with the deep feminine. A woman raised with positive female figures, on the other hand, embraced within the motherline, would be less likely to require a go-between.

The task Baba Yaga gives Ivan is apparently simple—to herd the mares in the fields and bring them back each day. The challenge is deeply symbolic. The horses galloping in all directions dramatize the many competing demands placed upon women, particularly today, when society expects them to become wives and mothers while succeeding in their careers. Women juggle many competing values, desires, obligations, and ambitions. (In contrast to men, who traditionally focus all their energies on one thing, usually a career; metaphorically, men harness their horses and force them to move in one direction, while women herd their horses.)

Herding animals is a common theme in fairy tales about women, but not about men. This suggests that herding is more feminine than masculine. Women, in fact, often refer to herding in describing how they think and act.[9] Herding is inevitable in raising children because mothers must be constantly vigilant to make sure that children do not wander off. Yet too much control will stifle a child's growth. Mothers learn to balance order with spontaneity. In the process, women learn to cope with constant distractions—an inevitable aspect of herding. Particularly with young children, just when a mother starts to concentrate on one task, some disruption occurs requiring her immediate attention elsewhere. Herding horses could not be more difficult!

Herding horses also offers a new image of the psyche. The horses concretize feelings, impulses, images, or inspirations, which arise from the unconscious. The challenge is to maintain some order among them and bring them back home—to make the instincts and insights useful to conscious life. In traditional psychology, these tasks fall upon the ego and superego, which impose order by repressing or suppressing unacceptable impulses. Ego and superego keep the horses penned up in corrals, tethered, or otherwise harnessed, and the underlying goal is to break the horses, reflecting heroic and patriarchal tradition. In herding, horses are free to roam within certain limits. This approach reflects a more flexible, intuitive, creative, and less linear type of thinking—greater openness to the unconscious, tolerance of the irrational, trust in the spontaneous, and a willingness to go with the flow, while moving steadily toward a goal.

Besides providing a new model of the psyche, herding offers a new paradigm of management and leadership, as Mary Catherine Bateson, Sally Helgesen, Helen Astin, and Carole Leland note. Instead of dominating or coercing people, which is the heroic image of power, herding relies upon cooperation, group cohesion, persuasion, and the gradual evolution of many competing interests into one direction. Such herding skills are essential in today's workplace, when executives and managers deal with educated workers who make many demands and with individuals from many diverse cultural backgrounds.

EMPOWERMENT

Ivan succeeds in herding the animals only because he is helped by myriad birds, bees, and wild beasts. They nicely symbolize the unexpected intuitions, inspirations, and hunches that often solve personal difficulties. When some-one sleeps on a problem, for example, after struggling all day, a solution commonly emerges in the form of a dream, or simply upon awakening. Essential to the process is being open to the unconscious. Ivan spared the seabird's eggs, the queen bee's honey, and the lioness's cubs, and so the animals aided him. Psychologically, he respected the unconscious, and did not try to devour it. Here we come to a subtle but important point. In sparing the animals, Ivan denies his hun-ger and starves himself. This recalls how Koschey was locked up without food or water. Koschey personified the repression of bodily instincts. How does Ivan differ? He starves himself in response to messages from the unconscious, from nature. Koschey is restrained by chains, by social convention. Ivan's self-starvation involves balancing one instinct, hunger, with another, intuitions from the deep self.

On the third and last time that Ivan herds the animals, the queen bee tells him to steal a mangy colt rather than a large, healthy one and the colt later turns into a powerful mare. This introduces the concept of empowerment, a spirit of fos-tering the growth of other people. It offers an alternative to the conventional concept of power, based on trying to control or intimidate people—taking a large, strong horse and break-ing it. Empowerment focuses instead on training and educat-ing others, metaphorically feeding a small colt so it can grow into its full potential. Development rather than domination is the key. Childrearing, of course, is a paradigmatic experience of empowerment, but the concept applies to leadership in general—to work and to community issues.

THE SPLIT FEMININE

Both the queen bee and Baba Yaga are connected to great goddess figures in mythology, yet the bee thwarts Baba Yaga's efforts to kill Ivan. So we have two apparently conflicting aspects of the archetypal feminine. This split in the feminine is clear in youth stories, which involve an evil stepmother and a good fairy godmother, as in "Cinderella." In those tales, the split dramatizes the good and bad aspects of a mother, which children must learn to integrate. Maria Morevna's tale involves a deeper meaning. The conflict between Baba Yaga and the queen bee reflects a split in the feminine psyche, found in most cultures. The witch reflects a highly negative view of the great goddess and feminine energy—the misogynist prejudice that powerful women are evil witches. Women who follow the path of achievement and authority often internalize this message, because they identify so strongly with traditional masculine values. (Elizabeth I of England, for instance, believed that all women were childish and foolish—except herself, of course, since she was the sovereign.) To counter these negative stereotypes, the unconscious sends positive images of the feminine in the form of dreams, intuitions, visions—and fairy tales. The queen bee symbolizes these authentic, spontaneous, instinctual affirmations of the feminine, not yet distorted by human convention. A woman's task is to look for the queen bee and to heed her message.

When Baba Yaga chases Ivan, she travels in her magic mortar. This is a traditional theme in Russian fairy tales, but the image is subversive. Mortars would normally be used to grind grain or other foodstuffs—backbreaking work assigned to women who must stay home to do it. Baba Yaga uses the mortar to travel where she wishes. She takes a symbol of domestic drudgery and makes it an emblem of her power and freedom, mocking social convention in the process.

Ivan manages to kill Baba Yaga by weakening the bridge over the fire. He acts as Maria Morevna's agent in doing so, and this echoes the central theme from "The Queen and the Murderer"—sometimes a woman must kill off relationships in order to protect herself and continue developing as an individual. Baba Yaga may also be interpreted as a negative mother, as well as a woman's own internalized denigration of the feminine, both of which must be killed off.

After killing Baba Yaga, Ivan returns to Maria Morevna,

and the two flee on Ivan's mare. When Koschey finally manages to reach them, it is Ivan's horse who fells the evil sorcerer. Ivan only kills Koschey when the sorcerer is unconscious on the ground. The magic mare defeats Koschey, so once again feminine energy is crucial.

IVAN AS A NEW MALE

Thus far I have interpreted Ivan mainly as an animus figure, representing a part of Maria Morevna's psyche, but he can also be interpreted as a man in his own right. Here the story offers women insights about dealing with men. Ivan starts off as a gentle man who is loving, loyal, and nurturing to Maria Morevna, the kind of man many women often hope for as a husband or lover, and who appears frequently in women's novels and short stories. Annis Pratt calls these male figures "green world lovers," because they are usually associated with the forest or wilderness, far from tyrannical patriarchs and macho heroes.

Men like Ivan, women might exclaim, do not exist! Maria Morevna's story is a fairy tale, after all. But fairy tales are not just wishful thinking, they are utopian, and envision what life can be like, not how life usually is. Men like Ivan may be rare in competitive Western society, but they are more common in other cultures, such as those of Thailand, Bali, and Tahiti.[10] So we can interpret Ivan as a "new male," what a man ideally develops into, when informed by and in sympathy with the feminine. Today, these may be men who have been moved by feminism and who have nurtured their own feminine sides. Inviting as they may seem, though, "Maria Morevna" points out several problems with them.

Ivan, for instance, is naive and undisciplined at the beginning. After being warned not to open the forbidden closet, he impulsively opens it. Then he is moved by pity to give water to Koschey, never wondering why Maria Morevna had the man locked up so securely. Ivan is what Robert Bly calls a "soft male." In real life, women often discover that such men are really adolescents. They are what Jungians call puers, eternal youths, unable to make commitments or forge deep emotional bonds. They seek a mother figure to take care of them, and their gentleness often masks neediness rather than kindness. Women then become trapped into taking care of them. Women require men who develop on their own. Ivan does just that, gaining depth and strength in opposing Koschey and Baba Yaga. He becomes a heroic figure but does not act like a macho male, strutting about or trying to control Maria Morevna. When Ivan finds her imprisoned in Koschey's castle, for example, she reproaches him for opening the secret closet and releasing Koschey. Ivan apologizes and admits his mistake, something a macho hero rarely does. But Ivan also says they should not dwell on the past and instead should try to escape from Koschey. So he demonstrates a traditional masculine emphasis on problem-solving and action. Ivan is a post-heroic man, who integrates power and gentleness, heroism and relationship.

Here the Tsarina's story contains an important insight. "New males" like Ivan are not found ready-made. They develop only after a long period of time. Women need the skill to pick out men with the potential for such development—just as Tsarina Maria recognized Ivan's worth and married him.

In describing Ivan's adventures, "Maria Morevna" contains keen insights about men's development, and this is true of women's tales in general. The tales, though, do not imply that women are supposed to take care of men, sacrificing themselves for this purpose. To the contrary: in Maria Morevna's tale, Ivan must take care of her, and work toward her development. The story also emphasizes that they must both grow, with Ivan reclaiming his heroic side and Maria her nurturing energy. Only then can the two relate to each other on a deep, mutual, authentic level.

FINDING A NEW BALANCE

To summarize this discussion of "Maria Morevna," I turn to a dream which parallels the fairy tale. In her dream, "Karen" walked through an unfamiliar land. She came upon a building made of steel and glass where women, dressed in military uniforms, were doing calisthenics in a stiff, rigid manner. Karen felt repelled by them, and circled around the building without being noticed. She continued on her way and came to a large pool of filthy, stagnant water. She realized she had to swim across the pool, but hesitated, feeling disgusted, before finally plunging in. She then entered a cottage where a fire burned brightly on the hearth, near an old-fashioned four-poster bed covered with luxurious furs. Everything was warm, cozy, and delightful in the cabin. A woman then appeared, and told Karen this was a place of love. She longed to bring her husband, David, to the cottage for a romantic evening, and here she woke up.

Karen associated her dream journey with her life course, and her focus on achievement and career. The exercise class of military women, Karen felt, dramatized her fears of what she was turning into—a woman who left behind all kindness and capacity to care for others. The fact that the women were in a group, moving en masse in a military drill, suggested they represented a collective energy, a force of conformity rather than individuality. These women correspond in the fairy tale to Maria Morevna as warrior queen, wielding a traditionally masculine type of power. Like the Tsarina, Karen was also a father's daughter, feeling more affinity for her father and the masculine than her mother and the feminine.

In Karen's dream, the military women did calisthenics in a stiff, rigid way, which Karen linked to how she treated her own body. Karen followed strict, often unrealistic diets, until her hunger burst forth during moments of stress, and she binged. Her denigration and domination of the body corresponds to Koschey, locked up without food and water in the closet.

Karen interpreted the filthy pool of water as her shadow,

and all the dark things in and around her she would rather not face. These issues included conflicts with her depressed mother, who had seemed horrifyingly needy to Karen throughout her childhood; sorrow that her father, despite his general support of her, really did not understand her and could not talk about anything outside of business; as well as anger and shame at the many humiliations she had suffered during adolescence, in an all-girls' Catholic school. Karen's immersion in the foul pool is equivalent to Maria Morevna's imprisonment by Koschey. Both women were forced to face the shadow and descend into the underworld.

In Karen's dream, on the other side of the pool, she came to a cozy cabin. The cottage, Karen felt, symbolized love, relationship, sensuality, and relaxation—all the elements she had neglected in favor of competition and career advancement. In this magic place, Karen wanted her husband to be with her, and she quickly realized that he personified all the cabin's qualities: he was emotionally expressive, nurturing, and accommodating. David played the same role in Karen's life as Ivan did with Maria Morevna.

Karen's dream heralded a creative phase in her life. She took on new responsibilities at the university where she taught. But she handled her tasks in a different way. Instead of trying to control everything, as she was used to doing, she began to delegate work, encouraging discussion and cooperation. The result was more chaos than she was used to, but also more creative endeavors. She switched from control and competition to herding and empowerment as a model of leadership. With her new outlook, Karen felt much less exhausted by her work, and her binge eating ceased. She also silenced her inner critic, which had until then goaded her on in almost all areas of her life, like an evil witch. Metaphorically, she killed off her inner Baba Yaga. At home, Karen began to explore a more vulnerable and nurturing side of herself, openly admitting her neediness to her husband, something she had avoided doing before. She became more assertive and more accommodating, and her relationship with her husband blossomed and deepened. Like the Tsarina and Ivan, Karen and David arrived at a deeper, more authentic relationship, based on an integration of power and love, achievement and intimacy.

This integration is the ultimate message of "Maria Morevna"—a challenge and a promise. The story calls women, and men, to move beyond traditional gender roles, to find a new, deeper balance between masculine and feminine, power and love. The tale also offers guidance along the way and the reassurance that others have made the journey successfully and left their stories as markers for those who follow.

PART II

Wisdom

CHAPTER 4

"The Three Little Eggs":
The Power of Intuition

(a Swazi tale from Africa[1])

nce upon a time, a woman lived with her husband and their two children. The husband was cruel and forced his wife to work from dawn to dusk, beating her for no reason and even burning her with flaming sticks. Finally, the woman had enough. When her husband went to a festival, she mustered her courage, gathered her children, and fled into the mountains. There were many villages beyond the hills where she hoped she could find work to support herself and the children.

The woman walked and walked, her baby girl on her back and her young son at her side. She followed a stream, barely a trickle of water in the dry season. When she paused to rest, she noticed a bird's nest in a leafless tree. She picked up the nest, thinking it would be a good toy for her children, and found three small eggs inside even though it was winter. "Be careful not to break the eggs," she told her children, as she gave them the nest to play with.

The mother continued on her way until night fell. The woman looked around, saw no likely shelter, and became frightened. "What am I to do?" she asked herself, thinking of the wild animals that prowled at night and how she would protect her children. A tiny voice answered, "Take the path to the right." The woman was astonished because the voice had come from one of the eggs in the nest. And to her right was a path, nearly hidden in the underbrush.

The woman followed the trail, and came to a large hut. No one answered her greeting, but she went in and found the house filled with bowls of fresh milk and piles of ripe fruit. The woman fed her children, ate a hearty dinner herself, and then they all fell fast asleep, exhausted from their flight.

In the morning, the woman arose, roused her children, and resumed their journey through the mountains. When they came to a fork in the road, the woman puzzled over which path to take.

"Choose the left," a voice said, and it was the second egg that spoke. The woman followed the advice and arrived at a gigantic hut. Inside, the mother saw an ogre, so enormous that its snoring shook the earth. The beast was covered with reddish hair, sported two enormous horns, and had a long tail. All around him lay pots filled with blood. She dared not move, for fear the beast would awake and devour them all.

At that moment, the woman heard the third egg speak up. "Pick up the round white rock by the door, climb on the roof, and drop it on the monster!"

"The rock is too big!" she protested softly. "How can I lift it?"

"Do as I say," the egg insisted.

The woman lifted her children onto the roof to keep them safe, then grasped the stone beside the door, and, to her surprise, lifted it easily. She climbed on the roof, peered down the smoke hole, and prepared to drop the rock on the monster. Suddenly another ogre entered the hut, dragging the bodies of several people with him.

The woman stifled a cry, and put down her stone. "I cannot kill them both at once! One will surely catch us and eat us! What am I to do?"

All three eggs immediately whispered, "Wait until they sleep, then flee." So the woman kept silent and rocked her children to keep them calm. The second ogre sniffed the air a few times, shrugged his shoulders, cooked the dead people, and ate them. Finally he fell asleep.

When the snoring of both monsters shook the hut, the woman crept down from the roof with her children and fled. She ran until she could no longer see the ogre's hut, and then continued through the mountains. The path entered a thicket of bushes and the woman could hardly see anything ahead. Suddenly she rounded a bend and came to a clearing beneath an enormous evergreen tree. The mother stopped with horror. Under the tree slept a huge monster, even larger than the two ogres. The creature had thick, matted hair, the snout of a jackal, enormous horns, and a long tail.

"An ogress!" the woman whispered in terror. There was no way forward except past the monster, and the woman dared not turn back, fearful of the two ogres in the hut. "What am I to do?" she whispered.

The eggs spoke in unison. "Take the axe next to the ogress, climb the tree, and drop it on her head!"

The woman thought a moment, put her children high up in the tree to keep them safe, and then picked up the enormous axe. Shaking with fear, she climbed onto a branch over the ogress, and let the axe fall. It hit the monster's head, but the ogress only moaned, merely stunned.

"Quickly!" the eggs spoke up. "Climb down and use the axe to kill the monster before she wakes up!"

The woman jumped out of the tree and retrieved the axe. The ogress began to open her eyes, and the poor mother trembled in every bone of her body. She ran toward the monster, striking her with the axe. The beast shrieked, fell over, and died.

In the next moment, the body of the ogress split open, and out walked hundreds of women, men, and children, with their herds of cattle, pigs, and goats. The people gathered before the woman and bowed.

"You have freed us from the ogress," the people said. "She swallowed us whole, and we have lived in her belly for many years." Out of gratitude, they asked the woman to be their Queen.

The woman demurred. "It was not I who saved you, but

these three eggs!" she said, pointing to the bird's nest. At that moment, the earth trembled, the eggs vanished, and in their place appeared three great princes.

The eldest of the three men knelt before the woman. "By your courage," he said, "you have freed my brothers and me from an evil spell." Then he asked the woman to marry him. "You are free to do as you wish," the prince explained, "because your husband in your old village has died." The woman thought a moment and consented. So before the assembled people, the brave woman married the prince. She became Queen of the new land, and he, her consort. And from that day on, the new Queen, her husband, and her children lived happily and in peace.

OPPRESSION AND SELF-LIBERATION

The protagonist of this striking African tale is a woman abused by a cruel husband, amplifying the theme of women's oppression. The mother musters her courage to leave the abuse and a major factor is no doubt her two young children: in real life many brutalized women, beaten into thinking they are not worthy of anything and terrified of further attacks, leave their violent husbands only when their children are threatened.

By leaving her cruel husband, the woman does the best thing for herself and her children, removing them from danger, giving them a model of courage to emulate, and at the same time finding a new life for herself. By taking care of herself, she also helps her children, integrating assertiveness and nurturing. The task is particularly relevant today as women combine career and family. "Three Little Eggs" dramatizes the stressfulness of the situation: the mother must worry about her two children while she travels through unknown territory, and her journey is an apt metaphor for women making their way through the work world, juggling career and family, achievement and intimacy. As the Swazi tale suggests, there are many monsters lurking out there, but the key to a woman's success lies in her heeding the counsel of her true self, the wisdom of her soul.

THE BIRD'S NEST

On her journey, the mother finds a bird's nest containing three eggs. Eggs are an archetypal feminine symbol, and appear prominently in women's tales and in the rituals of many women's secret societies, such as the Lisimbu in Africa or the ancient Mordvins in Russia.[2] Moreover, the eggs in the story are unusual since the tale notes that it is winter, when birds usually do not lay eggs. The wintry season parallels the woman's predicament. She has left her old, familiar world, psychologically dying with respect to her former life, like the warrior wife in Chapter 2, who was shut up in the casket and thrown in the river. Yet in the midst of this dismal situation, new life emerges, symbolized by the eggs.

The woman picks up the bird's nest to use as a toy to quiet and comfort her children. Tired and frightened, they have presumably been clamoring for attention, rest, and food. Although the woman must focus on action—escaping from a husband liable to track her down—she does not neglect her children's needs. She balances action and feeling, motion and emotion, and provides a new model of leadership, which contrasts with the patriarchal paradigm and its dismissal of feelings. The mother integrates efficiency and empathy, decisiveness and tenderness, as most successful career women learn to do.[3]

THE INNER VOICE

When night falls, the mother is fearful of wild animals. (Remember, the story is set in Africa, with lions and hyenas, not just wolves, as in European stories.) In this dark moment, one of the eggs speaks to her. They can be interpreted as a feminine source of wisdom, a woman's deep self. In fairy tales about girls, this inner voice is usually associated with the mother—for instance, when a doll given by a mother advises her daughter during a crisis. The woman here has no mother to help, or any link to the motherline, and there are probably two reasons for this. First, the woman has moved from her family to live with her husband, which breaks contact with her mother. Second, the woman is an adult, and her task is to find her own inner voice and wisdom. Unlike girls in youth tales, it is not enough to turn to a mother for answers. She must find her own way.

What is crucial is that the woman pays attention to the advice of the eggs. The mother does not ignore them when they speak, nor does she think she is going crazy. She heeds the eggs, strange and irrational as that might seem, reversing the social conditioning imposed on most women. As Lyn Mikel Brown, Carol Gilligan, Mary Belenky, and their colleagues demonstrated, girls start ignoring their inner voices in adolescence, succumbing to relentless social pressures to listen rather than to speak, and to agree with others rather than to argue. After years of self-censorship, when a woman's true self speaks up, it often appears only as a small voice, which is easily overlooked or ignored. And what a woman's inner self says may seem crazy or strange at first, because it goes against social convention.

In the story, the eggs speak to the harried mother, and speech, hearing, and voice are major metaphors for women. Women struggle to find their voice, to speak their truth, and to be heard. (By contrast, men focus more on vision than voice, going on vision quests, for example. Many women also note that men tend not to listen!)

The mother finds the eggs in the wilderness, near a stream, a typical scenario in women's tales. Women find help in the wild, from the unconscious, not from civilization and social convention. The help is also specifically associated with water, pointing to the fluid life-giving realm of feeling and intuition. The story adds that the stream is barely a trickle, since it is the dry season. Metaphorically, feminine wisdom and vitality have almost been destroyed, but even a trickle is enough, as the story reveals.

THE SANCTUARY

After following the first egg's advice, the woman finds a hut full of food, with no one around, so she and her children eat hungrily and spend the night. Remarkably, the owner does not return, and no one challenges the woman. In real life, of course, no homeowner would leave a house full of food unguarded in the wilderness—animals would surely find a way in and eat everything in sight! The hut is thus a magical place, and its appearance may seem to be mere wish fulfillment. But the theme recurs in other women's stories and is psychologically accurate. Many women find sanctuary and renewal in nature, by taking solitary walks or gardening. Away from other people and freed from social demands, women can hear the counsel of their true selves. (By contrast, in fairy tales, male protagonists typically struggle and suffer in the wilderness, without conventional male prerogatives.)

In the morning, the woman and her children leave their refuge and continue on their journey. The woman is not tempted to stay in the magical hut, comfortable though it may be. Instead, she strikes out once more into the unknown, facing danger. One reason she does so might be fear of her husband tracking her down. But I suspect that she also perseveres because a deep part of her knows what she must do and recognizes that she has not reached her final destination.

THE TWO OGRES

When the mother comes to a fork in the path, the second egg leads her to a gigantic hut, where a monster lies sleeping. The ogre is male and a cannibal—his partner appears later and eats several people for dinner. The ogre also has red hair, and is surrounded by pots of blood, presumably human. The color and blood underscore the monster's aggressiveness and violence. So he is another example of the ominous animus. Like the woman's abusive husband, the ogre makes a good symbol for violent men and social forces in competitive societies which often attack women.

The third magic egg advises the woman to kill the ogre by dropping a rock on him. The safe, easy thing to do would be to flee, avoiding the ogre entirely. Yet the woman's inner voice pushes her into a confrontation. In real life, this reflects an important stage in a woman's journey, when she recognizes the oppression she has suffered, becomes angry, and takes up arms against her situation. Since men are usually the established authorities, they become the targets of women's outrage—and appear to be ogres.[4]

The woman hesitates to pick up the rock, saying it is too heavy. The egg insists, so she tries to pick the rock up and finds she can do it easily. She assumed that the task was too much for her, but discovers she is much stronger than she thought. This is a major function of her confrontation with the ogre—she begins to learn about her own strength and resources.

Dropping the stone on the ogre is an indirect but wise strategy. The mother is clearly no physical match for the ogre and she must look out for her children, so she uses her wits instead. This introduces a vital theme in women's tales— women's wisdom—which other stories will develop further. Dropping the stone on the ogre also uses the force of nature— gravity—rather than her own strength. Or to put it another way, nature amplifies her strength. The stone is also white and round, and so resembles an egg. Many African cultures use such white stones as part of initiations into women's societies, suggesting that the mother's ordeal is an initiatory experience.

Just as the woman is about to drop the stone on the ogre, another fiend appears and the woman quickly realizes that her plan will not work. If she kills one monster, the other will attack. The mother is not aggressive in a mindless way, attacking impulsively. She is reflective, adaptable, and flexible. The story counters an unconscious fear many women have— the fantasy that if they are assertive, they will become aggressive or damaging, unable to control themselves. This does not occur when a woman heeds her inner voice.

In retreating, the mother breaks with the traditional heroic model of power. A hero is usually a solitary warrior who fights to the death—but he has only himself to worry about. The woman has her two children to protect. Heroic aggression is typically the province of unmarried males, who have no other responsibilities. Wisdom, on the other hand, focuses on responsibility to family, friends, and community. And it is wisdom that the mother exemplifies.

By quietly leaving the ogres and continuing her journey, the woman symbolizes a new phase in women's development. After becoming angry with an oppressive situation, seeing men and society as ogres and fighting with them, women usually move on, taking the anger and using its energy to build a new, more rewarding life. Women shift their attention from social demons to what they need and want. The story illuminates the issues that emerge next.

THE OGRESS

The woman comes upon an ogress, and the magic eggs advise her to kill the ogress. The task has many meanings. For instance, the ogress wields an axe and devours people whole, making her a figure of unbridled aggression and violence— just like the male ogres. But the story says that the ogress is larger and more terrifying than the male ogres. This reflects a belief in most cultures that aggressive women are monsters while aggressive men are heroes. Many women therefore imagine that their assertiveness is hideous and that an ogress lurks deep within their souls.[5] Women must slay this misconception.

As a female monster, the ogress also represents the shadow side of women. Confronting the shadow, after all, is a gender-neutral task. Note that the ogress appears after the two male ogres, suggesting that women must confront men's shadows first, and then turn to their own. The sequence is realistic. Most cultures blame women such as Eve and Pandora for humanity's misery. Husbands and bosses follow suit, so women tend to blame themselves when things go wrong. "Three Little Eggs" insists that women stop this false self-blaming and instead confront the ogres of oppressive stereotypes. The next step, though, is to confront the feminine shadow, the ogress.

At the end of the story, many people and animals—enough for a whole new kingdom—emerge from the ogress's body. So she gives birth to a new world, and this brings up the archetype of maternity and motherhood. As a dangerous character, though, the ogress focuses on the shadow side of the archetype. In real life, many women feel devoured by maternal stereotypes—the expectation that they be ever patient, self-sacrificing, and always available for others. Women must slay this monstrous stereotype.

In the story, the ogress is the last obstacle that the woman faces, and appears just before the woman achieves a great triumph, freeing a whole country and becoming queen. The link between "ogress" and "success" brings up an important issue—women's "fear of success," or, more accurately, the fear that being successful means sacrificing family and relationships.[6] Successful women also encounter many prejudices, such as the belief that career women are "unfeminine," cold, or ruthless—that is, some kind of ogress. Women must defy these negative feminine stereotypes. As a negative mother figure, the ogress also dramatizes how maternal issues often emerge when a woman is on the verge of success.[7] Women, for example, may feel guilty about achieving something their mothers could not, or they may fear that their mothers will reject them if they are successful.

KILLING THE OGRESS AND FREEING THE WORLD

The eggs advise the woman to attack the monster while she sleeps, taking the ogress's axe and dropping it on her. Once again, the woman's inner voice suggests an indirect approach. Here she must use the power of the ogress, symbolized by the axe, against the monster herself. This is psychological aikido, the martial art that focuses on redirecting the enemy's own energy against him or her.

When the woman drops the axe, she fails to kill the ogress and must then attack her directly. In doing so, the woman carries out the traditional role of the youthful male hero, who battles and kills an evil monster. The story thus emphasizes that heroism and courage are not "masculine," but simply human, and that wisdom is needed to determine when to be heroic and when to retreat, when to make a direct confrontation and when to be indirect. That knowledge, the story reveals, comes from a woman's deep self in time of need.

After the woman kills the ogress, hundreds of people emerge from the monster's body. On a psychological level, by killing the ogress the woman breaks through the last obstacle to reclaiming her true self. The people and animals that emerge symbolize her vitality and strength, previously obstructed by negative mother issues and oppressive stereotypes of motherhood. There are also societal implications to the ogress's death. By reclaiming her own strength and developing as an individual, the woman awakens a whole world from a long sleep, just like the protagonist in "The Queen and the Murderer." Both women symbolically create a new social order. If the outcome of women's individuation is waking the world, it is a result, not a duty. The brave woman kills the ogress to protect herself and her children, only later discovering the unexpected outcome—the liberation of society.

THE PRINCES

After their liberation, the people thank the woman, but she credits the advice of the magic eggs. Women often downplay their successes in public because most cultures ostracize women of accomplishment, as Carolyn Heilbrun notes. In misogynist cultures, many women learn to denigrate themselves: "If I did it, it could not be a major achievement." Only when writing in private diaries do women take credit for themselves. Yet feminine modesty reflects wisdom, too. Women are usually very sensitive to relationships, and recognize the need for cooperation. So women often realize that credit for accomplishments must usually be shared among many individuals.

When the woman praises the eggs' wisdom, they suddenly turn into three handsome princes who thank her for freeing them from an evil spell. The eldest marries the woman, and they become rulers of the new country. Again, it is the woman who frees a helpless prince—and in this case, actually three of them.

As inner characters, the princes are animus figures and illustrate how the masculine evolves in a woman's experience: in the story, the abusive husband appears first, followed by the monstrous ogres and finally the kind princes. As women reclaim their strength,[8] they feel less threatened about being assertive and outspoken, so the malevolence of the animus diminishes. The sequence is clear in women's dreams, as Karen Signell, Polly Young-Eisendrath, and Florence Widermann observed.

The three princes can also be interpreted as outer figures, representing men in a woman's life. Helpful and supportive, the princes are "new males," like Ivan in "Maria Morevna." But the brave woman must release them from their spell—from traditional patriarchal privileges and macho ideals. A woman's inner journey, in fact, often forces men to develop.

The fact that princes emerge from the eggs is something of a paradox—male figures from a feminine symbol. This does not imply that the center of a woman's soul is masculine. It suggests, I think, that deep within the feminine psyche is an interest in "the other." This focus usually manifests itself in attention to relationships, but "the other" could also involve ideas, images, nature, and art.

EMPOWERMENT

The woman began as an abused wife and ends up as queen of a new realm, but the whole process begins with a small action: she picks up a bird's nest to use as a toy for her children. Her act of nurturance leads to wisdom, energy, and liberation. This is empowerment, the power of love and care, a central theme in the stories to come.

CHAPTER 5

"The Wise Wife":

Cleverness and Courage

(from Iraq[1])

 nce upon a time, a saddler and his wife lived with their three daughters. The man worked hard, and over the years saved a hundred gold coins, which he sewed for safekeeping inside a saddle. Sometime later, he sold the saddle by mistake, and only discovered his error after the customer had left the shop and the city.

A year later, the customer returned to have the saddle repaired. The craftsman could not believe his good fortune when he found his savings still in the saddle. He retrieved his treasure and made up a little song to celebrate his luck, singing it every day:

> "I hid it and lost it.
> I waited and found it.
> It's my little secret,
> And no one will ever know."

One day, the Sultan passed by the shop and heard the song. "What is your secret?" the Sultan inquired.

"If I told you," the saddler said, "would it be a secret?"

The monarch frowned. "I am the Sultan. Tell me your secret." The saddler refused, so the Sultan demanded angrily, "Do you have a family?"

"A good wife and three beautiful daughters, not yet married," the saddler answered.

"In that case," the Sultan commanded, "bring your daughters to my palace tomorrow morning, and make sure all three are pregnant by then. Otherwise I will cut your head off!"

"But, Majesty!" the father exclaimed in horror. "My daughters are virgins! How can they become pregnant? And if they do, how will they marry? They will be ruined for life!"

"That's for you to figure out," the monarch laughed as he rode off.

The poor man returned home in despair. His youngest daughter, the wisest of his children, noticed his distress. "What troubles you?" she asked him, and her father explained the problem.

The daughter thought a moment and then said, "Do not despair, Father. Just buy me three water pots, and I will show the Sultan how three virgins can be pregnant!"

The next morning the youngest daughter put a pot under her dress, told her sisters to do the same, and coached them in what to say. When the maidens appeared before the Sultan, he asked the eldest, "How long have you been pregnant, and what do you crave?"

The eldest daughter bowed and said, "I am three months pregnant, sire, and I yearn for salted cucumbers." The Sultan asked the middle daughter the same questions, and she explained, "I am six months pregnant, sire, and I crave pickled eggplants." When the Sultan asked the youngest daughter, she replied, "I am due any day now, and I crave fish roasted under the seven seas."

"But how can one roast fish underwater?" the Sultan protested. "That is impossible!"

"The same way a virgin can be pregnant," she retorted, and the three sisters quickly left the palace.

The next day the Sultan summoned an old woman, gave her a purse full of gold, and sent her to the saddler's house to ask for the hand of the youngest daughter. "Such a clever woman," the Sultan thought to himself, "should be my wife." When the old woman looked in the purse and saw the gold, she stole two coins. Then she made her way to the saddler's house where the youngest daughter opened the door.

"Is your mother home?" the old woman asked.

"No," the youngest daughter replied, "she is away changing one into two."

The crone could make no sense of the answer, so she said, "Well, then, let me see your eldest sister."

"She is changing black into white," the youngest daughter explained.

The old woman persisted. "Is your middle sister in?"

"She is out picking roses," the daughter replied.

"But it is winter," the old woman protested. "There are no roses anywhere!" She shook her head, thinking the maiden was crazy. "Here is a gift the Sultan sent to you," the crone muttered, handing over the purse.

The youngest daughter counted the gold coins and turned to the old woman. "I have a message for you to take back to the Sultan. Ask him this, 'When giving a lamb as a gift, does one cut off the tail?' "

The old woman shook her head again, returned to the Sultan, and reported everything the maiden had said. "I fear she is mad," she sighed. The Sultan thought for a moment and smiled.

"She is not, old woman," the Sultan said. "She is truly wise—fit to be my wife! When she said her mother was out changing one into two, she meant her mother was a midwife, delivering a baby. The sister who was making black into white is a beautician, removing hair from a woman's body. And the sister picking roses in winter was embroidering flowers on cloth." Then the Sultan grew stern. "As for the lamb without the tail, she meant that you stole money from the purse I gave you! Never do that again, or I will punish you!"

The next day the Sultan sent the old woman back with another marriage proposal and this time the saddler and his youngest daughter accepted. The wedding was soon celebrated, but on that very day, as the new wife waited in the bridal chamber, the monarch rode off to wage war in the land of Siin. The woman waited and waited for her new husband. When he did not appear, she asked the servants where he had gone, and sat thinking a moment. Then she took off her wedding finery, put on the uniform of a general, assembled an army, and set off after the Sultan.

Several days later, she found her husband's troops encamped by a river. She assembled her army on the other bank, as if she were an enemy. Then she sent a messenger to the Sultan, challenging him to a chess game, and the Sultan took up the contest. When the two met, he did not recognize his wife, and she won the first round of chess. As a prize, she demanded the Sultan's jeweled dagger. He gave it up, played another game, won it, and demanded his dagger back.

"I suggest a better prize," his wife said. "I have a beautiful slave who is a virgin. I will let you spend the night with her." The Sultan agreed.

The wife departed, took off her uniform, adorned herself with jewelry and perfume, and went to the Sultan. The monarch was delighted at her beauty and not once did he recognize his wife. The next day, she returned home with her army, while the Sultan went to war in Siin.

Nine months later, the wife gave birth to a beautiful baby boy, and she named him Siin. Two years after, the Sultan returned from his war, but he greeted his wife only briefly before departing for another battle in the land of Masiin. The next day, the wife took off her gowns, donned the uniform of a general, and marshaled her own army. She followed her husband, set up camp nearby, and sent a herald to the Sultan, challenging him to a chess tournament.

He accepted and when the two met, he never recognized his wife. She won the first game and claimed the Sultan's prayer beads as a prize. The Sultan won the second match and asked for his beads back. "I have a better offer," his wife countered, "a beautiful slave woman who has known a man only once. If you like, you can have her for the night." The Sultan agreed, so the wife left, adorned herself, went to the Sultan, and they spent the night together. The next day, the Sultan departed for Masiin while his wife returned home with her army. Nine months later, she gave birth to another beautiful baby boy and named him Masiin.

Over a year afterward, the Sultan returned from his war, laden with booty. He hardly glanced at his wife, recruited more troops, and departed for a campaign in far-off Gharb. So she dressed as a general once more, assembled her troops, and pursued the Sultan.

When she caught up with him she sent a messenger inviting him to play chess. He accepted and she won the first round, claiming the Sultan's headcloth as a prize. He prevailed the next time and asked for his headcloth back.

"I have a better idea," the wife suggested. "I offer you a beautiful slave woman who knows all the arts of love. You can spend a night with her." The Sultan agreed, so she left, dressed in a beautiful gown, and went to her husband. The next morning, the monarch departed for his war in Gharb, while she returned home with her troops. Nine months later she gave birth to a beautiful baby girl, whom she named Gharb.

Three years passed before the Sultan returned from his war. He did not speak to his wife because he had decided to take a new bride and planned to marry a princess, more fitting to his royal station than the daughter of a saddler. When the wedding day arrived, the first wife dressed her three children elegantly, and gave the elder son the Sultan's dagger to wear. She put the monarch's prayer beads in the hands of the middle child, and his headcloth on her daughter. Then she taught the three children a song.

Just before the wedding began, the children appeared before the Sultan and sang:

"He wins in war,
He wins in chess.
He wins at love,
He wins on quests.
Our little secret,
Will he guess?"

The Sultan looked at the children, and recognized the dagger, prayer beads, and headcloth. Then he stared at their mother and finally realized what she had done. "You were the generals who challenged me, and the slaves who slept with me!" he exclaimed. "And these are my children?" His wife nodded.

The Sultan canceled the new wedding, sent away the princess, and turned to his wife. "You are more wise than any woman in the world. I will have no one else for my wife!" The Sultan and his wife embraced, and the monarch hugged his three children. Then he ordered a feast for his true wife and newly found family. And from that day on, they all lived in happiness, love, wisdom, and peace.

FATHER AND DAUGHTER

The protagonist of this Iraqi tale is clever, wise, resourceful, strong, sexual, and brave. Nor is she unusual, because other stories from around the world are almost identical.[2] The tales celebrate the vitality and wit of adult women. Yet like other women's stories, the tale begins by focusing on a man, the father of the wise woman, before shifting to her, the real protagonist.

The father loses his gold because of a blunder and regains it by good fortune. The father is lucky, and the point is important. In a strongly patriarchal society like Muslim Iraq, a father who has no sons is counted terribly unlucky. The tale repudiates this convention by insisting that the saddler is blessed with good luck and showing what his true treasure is—his wise daughter.

Delighted by regaining his gold, the father makes up a song about the event, then refuses to explain it to the Sultan. The father is stubborn here and endangers his daughters. His fault causes problems for them, just as occur often in real life. The youngest daughter must then remedy the situation.

The angry Sultan orders the saddler to send his daughters to the palace, pregnant. This would ruin the women, since brides must be virgins in Muslim tradition. The Sultan's action thus brings up a familiar theme—women's oppression.

The father despairs, but his youngest daughter notices his distress; she is sensitive and perceptive. When he explains the problem, she tells him what to do and *he heeds her*. Part of her confidence and courage later in the story no doubt comes from being respected and validated by her father. Other women's tales emphasize the point—successful women have empowering fathers and mothers.[3]

THE POWER OF METAPHOR

The youngest sister coaches her two siblings, and the three maidens present themselves to the Sultan with water pots under their dresses to look pregnant. The elder sisters mimic the odd cravings of pregnancy and say they hanker for salted cucumbers and pickled eggplants, while the youngest explains that she longs for fish roasted under the seven seas. When the Sultan asks how it is possible to roast fish underwater, the youngest daughter fires back with her carefully planned retort—"The same way a virgin can be pregnant."

Like her father, the daughter is brave in defying the Sultan to his face. But she uses oblique means, relying on a metaphor, so the Sultan can ignore her criticism if he wishes. She is also extremely clever, maneuvering the Sultan into asking how fish can be roasted under the sea, and so forcing him to shift from his usual mode of operation, which is to demand and command, as patriarchs usually do. Only when he becomes open-minded and listens, if only for a moment, does the wise woman introduce her point of view. She also has the Sultan assert something similar to what she wants to say. The monarch declares that it is absurd to talk about roasting fish underwater, so she points out that it is equally ludicrous to expect virgins to be pregnant.

The use of such clever allegories surfaces repeatedly in women's literature, art, and craft.[4] Women writers in the past relied on irony, satire, parable, and allegory, just as the clever daughter did, using a double voice, one conventional and obvious and the other hidden and subversive. Even traditional nursery rhymes contain these double meanings: the music is soothing, but the lyrics often reflect a mother's ambivalence about the conventional childrearing role, and a desire to be free of her child.

In using metaphors with the Sultan, the wise daughter offers a practical model for women today who are trying to communicate with men. Raised in traditional ways, many men avoid the emotional sharing important to women. The fairy tale suggests that women can nevertheless communicate through parables and stories. "Barbara," a businesswoman in her late fifties, provides an example. She and her husband had difficulties with their youngest son, who spent most of his time in college "partying." Barbara tried to talk with him, but their exchanges always ended up in terrible fights. She asked her husband to deal with their son, but he insisted the young man was just going through a phase. Then Barbara had a remarkable dream, in which she saw a navy ship at port with its crew sitting idly on deck. The ship was leaving soon on a training voyage, and the novice crew was waiting for the training officers. She tried to approach the ship, but military police escorted her away. When Barbara woke up, she realized the significance of her dream, and told her husband about it. He understood the message, too: their son struggled with issues of male initiation and needed male leadership. The dream galvanized Barbara's husband, and he made a concerted effort to talk with their son. The young man's difficulties gradually improved. Barbara's dream provided a powerful metaphor that her husband and son could heed.

THE MOTHERLINE

The Sultan is intrigued by the youngest daughter's allegories and sends an old woman to propose marriage on his behalf. She turns out to be greedy and unable to understand the young woman's riddles. On one level, she provides a warning: if girls do not exercise their creativity and wit, they may end up as foolish old women. On a deeper level, the crone personifies the Sultan's feminine side, which is undeveloped. Accustomed to power, the Sultan is not sensitive to relationships or feelings.

The youngest daughter tells the crone that her mother is changing one into two, her eldest sister is turning black into white, and the other sister is picking roses in winter. The metaphors confirm that the youngest daughter is clever and wise. She is also practical and correctly guesses that the old woman stole money from the Sultan's purse.

The mother and sisters engage in traditionally feminine tasks—delivering babies, beautifying other women, and embroidering. Although they are not powerful figures in the story, they provide a womanly background—the motherline. This feminine wisdom helps explain a detail earlier in the story. The clever daughter used water pots to mimic pregnancy. Since it would be more comfortable to use pillows, the choice must be symbolic. Pots containing water, of course, make a good metaphor for wombs, filled with amniotic fluid. But there is a more concrete meaning. Although we take it for granted now, pottery was a major technological advance early in human history, and was probably invented by women. (Ancient pottery shards are more likely to have women's finger markings than men's or children's.) Pottery permitted the long-term storage of liquids, which made fermentation possible, and the creation of cheese, beer, and wine. Pots are also heat-resistant and permit boiling and stewing, which changes many poisonous or indigestible plants into nutritious foods. So pottery, like embroidery and midwifery, alludes to ancient feminine ingenuity.

THE WOMAN WARRIOR

Impressed by the youngest daughter's defiance and wisdom, the Sultan decides to marry her. This is extraordinary. In folktales and folksongs, the usual outcome for a strong woman is death or ruin,[5] reflecting social conventions which favor submissive females. "The Wise Wife" rejects the stereotype.

After the wedding, the Sultan immediately goes off to war, and the wise wife finds herself emotionally abandoned: the Sultan prefers glory and booty to wife and home, reflecting a traditional heroic ideal of manhood. The new wife does not despair of her situation. She goes after her husband.

The wise wife mobilizes her resources, dresses like a soldier, and assembles an army. She masquerades as a man and becomes a warrior, just like the protagonist in "The Warrior Wife." The clever wife must wear men's clothing because as a woman she cannot wield power in public. Even today, women often must adopt masculine clothes and modes of behavior to advance in their careers. Professional women, for example, quickly learn that if they wear playful, colorful, or feminine clothes, they are dismissed as frivolous.

THE WARRIOR OF LOVE

If the wife dresses like a male warrior, she does not become one. She never kills anybody and her motivations differ sharply from the Sultan's. He goes off to war seeking glory, while she aims to reclaim him. The Sultan wants to take what is not his by invading a foreign land, while she seeks what is rightly hers. She is, in short, a warrior for love, not power, for communion rather than conquest. Indeed, she ingeniously adapts the warrior role to fit her own needs and values by challenging the Sultan to a game of chess. She turns their conflict into a symbolic one, shifting the deadly warrior ethic, based on force, to the sociable attitude of a game.

When the wife wins the first chess game, she asks for the Sultan's dagger as the prize, and later takes his prayer beads and headcloth. The dagger symbolizes aggression, a traditional heroic trait, so in asking for it, the wife really demands that the Sultan give up his violence. The prayer beads, in turn, symbolize a connection to Allah, the Great Father. In claiming the beads, she symbolically compels him to share his connection to the divine with her, giving up the patriarchal view that a woman must reach God through a man. Similarly, the Sultan's headcloth is the equivalent of a crown, a symbol of his authority, so in asking for it, she has the Sultan share his power with her, surrendering the traditional view that only men can wield authority.

THE SLAVE

After winning the Sultan's dagger, the wise wife loses the second chess game—apparently by choice, since she always wins the first game and "loses" the second. She then offers him a night with a beautiful virgin, adorns herself, goes to the Sultan, and spends the night with him. This episode is extraordinary! First of all, the Sultan does not recognize his wife. He is psychologically asleep, and the scene dramatizes how patriarchal cultures are ignorant of the feminine, blind to women's real identities, desires, and needs. However, in choosing the night with a beautiful woman as his prize, rather than regaining his dagger, the Sultan shifts away from a traditional masculine emphasis on aggression to a feminine focus on love and intimacy. So the wife succeeds in changing him a little.

In switching roles from general to slave so skillfully, the wise wife reflects a trait of many women in leadership positions today. As one woman executive said, "Sometimes, it's like I'm in a play. I have different roles with different scripts, but I'm the same person. It's the same actress in those parts."6 This flexibility is necessary for women moving into conventional institutions that are not attuned to feminine values or women's needs.

By going to the Sultan as a sex slave, the clever wife voluntarily gives up her virginity. She refused to do so at the beginning of the story, when the Sultan demanded it; she relates to him on her own terms and thus stays true to herself. She remains a virgin in the original meaning of the word—

not as a woman who has never had sex, but as a woman who belongs to herself, who is one in herself, as Esther Harding put it. The wise wife may be a warrior for love, but she does not lose herself in relationships. She balances integrity and intimacy.

TRICKS AND WISDOM

The story presents the wife's trickery in a positive light. This breaks with tradition because most cultures condemn women's wiles. (Yet women's wisdom is too important to ignore, so many cultures also create an abstract image of feminine wisdom, like Hokmah in Jewish tradition, or Sophia, the Christian equivalent, honoring the abstraction, while devaluing real women.) In fact, trickery is essential for women to survive in most societies, as Mary Bateson observes.[7]

The wife's clever ruses recall an archetypal figure in folklore—the Trickster. In mythology, though, Tricksters are almost always male, and inventing tricks is an end in itself, their purpose in life. In folktales about women, trickery is a tool rather than a goal, a momentary strategy instead of a life purpose. To put this another way, women use the Trickster's energy, but do not become Tricksters.

The wife pursues and challenges the Sultan three times.[8] Many women may ask why the wife runs after him, and why not just enjoy life on her own in the palace? She is so wise, insightful, and perceptive in everything else, we must assume that she pursues her husband for a good reason and sees some potential in him. She dramatizes an issue most women face at some time in life—deciding whether they deal with a dangerous villain, as in "The Queen and the Murderer," or a man who can change, like the Sultan. In this situation women must consult the wise wife within themselves, that part of them that is clear in judgment, intuitive in perception, questioning of convention, and insistent on truth. Women's tales help by laying out different options for women, and in none of them does a wife return to a submissive role with her husband.

There is another meaning to the wife's pursuit of the Sultan. As a ruling monarch, he represents conventional society. In trying to gain his recognition, the wife symbolizes women today, working to change old, oppressive customs and institutions.

THE REMARRIAGE

Each time the clever wife sleeps with the Sultan, she bears a child. The first two are sons and the third a daughter, so there is a symbolic shift from the masculine to the feminine. Until now, the Sultan has had all the privileges in his marriage. He came and went as he pleased, ignoring his wife's needs and desires. This soon changes in the story, as the wise wife gains greater equality with the Sultan. So the birth of the daughter anticipates an evolution toward a more balanced world.

Upon returning from his third war, the Sultan repudiates the wise wife and prepares to marry a woman of greater social standing, a princess. The wise wife, after all, is only the daughter of a saddler. (The princess is also presumably younger than the wise wife.) In this precarious situation, the wife does not despair, but turns to her own counsel and resourcefulness. Just before the wedding, she gathers her three children and gives them the Sultan's dagger, prayer beads, and turban, which she has wisely kept for exactly this kind of crisis. The children appear before the Sultan singing a clever song, and he finally realizes that the generals he played chess with and the slave women he slept with were none other than his wife. Psychologically, he wakes up.

The Sultan cancels his new wedding and affirms the clever wife as his only one. This is surprising, because in Muslim tradition, a man may have many wives, and from a conventional viewpoint, the Sultan would do best to keep both women. His first wife offers him wisdom, while the royal princess would give him status—and probably a large dowry. In voluntarily abandoning polygamy, the Sultan symbolically shifts to a more egalitarian relationship with his wife. He affirms feeling and relationship after years of seeking power and glory through war.

Where tales of youth end with a sacred marriage, stories of mature men and women end with a spiritual remarriage.[9] The same theme emerges in today's movies. As Carolyn Heilbrun points out, many films from the 1930s onward portray husbands and wives at midlife moving toward greater equality, mutuality, and respect for each other. Fairy tales and Hollywood romances may seem unrealistic, the stuff of wish fulfillment, but there is a deeper truth in them because the stories remind us of our highest potential, what we can become, rather than how we commonly end up.

CHANGING SOCIETY

In prompting the Sultan to reform, the wife symbolically changes society. She acts as a midwife to a new social order. In a sense, she takes a traditional feminine craft—her mother's profession of midwife—and applies it to society. She does the same with her sisters' crafts—embroidering and cosmetics. Instead of embroidering cloth, the clever wife stitches together metaphors, riddles, and tricks. Her metaphors prompt the Sultan to become open-minded and nurturing. She cleans up some of his shadow side, especially his initial, callous disregard for her. Symbolically, she changes black into white, just like her beautician sister.

The application of traditional feminine skills to the whole world is an important theme in women's art. A striking example comes from Remedios Varo, a visionary artist. In her painting *Embroidering Earth's Mantle*, Varo portrays a group of women weaving and embroidering in a tower. The fabric they create spills out the window, and as it unfolds, it becomes the landscape—the earth and all its human settlements. The women literally weave the world. The wise wife does the same. She weaves a new world with all her clever stratagems, awakening the Sultan's heart. This is the ultimate result of her adventures—not just private gain, but the transformation of the Sultan and society; not individual fulfillment, but the release of soul in the community.

PART III

Nature

CHAPTER 6

"The Handless Woman":

Healing and Wilderness

(from Japan[1])

 beautiful girl once lived happily with her parents, but her mother died when the girl was only four years old. After a few years her father married again, but his new wife was jealous of the girl and made life hard for her. The girl grew into a lovely maiden, which made the stepmother hate her even more. So the wife began saying evil things about her to her father, and slowly turned his heart against his daughter.

Shortly after the young woman turned fifteen, the stepmother threatened her husband: "I cannot stand living with your wretched daughter! I am going to leave you!" The husband begged his wife to stay. "Then get rid of your daughter," she demanded. He promised to do so and came up with a plan. He invited his daughter to go with him to a festival, and gave her a beautiful kimono to wear. The daughter was delighted to go, but became puzzled when her father led her into a forest.

"Where is the festival?" she asked.

"A little farther," he replied. Then in the middle of the wilderness, they stopped for lunch, and the maiden fell asleep, exhausted from their long walk. This was the moment her father had waited for. He picked up his axe, went to his daughter, and chopped off her hands. His daughter awoke and cried out. "Father, what are you doing?" He quickly left her and so she ran after him, stumbling and rolling down the mountain. The father quickened his pace and abandoned the poor girl.

All alone, she crawled to a stream and washed the stumps of her arms. Having no place to go, she remained in the woods, picking berries and nuts with her teeth, just like the beasts, and sleeping on the earth.

One day, a handsome young man went hunting in the forest. He came upon the handless maiden and exclaimed in surprise, "You have no hands, yet you look human! Are you a demon or a ghost?"

"No," she replied, "I am a woman forsaken by all." She said nothing about her father.

The young man took pity upon her, put her on his horse, and took her home. "I found this poor creature in the mountains," he explained to his mother. The old woman was kind and took the handless maiden in, bathing her and giving her new clothes. Clean and fresh, the handless maiden was as beautiful as sunrise and sunset, and the young man fell in love with her. He proposed that they marry, his mother approved, and the young couple were soon wedded.

In due time the handless woman expected a child. Her husband had to leave on an extended trip, and entrusted his wife to his mother: "Look after her as you would me."

"I will," the mother promised. "I love her as dearly as you do." Soon afterward, the handless wife gave birth to a beautiful baby boy. She and her mother-in-law rejoiced, and the old woman quickly wrote a letter, saying, "Your wife gave birth to a handsome boy. She is doing well and we eagerly await your return." The mother sent a messenger with the letter to her son.

The courier put the note in his purse and walked all day. Finally he went up to a home and asked for water. A woman came out, gave him a drink, and started talking. "Where are you going in such a hurry?" she inquired.

WAKING THE WORLD   99

"I am carrying an important message from a rich family," he replied. "It is from a handless woman, who just gave birth to a boy, and she is sending a letter to tell her husband the good news."

Now this woman was none other than the evil stepmother. She immediately figured out that her stepdaughter had not died in the forest. Filled with hatred, she came up with a plan. "You must be tired," she said sweetly to the messenger. "Have a drink and relax." She poured him wine and the courier drank until he fell asleep. The stepmother opened his purse, read the letter, and then wrote a note of her own.

"Your wife gave birth to a horrible monster that looks like a snake and a dog! What am I to do?" She put her letter in the courier's wallet, and when he woke up, gave him some food and wished him well. "Please stop by on your way back," she said.

The courier resumed his journey and finally delivered the letter. The husband read the note with horror, thought a moment, and wrote a reply to his mother. "Please take care of my wife and son until I return, no matter what the baby looks like. I will be back as soon as I can." The courier set off with the letter and stopped at the stepmother's house, hoping for some wine.

She greeted him warmly and served him wine until he fell asleep. Then she opened the letter and replaced it with one that said: "Get rid of my wife and child! I do not want such monsters in my family. I will not return home if they remain there!" When the courier woke up, she sent him on his way, wishing him well.

The messenger delivered the false note and the mother-in-law read it with disbelief. "This cannot be! My son would not send his wife and child away!" She asked the messenger, "Is this the right letter? Did you carry others, or did you stop anywhere on your way here?"

"No," the messenger insisted.

The mother-in-law decided to wait for her son, but as the days went by, she feared he would not return, just as the letter threatened. Finally she showed the note to her daughter-in-law. The handless wife was heartbroken. "If my husband does not want me, I will not stay," she said. The two women wept bitterly and the handless woman left the house, carrying her child in a sling on her back.

The poor woman had nowhere to go, so she returned to the forest. She was thirsty from her walking, and knelt beside a stream. When she bent over to drink, the baby began to slide off her back. "Help! Help!" she cried, desperately trying to hold her baby. But she had no hands to catch him, so the child slipped into the stream. She grabbed desperately for him, plunging the stumps of her arms in the water. Suddenly her hands grew back, and she plucked her baby from the stream. "My baby is safe and my hands are back!" she exclaimed in astonishment. Then she knelt on the ground and thanked all the gods and spirits, weeping with joy.

Meanwhile, her husband returned home and was shocked to discover his wife and child missing. "But you told me to send them away!" his mother scolded.

"What are you talking about!" he exclaimed. Mother and son soon figured out someone had switched their letters, so they summoned the messenger, who confessed that he had stopped along the way.

The husband immediately set off into the woods to look for his wife and child. He searched long and hard, vowing not to rest until he found them. Then he came to a stream, and saw a woman praying beside a shrine, holding her child. "She looks like my wife," the man thought, "but she has hands!" He went up to her, and saw that she was indeed his wife.

"My wife!" he cried out.

"My husband!" she exclaimed, and they embraced. He explained how their letters had been switched and she told him how her hands had miraculously grown back, for the first time revealing how her father had chopped them off. Then they embraced anew, weeping with joy, and where their tears fell upon the ground, flowers sprang up. Hand-in-hand, the wife and husband returned home, carrying their child, and as they walked through the forest, all the trees burst into bloom. When they arrived home, the husband went to the authorities and told them about the stepmother and father. The police seized the wicked couple and the judge threw them into prison. And so the once-handless woman and her husband lived happily for the rest of their days with all their children.

MANY VERSIONS, ONE DRAMA

The tale of the handless woman brings up horrifying themes. Many psychologists have analyzed the drama, relying on the German version from the Grimm brothers. I have avoided their version because the Grimms revised the story extensively to fit conventional, middle-class values, and I wanted to emphasize the cross-cultural nature of the story. The Japanese version starts off like "Cinderella," with an evil stepmother persecuting an innocent young girl. The wicked stepmother is a familiar figure in fairy tales and brings up two themes. First, women can be persecuted by women, not just men, and other versions of "The Handless Woman" show the protagonist being attacked by resentful sisters, an envious sister-in-law, even a jealous nanny. Second, the stepmother can be interpreted as a negative mother figure, symbolizing mother-daughter conflict. (Many fairy tales originally had a mother persecuting a daughter, but editors substituted a stepmother to sanitize the tales.) The present story highlights these conflicts in two details. The tale says that the handless maiden's mother died when the girl was four, the age, psychoanalysts tell us, when a girl often begins competing with her mother for her father's attention. To the daughter, the mother often seems like a dangerous rival, metaphorically, turning into an evil stepmother. Mother-daughter conflicts reappear dramatically in adolescence, as the story indicates: it is when the young woman turns fifteen that the stepmother demands that her husband choose between them. When a young woman becomes sexually mature and attractive, the mother may feel envious, or become more intrusive and controlling. Emotionally, mother and daughter sometimes feel there is room for only one of them.

AMPUTATION AND HELPLESSNESS

When the father takes his daughter to the woods, the girl becomes concerned and asks where they are going. Her instincts warn her that something is wrong, but she silences that inner voice after her father reassures her, and disaster occurs. Note that the father attacks his daughter only after she falls asleep: he can harm her only when she is unconscious and cannot rely on her natural wisdom.

When the father chops off his daughter's hands, the deed is so atrocious it is hard to understand. The father could just leave the girl in the woods, as in "Hansel and Gretel"—why maim her so cruelly? There must be deeper symbolic meanings here.

Without hands the young woman is completely helpless. This graphically illustrates women's plight in many cultures, where women are confined at home and prevented from doing what they want or need to do. Something similar happens in modern Western culture, where social pressures discourage adolescent girls from speaking up or asserting themselves. They are prevented from reaching for their dreams; society chops off their hands psychologically.

Cutting off hands conjures up images of amputating other body parts, bringing up the notion of castration. Here we come to a theory of feminine psychology dear to Freud. According to him, when little girls discover that boys have penises and girls do not, the girls imagine that they, too, once had penises, but lost them somehow. So girls believe they were castrated and feel inferior to boys. Few defend this theory today, but the fairy tale reveals the deeper meaning behind the castration imagery. In most cultures, girls are indeed castrated, but they do not lose a penis, they lose their hands, the ability to master the world and to reach for their dreams. The castration is socioeconomic, not anatomic.

The handless motif emerges clearly in women's dreams, as psychologist Claire Douglas illustrates.[2] In one of her dreams, Douglas saw her mother on a pier and knew that her mother was possessed by a ghost. Douglas went to her and turned into a twelve-year-old girl. Her mother then told her that the custom of the land was to cut off the right arm of every girl, to make her more manageable and marriageable. She added that this amputation was essential for brainy, troublesome girls like Douglas. Horrified and outraged, Douglas ran to an older woman sitting on a nearby pier, who jeered at Douglas's mother.

The dream clarifies the major themes of "The Handless Woman" by noting that the purpose of cutting off girls' hands is to make them "manageable" and "marriageable," forcing them to fit unhealthy feminine stereotypes. The dream also explains that Douglas's mother was possessed by a ghost, and this is equivalent to having the evil stepmother replace the good mother in the fairy tale. The ghost presumably is a metaphor for powerful social conventions.

THE DEVIL

Other versions of the story add further insights to the maiming theme. In the Grimms' retelling, it is the devil rather than a wicked stepmother who forces the father to cut off his daughter's hands. The devil personifies extreme evil, and many versions of "The Handless Woman" reveal exactly how extreme: the father cuts off his daughter's hands because she rejects his incestuous advances, his attempts to rape her. Susan Gordon observed that women who have survived incest and rape react with profound emotion when they hear "The Handless Woman." The unthinkable horror of having one's hands cut off captures the unspeakable trauma involved in rape and incest.

The father cuts off his daughter's hands shortly after she turns fifteen, or at about the time of menarche. In fact, as part of girls' puberty rites, many societies enforce female circumcision, a horrendous practice involving the excision of a girl's clitoris and labia, followed by sewing her vagina almost completely shut. The mutilation is unimaginably painful, makes intercourse an ordeal, and leaves women vulnerable to recurrent infections. The amputation theme in the fairy tale is no fantasy.

QUESTIONS AND SILENCE

Even after her father chops off her hands, the daughter runs toward him and cries out for help. The episode is heartrending but literally true, because children who have been abused and even raped by their parents remain attached to them.

Bleeding from her wounds, the poor girl crawls to a stream and washes her stumps. The tale does not explicitly say so, but presumably the water heals her wounds. Thus we have the wilderness theme again—nature, and particularly water, offers healing and sanctuary to women, and the story elaborates the point a little later.

After living alone in the forest, the handless maiden meets a young man. He is shocked to see a woman without hands and does not realize that being maimed and handless, both physically and psychologically, is a common state for women in most societies. Nor can he understand how such a helpless woman could survive in the wild, not knowing women's ability to sustain themselves in adversity.

The young man asks the handless woman if she is a spirit or human, and the question appears in most versions, reflecting its importance. He wonders whether she is real or not, and whether her horrible mutilation is a reality or a fantasy. The issue remains today in cases of incest. Is the report true or imagined? Is the recovered memory reliable? The same questions come up with rape and sexual harassment. In the case of Anita Hill and Clarence Thomas, the United States Senate decided that Hill's experience was imaginary rather than real.

The handless woman says nothing about her father cutting her hands off. Other versions of her story are even clearer about her silence. In one variant the maiden says that animals ate her hands, keeping her father's atrocity secret, while another version has the maiden say she does not remember what happened. These stories dramatize how a trauma is often so great a woman cannot speak of it. Or she may have learned to keep silent because nobody believes her. For some women, the horror causes the psyche to fragment, so they lose a continuous sense of self. They experience the world in disjointed episodes, with terrifying gaps in between: like the handless maiden, they may not consciously remember what happened. Some victims say nothing so as to protect the rapist, especially if he is a family member. Many women also feel intensely ashamed, as if they were responsible for the abuse and rape—a position many societies reinforce. Women not only have their hands amputated, their tongues are chopped off, too.

RESCUE

The young man takes pity on the handless maiden, brings her home, falls in love with her, and they marry. This is the typical "Cinderella" plot—an abused maiden is rescued by a brave hero, and they marry and live happily ever after. But "The Handless Woman" is only halfway through! Romantic rescue is only a temporary phase on a woman's journey through life.

Curiously, the young man lives with his mother, unlike most heroes who have left home. The young man's father is not mentioned, so the story emphasizes the motherline rather than the fatherline, and hints at ancient matrilineal tradition. This motif helps explain why the young man's mother is kind to the handless woman. In cultures where men have power, a mother-in-law and daughter-in-law fight over who influences the man of the house. In matrilineal cultures, women have their own sources of authority, so mother and wife do not fight over the son-husband.

When the handless woman becomes pregnant, her husband goes off on a journey, becoming physically and emotionally absent just when she needs his support the most—like many men who conventionally devote themselves to their careers. When the handless woman gives birth, she and her mother-in-law send a joyful message to the husband, but the wicked stepmother reappears and switches letters. In other versions, it is the devil rather than the stepmother who switches letters, but the meaning is the same—some shadowy element creates trouble between the husband and wife. In real life, these conflicts often involve "projection." A husband, for instance, might accuse his wife of being infantile when she is angry, while he is really the one who has tantrums. He blames his wife for his faults, projecting his vices on her. These projections proliferate in the absence of good communication, as the story stresses by having the messages mixed up when the husband and wife are physically separated; unable to communicate directly with each other, devilish troubles ensue.

The birth of children often precipitates more miscommunication between spouses. A husband may feel jealous of the attention his wife gives to the child, stirring old memories of not being nurtured by his own mother, so that he unconsciously feels the new baby is a monster. A wife for her part may feel overwhelmed by the care required by her new child. To her psyche, the new child may seem like a demon, threatening to devour her life. The image of a monstrous baby, contained in the stepmother's letter, is psychologically accurate.

EXILE AND HEALING

When the husband sends a reply to the first false letter, asking his mother to take care of his wife and child, the stepmother substitutes another letter, saying the opposite. The man's mother does not believe the second message, but eventually gives in and obeys the letter. Her natural instincts are overcome by the social conventions which make her son the head of the house. When the handless woman reads the letter, she, too, obeys. She does not protest, but simply goes into the wilderness with her baby, underscoring how much she has been silenced.

In the forest, the newborn baby falls from his mother's back into a stream. The woman calls for help, reaches out to retrieve her child, and her hands miraculously reappear. Other versions reiterate the drama, underscoring its symbolic significance. Notice, first, that the handless mother is healed in the forest, far from civilization: nature provides healing for women, in the same way it provides sanctuary, as we saw in "The Three Little Eggs" of Chapter 4. Women's art and literature repeat the healing motif,[3] and reverse a tradition in many cultures, where women and nature are associated as a source of life for the benefit of *others*. Woman's tales emphasize that nature is a source of renewal for women themselves. The theme is clear in dreams, and Clarissa Pinkola Estés provides a dramatic example: A woman dreamed that she had open-heart surgery and was conscious during the procedure. She saw that the operating room was open to the sky above, and as the surgeons exposed her heart, a ray of sunlight fell upon it, healing her instantly. The surgeon then declared that nothing further was needed.

Nature can be profoundly healing even for women wounded early in life, by their own mothers. The bounty and beauty of the wilderness can substitute for a neglectful or destructive mother. Psychoanalyst Jane Wheelwright, for example, describes how she grew up in a wilderness area with a mother who was neither attentive nor warm.[4] Wheelwright found comfort, nurture, and inspiration in nature. The wilderness became Mother Nature to her and a source of healing.

THE WATER OF LIFE

The handless mother is healed when she plunges her arms into a stream, and other versions repeat the water imagery. These tales reiterate an ancient link between water and the deep feminine. The Chinese notion of yin, the cosmic female principle, for instance, is tied to moist, fertile valleys, while the Celtics associated pools, rivers, and springs with female spirits. Language reflects the association, too: in French the word for "water" is feminine. The link between water and the feminine is not surprising because the qualities of one reflect the virtues of the other. Water is flexible—when blocked, it simply flows around the obstacle with quiet, steady energy, gradually wearing down the obstructions. Water can also be astonishingly powerful, emerging in a flood that clears everything in its path. The power of water is often overlooked, though, because it seems so ordinary and mundane—just like feminine vitality. Yet water is life-giving, nurturing, and generative, whether as amniotic fluid or as rain bringing crops to fruition.

In real life, water themes often play a prominent role in women's experience of wholeness. Meinrad Craighead offers an example. On a hot summer afternoon, she sat with her dog in the garden: "As I looked into her eyes I realized that I would never travel further than into this animal's eyes. They were as deep, as bewildering, as unattainable as a night sky. Just as mysterious was a clear awareness of water within me, the sound in my ears, yet resounding from my breast. I gazed into the dog's eyes and listened to the sound of rushing water inside me. I understood, 'This is who God is. My Mother is water and she is inside me and I am in the water.' "[5]

Craighead's epiphany was mediated by an animal and by water—by nature. Her vision also occurred when she was only seven years old, before she knew anything about goddesses and before they became a popular topic. The revelation also diverged sharply from the Christian tradition in which she was raised, emphasizing how spontaneous and archetypal her vision was—it arose from her inner being, from the deep feminine.

THE DEEP FEMININE

In showing how nature and water heal the handless woman, the tale emphasizes that women's wounds can be healed only by the deep feminine. Conventional feminine roles, like being a beloved wife, do not work: as the story suggests, the husband cannot heal his handless wife. Nor does the wife find wholeness in just being heroic, surviving in the wilderness. Reclaiming her masculine side, her animus, is not sufficient. Men and the masculine cannot heal the wounds women receive from society. Only the deep feminine can. However, the experience can be arduous, as the story indicates. It is only when the baby falls into the stream, leaving the women helpless and frantic, that she is healed. Significantly, she does not give up, but reaches out for her child. This is essentially a death-rebirth process, familiar from previous tales: in the midst of a hopeless situation, a woman finds new life. Indeed, the infant can be interpreted as a symbol for the woman's true self, drowning in oppressive social conventions and rescued in the nick of time. The story holds an implicit warning here: if a woman does not reach out with all her strength, even when it seems useless, her true self will drown; but if she does, she will find healing and wholeness.

The handless woman regains her hands on her second sojourn in the wilderness. Her first stay occurred immediately after her hands were cut off, when nature provided her with food and safety, but not with complete healing: she did not regain her hands. It is only at midlife—after she has married and become a mother—that she finds true healing and wholeness.

One reason for this is that young women, like young men, often follow romantic ideals, where a beautiful princess falls in love with a handsome prince. Women must break free from these romantic conventions before they can gain full access to the deep feminine. Moreover, the deep feminine is powerful and can be overwhelming when first encountered, so a sturdy ego is necessary to explore the mysteries of the feminine, and women gain this strength from life experience.

WOMEN'S SPIRITUALITY AND THE BODY

After the woman regains her hands, she prays at a shrine near the stream, giving thanks to the gods. This highlights the spiritual aspects of her story, and the theme appears in other versions of the tale. "The Handless Woman" is not merely about women's psychological development; it also portrays women's spiritual journey in life. All versions also agree that women's spirituality is tied to nature, not civilization. A German version of "The Handless Woman," not from the Grimms, makes the point in a poetic way. When the handless mother flees with her baby into the wilderness, she meets two men named Peter and John by a stream. They are most likely the Apostles, and offer her three wishes, reminding her not to forget the most precious thing to ask for, by which they presumably mean eternal salvation. The handless woman first asks for shelter and food for herself and her infant. Peter and John grant the wish and remind her again of the most priceless thing to ask for. The mother wishes to see her husband one more time and the two Apostles agree to it, repeating their advice about wishing for the most important gift of all. The mother thinks a moment, and then asks for her hands back. She regains them and soon afterward finds her husband. They reconcile and live happily ever after with their family.

Here the handless mother does not ask for what is conventionally considered "the most precious thing"—eternal salvation. She wants her hands back instead. She demands her ability to act in this world, and does not settle for a vague promise of bliss in the next one. She prefers practical, material healing, rather than abstract, theological benefit. The tale thus hints at the embodied nature of feminine spirituality, a theme stressed by theologians and thinkers from Mary Daly to Naomi Goldenberg.

RECONCILIATION

When the husband returns home and learns about the false letters, he immediately goes in search of his wife and child, and in many versions he does so for a number of years, without rest, undergoing great hardships. It is his turn to suffer, a theme which also appears in men's tales. Fairy tales thus show women enduring great oppression in youth, but finding liberation and healing at midlife. Men, on the other hand, enjoy privilege and power in youth, and then suffer a calamitous downfall at midlife. The stories portray a role reversal, which equalizes men and women, so that they can return to each other later in a balanced, egalitarian relationship.

In searching for his wife, the husband demonstrates how much he values their relationship. He is a "new male," like Prince Ivan in "Maria Morevna." Yet when he comes upon his wife in the forest, he is not sure that he recognizes her, and other versions are even more dramatic. The husband's failure to recognize his wife is another example of men being unconscious and having to wake up. "The Handless Woman" adds a new twist: the husband has trouble recognizing his wife after she regains her hands; that is, he does not recognize her as a whole, healed, integrated individual. In real life, when women reclaim their repressed vitality, husbands and male co-workers often cannot accept the changes and a conflict results. This all-too-common reality helps explain why many women find it inexplicable or offensive for the wife in the story to return home with her husband. What makes reunion and reconciliation possible is that the husband changes as much as the wife. He recognizes and affirms her as a whole, healed person and they return as equals. This is the ultimate goal of the drama. Women's tales portray not only a woman healing her wounds, but also a newly awakened male, a post-heroic man, who welcomes her in all her strength and vitality.

CHAPTER 7

"The Woman from the Egg":

Resurrection and Nature

(from Germany[1])

young man once went searching for a wife, not liking any of the maidens in his village. "Well, go looking if you must," his mother said, "but surely hunger will bring you back—or thirst!" As the young man traveled through the forest, his stomach soon began rumbling and his throat felt parched. He spied a bird's nest high in a tree and climbed up, looking for eggs to eat. He found three and, back on the ground, broke one open. To his surprise, a beautiful maiden appeared before him.

"Give me water," she said, "and I will be yours, and you will be mine."

The young man had no water, and so the woman vanished. He broke the second egg, and a maiden even more radiant appeared.

"Give me water," she declared, "and I will be yours, and you will be mine."

Before he could find water, the maiden vanished. Sadder but wiser, he searched for water before opening the last egg. He found a well in a garden, filled a goblet with water, and then broke open the egg. A maiden as beautiful as the sun and moon appeared, dressed in a golden gown. In an instant, the young man fell in love with her.

"Give me water," she said, "and I will be yours, and you will be mine."

The young man offered her the goblet of water, and she drank from it, saying, "Now I am yours and you are mine."

The young man was loath to have the beautiful woman walk back home, so he told her, "If you wait here by the well, I will fetch a carriage for you!"

The woman agreed, and waited at the well. Soon afterward, a witch walked by with her hideous daughter. The witch saw the beautiful woman and asked, "Why do you sit here all alone?"

The woman from the egg replied, "I am waiting for my new husband to fetch me in a carriage."

The hag hissed, "That's what you think!" She seized the beautiful woman, yanked off her golden dress, and cackled, "It will be my daughter your husband takes home, not you!"

The woman from the egg leapt into the well, turned into a fish, and swam out of sight. The witch dressed her ugly daughter in the golden gown, told her what to say when the young man returned, and departed.

Some time later, the young man arrived with the carriage. When he saw the ugly woman, he was taken aback. "What happened to you?" he asked. "You were so beautiful when I left!"

"Alas," the witch's daughter replied, "you left me exposed to the sun, and so I turned black! But if you take me home, I will bathe and look as beautiful as before."

The young man returned home with her, but when his mother saw the woman, she exclaimed, "Your bride is a vagabond!"

The witch's daughter bathed herself and the young man married her, but she still remained hideous. So she pretended to be sick and took to bed. "Only one thing can cure me and restore my beauty," the ugly wife told her husband. "A magic fish lives in the well where I waited for you. If I eat it, I will be cured."

The young man returned to the well, emptied it of water,

and caught the only fish there. He brought it home and his wife ate it with relish, throwing the bones into the yard. But she remained as ugly as before.

The next day, a duck wandered over from next door, where there lived an old woman who worked for the young man. The duck saw the fish bones in the yard, gobbled them up, and returned to the crone's home. In several days, the duck grew golden feathers. The old woman was amazed to see the shining quills, so she plucked them and put them in a small pot.

The next day, the old woman went to church as she usually did. When she returned home, she was surprised to find that the dinner she had made was gone. Someone had eaten it! The same thing happened the next day, and the one after that. So the following morning, the old woman pretended to go to church as usual, but she quietly returned home and peeked through the keyhole. To her amazement, she saw a beautiful woman arise from the pot of golden feathers—the woman from the egg.

The old woman hastened inside and touched the egg woman, and this set her free. From then on, the two lived together. Each morning, the old woman went to work for her neighbor, the young man, helping with the farm chores. One day, the woman from the egg said, "Let me take your place today, and go to work at our neighbor's."

The elder woman shook her head. "If you go, the master of the house will see you, and he might want to keep you!"

"Well," said the woman from the egg, "I will wear dirty, old clothes, so he will not take a second look at me." She dressed in rags and went next door.

When she walked in, the husband glanced at her and then took a second look. He recognized her, thought a long moment, then asked the women to each tell a story to pass the time. First his mother told a tale, and then the ugly woman, but when it was the turn of the woman from the egg, she said, "I have no stories to tell, only a dream."

"Well," the husband said, "a dream will do fine."

So the woman from the egg began, "Once I dreamed of a young man who did not like any of the maidens in his village.

So he went looking for a wife elsewhere. As he walked in the forest, he found a bird's nest with three eggs. When he broke open the first egg, a maiden appeared . . ."

The ugly wife began pacing. She turned to her husband and asked, "What are you doing here with all these women? Why don't you rest and get some sleep?"

"I want to hear her story," the husband insisted, so the woman from the egg described the three maidens, and how the young man gave the last one a goblet of water. "Then," she said, "he went to fetch a carriage for his new wife. Here I woke up," the beautiful woman concluded, "so I do not know how the dream ended."

"Try to remember," the husband urged, and the woman from the egg resumed her story, describing how the witch substituted her ugly daughter for the new bride. Hearing that, the husband seized the hag's daughter and locked her in a room. Then he went to the witch's house.

He asked her, "What do you think of somebody who steals a man's wife, tries to kill her, and substitutes a hideous toad in her place?"

The witch replied, "Why, such a person should be shut up in a barrel full of nails and thrown from the highest mountain. And the false wife, too!" So that is exactly what the husband did. Then he married his real wife in the church, and the two of them lived happily for the rest of their days.

THE YOUNG MAN

This German fairy tale begins with a young man looking for a wife. Yet the woman from the egg is the real protagonist, as the title of the story implies. Moreover, the drama revolves around women—the woman from the egg, the witch, the witch's daughter, and the wise old woman. Like other women's tales, this one begins by focusing on a man and then shifts to the woman protagonist and her development.

The young man was not satisfied with any of the eligible

women in his village, and so went searching elsewhere for a wife. He may simply believe, like many young heroes, that he is special and deserves a unique wife. On the other hand, in seeking something beyond convention, he may be able to move beyond traditional gender roles and become a "new male."

While journeying through a forest, the young man comes upon a bird's nest with eggs and the latter are archetypal symbols of the feminine. Other versions of the tale do not feature eggs but use equivalent feminine symbols. The Italian story "The Pomegranate Maiden," for example, substitutes pomegranates for eggs. But pomegranates are associated with the feminine in many cultures, such as in Greek, Hebrew, and Chinese tradition. If the particular symbols differ between stories, the symbolism remains the same.

When the first beautiful woman leaps out and asks for water, the young man has none, and she vanishes. Since water is an ancient symbol of the feminine, in demanding it the egg maiden asks the young man if he has a connection to the feminine and if he affirms the importance of the feminine. Like many other young men, he does not. So the egg maiden leaves him.

The young man learns. After the second maiden disappears, he goes in search of water and finds a well in a garden. The well is unexpected, since the young man is in a forest. A stream or lake would fit the wilderness setting more, suggesting that the well is symbolic. The implication is that water, symbolizing feminine vitality, is not freely available any more and comes only from an artificial source. That is, something has blocked access to the feminine and this is most likely civilization. As a number of historians and anthropologists, such as Marija Gimbutas, Gerda Lerner, and Peggy Sanday, have pointed out, heroic, male-dominated cultures overran early matrilineal societies which honored the feminine. Thus much work and effort, symbolized by the well, is needed to tap into the feminine realm. Women's tales offer just such access.

THE MARRIAGE

In asking for water, each egg woman says, "I will be yours, and you will be mine," implying that by giving her water, the young man will marry her. The egg maidens do not simply say, "I will be yours," surrendering themselves to him. They demand an equal, mutual relationship. A small detail highlights the marriage theme. The young man fills a goblet with water and offers it to the third maiden. He does not simply scoop water up with his hands, or even use an ordinary cup. He utilizes a ceremonial drinking vessel common in marriage ceremonies around the world, implying that they celebrate a soul marriage.

If we interpret the three women to be different aspects of the same female protagonist, the story takes on further meaning. The woman from the egg must try several times before the young man figures out his task—honoring feelings and the feminine. The story implies that "new men" who celebrate the feminine and affirm women as equals are not found ready-made. They develop, and women must often wait for them to do so.

THE CARRIAGE AND THE WITCH

The husband tells his wife that she should ride home in style, and he goes to fetch a carriage. He falls prey to traditional social concerns—status and prestige—and may even revert to the old view of wife as ornament. It is then that the witch and her ugly daughter appear. Symbolically, when a wife and husband are alienated in some way, whether from pride, social convention, or poor communication, the shadow creeps in and works its mischief, just as "The Handless Woman" suggested earlier.

The witch and her ugly daughter point to mother-daughter conflicts which often arise when a woman enters an intimate relationship, like marriage. The depth of a woman's connection with her lover or husband recalls the original, deep communion between mother and daughter, and this brings up all kinds of childhood issues.

The woman from the egg explains to the witch that her new husband has gone to fetch a carriage. She never suspects that the hag might attack her, and does nothing to protect herself when assaulted. She dramatizes the reaction of many women when first attacked by another woman—disbelief, shock, and paralysis. The victim wonders, "How could another woman do this to me?" Often self-doubts arise: "Perhaps I provoked her?"

The story hints at one cause for these conflicts between women—jealousy or rivalry. In most societies, women cannot exercise power or gain status on their own account— only through their husbands. So it becomes imperative for women to marry well, and they must focus their rivalries on that task. The witch attacks the woman from the egg so that her daughter can move up in the world.

THE TRUE SELF AND THE FALSE SELF

The egg woman is surpassingly beautiful in all versions, and even numinous in some way. Her luminosity reflects, I suggest, her natural self, her inner beauty. She has not yet been wounded by social conventions, nor has she distorted herself to gain external approval. Emerging from an egg in the forest, she shines with the splendor of her deep self, and this innocence and wholeness draw the witch to her.

When the hag attacks, the wife jumps into the well and turns into a fish. This is intriguing. Why would she jump into the well, rather than run away? And how did she turn into a fish? The story says nothing about the witch casting a spell, so the woman apparently changed spontaneously. What does that mean? A clue, I think, lies in what happens immediately afterward.

The witch's daughter replaces the beautiful woman, bring-

ing up a major theme in fairy tales about women—the contrast between a "true" wife and a "false" one.[2] The motif is
specific to women's tales—there are few stories about a true
groom and a false groom—suggesting that the impostor wife
reflects an issue in feminine psychology.

The false wife personifies a false self, which women are
forced to develop in most cultures. Young girls usually know
who they are and what they want or need. But during adolescence, girls are pressured to conform to conventional feminine roles, suppressing their true natures and developing
false selves to present to the world. The fairy tale dramatizes
this painful process when the egg woman jumps into the well
and turns into a fish. The true self vanishes into the unconscious and is totally silenced—fish cannot speak or cry out.
Yet the fish remains alive, hidden in the water: a woman's
true self remains intact, protected by the unconscious.

The dream of a woman, retold by Linda Leonard in *Meeting
the Madwoman*, dramatizes this suppression of the true self. In
the dream, the woman became a little girl whose mother ran
a brothel for Nazi S.S. officers. The dreamer was horrified at
the situation, but her mother injected her each day with a
drug to numb her feelings. The girl finally ran away, but had
to return eventually for another injection, having become
dependent on the drug. When she returned, defeated and
humiliated, the Nazi officers laughed at her.

As a result of the injections, the girl is numbed and becomes a zombie—a false self. The drug suppresses her true
self. The dream depicts the woman's mother as a villain, just
like the evil witch in the fairy tale, but the real culprits are
destructive social conventions, aptly personified by the Nazis.

The fairy tale emphasizes how ugly the false wife is, and
the motif appears in other tales. The false self is ugly because
it reflects an evil situation—the repression of a woman's true
self. Along with such repression comes depression, which the
present tale hints at by giving the ugly false wife a dark face.
Her color expresses the inner despair that haunts women
forced to fit confining feminine stereotypes. Anna Fengel, the
German painter, offers a riveting image of this split in a painting entitled *The Subterranean Goddess*. Fengel portrays a

woman's pale, white face looking lifeless, chalky, and hideous as it lies upon the earth. Beneath that face, hidden under the ground, is another one that is red and vibrantly alive.[3] The contrast between an empty self and passionate self, the false self and the true self, could not be clearer.

G O I N G '' H O M E ''

When the husband returns with a carriage, he is perplexed to find his beautiful wife looking ugly and does not realize that he deals with an impostor! He is ignorant, psychologically unconscious, and must be awakened. Moreover, his immediate reaction to the false wife concerns her lack of beauty, suggesting that beauty is what he values most in a woman.

The false wife explains that the sun made her ugly; that is, nature ruined her. Here she follows patriarchal convention, which views nature as dangerous and something to be conquered. This contradicts women's tales, which insist that nature is a sanctuary and place of healing for women. The contradiction is only apparent because the false wife is a false self, so presumably says false things.

Despite her ugliness, the husband takes the false wife home. He does not abandon her and flee, implicitly recognizing that he made a commitment to her. This suggests that he is on the way to becoming a "new male." When the false wife arrives at her new home, the husband's mother immediately suspects something is amiss. But her son goes ahead with a wedding anyway. Similar events occur in other stories: older women are not deceived by pretenses; they see the truth. Unfortunately, men do not believe them until much later, when they wake up.

When the young man marries the ugly woman, the false self, he makes her his legal or official wife. Symbolically, it is often a woman's false self that society recognizes and honors, not her true self. Women are rewarded for being thin, beautiful, nurturing, and accommodating—not for speaking their minds, insisting on what they want, or heeding what their bodies need. The toll this takes on a woman's soul is horrifying, as the tale reveals.

EATING THE FISH

The false wife takes to bed, pretending to be sick, and declares that she will be cured, regaining her beauty, only if she eats the fish from the well in the forest. Note that she equates being cured and becoming beautiful, reflecting a painful conviction for women in today's culture. From adolescence onward, many women are told by advertisements, "If only you were prettier, you would be happy and whole."

The husband catches the fish by emptying the whole well of water. This is an odd and rather extreme way to catch a fish, so the deed must be symbolic. Metaphorically he destroys access to the fluid, feminine realm, not knowing the significance of his actions—that he is killing his true wife. Once again, he is psychologically asleep. Today, many men devalue or attack the feminine and women in this unconscious manner. Men are often surprised, for instance, to learn how many of their gestures and actions at work are experienced by women as sexual harassment. In having the husband empty the well, the story also sums up the cumulative effect of centuries of male-oriented culture—the deep feminine is dried up.

When the husband gives the fish to the false wife, she promptly eats it. The image is gruesome, since it implies cannibalism. Yet the act is profoundly accurate in portraying the false self devouring the true self. In real life, when a woman has no chance to express her inner nature, and when she is rewarded by society only for conforming to feminine stereotypes, she risks losing contact with her deep self, her soul—the false self devours what is unique and priceless in her.

Even when a woman's true self is devoured by the false one, however, not all is lost, and this is surely one of the most important messages in the story.

TRANSFORMATIONS

The false wife spits out the fish bones, a duck gobbles them up and grows golden feathers, and then an old woman plucks the feathers and keeps them in a pot. From the feathers the egg woman reappears. So the true wife changes into a fish, fish bones, and golden feathers on a duck, and then regains her human form. Such transformations are common in women's tales but rare in men's stories, suggesting that shape-shifting symbolizes something unique about the feminine. On one level, the egg woman's transformation symbolizes how women pass through many roles and identities in life: for instance, they often focus their energies on family early in life, but after their children leave home they return to school, start professional careers, or launch businesses. This pattern applies not just to modern society, but to Victorian England, imperial China, and many tribal cultures around the world.[4] Native Americans of the Southwest celebrate this feminine fluidity in the mythic figure of "Changing Woman." Other cultures use the moon goddess to convey the same motif, with constantly shifting lunar phases.

In becoming a fish, the egg woman feels and sees things as a fish would. She enters a new world and dramatizes a trait closely associated with the feminine—the ability to empathize deeply with other people, to feel and think as they do, to enter their worlds. The egg woman's tale suggests that empathy can extend beyond people to include nature. To the feminine psyche, relationships are possible not just with human beings, but with animals, and plants, too. The theme appears in other women's tales and surfaces in the work of women artists. Leonor Fini provides excellent visual examples[5] because her early work included many paintings of women who are half human and half plant or animal. Similar images emerge in the paintings of Remedios Varo, the poetry of Diane Wakoski, and the visions of Christiana Morgan.

In traditional psychology, empathizing with animals or plants is called "animism" and is considered immature—characteristic of children and primitive peoples, but not modern adults. This reflects conventional Western thinking, which sees nature as a thing to be used and exploited. Eco-feminism rejects this view and insists that human beings must relate empathically to animals and plants. In fact, empathizing with nature and shape-shifting reflect ancient shamanic traditions, and the egg woman's journey through various animal forms constitutes a classic shamanic initiation. Shamans usually describe their initiations in similar terms, saying that they descend through some opening in the earth, like a spring or a cave, the way the true wife dives into the well. The shaman then meets a spirit guide, often in the form of an animal. Or the shaman turns into an animal, paralleling the egg woman's transformation into a fish. At some point, the shaman is killed, or devoured by demons, and is reduced to a skeleton. But from the bones, the shaman is resurrected, just as occurs with the woman from the egg. The shamanic theme is significant because shamanism is probably the oldest form of human spirituality and healing. It antedates warrior tribes and patriarchal states by many millennia and reflects ancient egalitarian cultures—both women and men could be shamans.[6] So "The Woman from the Egg" draws on truly ancient traditions.

In shape-shifting, the woman from the egg changes physically—her whole body is altered. Here the tale highlights an important aspect of the deep feminine: it is closely linked to physical experience. Women, of course, undergo monthly physical changes with menstruation, and even more dramatically with pregnancy and childbirth. Patriarchal cultures usually view the body with distaste and distrust, claiming that the world of flesh is feminine and corrupt. "The Woman from the Egg" decisively rejects this notion, but in a subtle way. The story condemns the witch and her daughter, who do not shape-shift or alter their bodies. Yet the egg wife, who does, is rewarded and portrayed in a positive light. The witch and her daughter actually follow conventional patriarchal values—they are competitive and ruthless, seeking social prestige and power. So the story condemns civilization and culture, not nature and the body.

Overthrowing stereotypes about the body and attending

to bodily needs can be deeply healing for women. Sylvia Perera and Marion Woodman, for example, emphasize how women often benefit from "bodywork"—embodied forms of therapy, like dance, massage, or body manipulation. Talking things over in traditional psychotherapy often has limits and deeper, pre-verbal modes of change based on bodily experience are sometimes necessary. The egg woman's tale conveys the point in metaphorical language: she changes her physical form several times, moving from human to fish to fish bones to duck feathers, before she becomes fully human, fully herself. In reshaping her body, she reshapes her psyche, and she does not talk during the process, she simply experiences it.

THE DUCK AND THE GODDESS

The woman from the egg emerges from the golden feathers of a duck. The story might have used another farm animal, so the specific choice is significant. In ancient Egypt, the duck was specifically associated with Isis, the great goddess, suggesting that when the woman turns into duck feathers, she makes contact with a divine, feminine energy. In Native American tradition, the duck was considered a mediator between the sky and water, since it can fly and also swim. This link is central to the woman from the egg. She came from a nest, high up in a tree, near the sky and the heavens, but she later turns into a fish, living underwater in a well. So she unites sky and water, the celestial and the oceanic. The theme reappears in ancient goddess figures. Inanna, the Sumerian Queen of Heaven, for instance, was a celestial goddess, but she received much of her power from Enki, god of water. The Greek goddess Aphrodite was born from the sea when the blood of Ouranos dripped into the ocean, but Ouranos was a sky god, making Aphrodite the union of heaven and ocean. Within Teutonic tradition, particularly relevant to the German fairy tale, the goddess Holde (or Holle, or Hulda) was said to fly on the wind and disappear into lakes, streams, and springs. So she, too, crossed between sky and water.

In psychological terms, the watery underworld commonly represents the unconscious, while the celestial overworld often symbolizes a sublime, spiritual domain. The story thus suggests that the woman from the egg has access to the unconscious and to the divine, and this breaks with patriarchal religions with their duality of instinct and spirit. The former is associated with women and the underworld, while men and the masculine are considered celestial and spiritual. "The Woman from the Egg" insists that women have equal access to the spiritual and the instinctual, to sky and water. Indeed the story suggests that it is the deep feminine which heals the traditional schism between soul and body: through a woman's embodied experience, by symbolically becoming a fish and a bird, by empathizing deeply through bodily knowing, the feminine psyche unites spirit and matter.

THE WISE WOMAN

After the true wife turns into golden duck feathers, the crone recognizes how unusual and valuable the plumes are, plucks them, and keeps them in a pot. Later, the old woman notices that someone eats her food each day, and sets out to discover the culprit. She is observant, resourceful, and clever. In mythological terms, she is the wise crone, knowledgeable in the natural and supernatural. In fact, she completes what amounts to an initiation for the woman from the egg. The process began when the woman changed into a fish and duck, merging with nature and plunging into the deep feminine. For the transformation to be complete, the woman must return to everyday society, and this is what the wise crone accomplishes when she touches the woman, apparently allowing the egg wife to remain in her human form.

Because the old woman spies and interferes with what is going on, in a conventional view she would be dismissed as a nosy nuisance, meddling in other people's affairs. The tale rejects this stereotype and insists that her meddling and spying are essential and positive. In fact, in tribal societies, older women initiate young women into feminine mysteries by observing the young women carefully and intervening at the right time with rituals and training. Today's culture provides no such role for older women, or any instruction in how to become a ritual elder. The crone is not merely an inner figure, she is normally also an outer reality, carrying out an essential and honored social role.

RECOGNITION

Every day, the old woman goes to work for her neighbor, the husband of the egg woman. The crone plays the role of go-between, linking the woman and her husband and uniting different worlds, the deep feminine and conventional human society. One day, the egg woman decides to go to the neighbor in place of the crone. The crone is reluctant at first, saying that the man might want to keep her there. Her response has several possible meanings. She may simply be wary about men from her own experience, or she may fear losing the younger woman's help and company. But there is a third possibility, which is only hinted at in the present tale and which becomes clearer in others: a woman must often make a conscious effort to return to human society from the deep feminine.

When the woman from the egg goes to her husband's house, she dresses in dirty old clothes. She does not go directly to him and identify herself. This may be because she has been silenced for so long and has given up speaking for herself. Or it could be that she fears the power of the false wife. The ugly woman, after all, is a witch's daughter, and who knows what harm she could do to the true wife? In approaching the shadow, the dark side of the human heart, it is wise to be cautious and indirect. (The Greeks recognized this when they made offerings to Hecate, the goddess of the underworld—they approached her altar with their heads turned away.)

The woman from the egg may also be testing her husband.

So far he has not realized that the ugly wife is an impostor. Psychologically, he does not know that he relates to a false self, and if he does not wake up, the woman from the egg may well leave him forever, the way the first two egg women did. Other women's tales repeat the motif[7]: after a woman re-claims her true self, she returns to her husband in disguise and tests him to see if he can recognize her. These dramas reverse the "Cinderella" plot, where Cinderella must pass a test, namely, fitting her foot into the dainty shoe. In women's tales, it is the man who is tested. Is he conscious? Does he affirm women? The husband passes both challenges, recog-nizing his wife. He wakes up. Such new males, I might add, have been appearing more frequently in romance novels today.

WOMEN'S STORIES

When the husband figures out that the ugly wife is an impos-tor, he asks each woman in the house to tell a story. Like the true wife, he takes an indirect approach, not immediately confronting the false wife. This may be because he, too, is afraid of her power, but it could also mean that he adopts a more "feminine" perspective, giving up the reflex of young heroes to attack and kill a villain. In fact, by asking each woman for a story, the husband demonstrates an unconven-tional respect for women's talk. In most cultures, men dismiss what women say as gossip or old wives' tales. The husband rejects these stereotypes by listening to each woman's story.

When it is her turn to speak, the woman from the egg says that she has no stories, only a dream to recount. Having been silenced for so long, she may no longer believe in her own history, thinking her memories are false and fantastical. In fact, when a woman is forced to forget her history, the truth sometimes emerges only through dreams, and the initial clue that a woman was physically or sexually abused as a child, for example, may be terrifying dreams that are otherwise inex-plicable to her.

As the woman from the egg tells her dream story, the false wife asks the husband to leave and go back to sleep. As a false self, she needs the man to remain asleep and to live in false consciousness, like herself. The husband refuses. The true wife apparently does not give details of her experience of the deep feminine, and her transformation into various animals. One reason is probably discretion: women's mysteries are not to be exposed. Women in indigenous cultures are secretive in this way about their rituals, more than tribal men, who often tell anthropologists about male rituals. The experience of women's mysteries also cannot be easily reduced to words. As embodied, emotional experience, women's mysteries transcend verbal, intellectual knowledge.

RETRIBUTION AND RETURN

After hearing out his true wife, the husband goes to his mother-in-law, the witch, and asks her what punishment a person should suffer for trying to kill a man's wife and substituting a hideous impostor in her place. When the witch declares that such a villain, along with the false wife, should be shut up in a barrel full of nails and thrown from a high place, the husband does just that to her and her daughter. The husband lets the witch condemn herself. He evokes the witch's harsh, vindictive nature and turns it against her. In using the witch's own meanness against her, the husband practices a sort of psychological aikido. This is an indirect, clever approach, recalling feminine wisdom.

In punishing the witch and her daughter, the husband rescues his true wife. Yet this does not bring up the old fairy tale theme, where the brave hero saves a helpless woman and the two marry, with the wife eternally grateful and submissive. Killing off the witch and the false wife is better interpreted as killing off conventional stereotypes of women. Only when a man does this can a woman have an authentic relationship with him. Here the duck symbolism in the story takes on new meaning. In Chinese and Japanese mythology, ducks symbolize marital fidelity, since many species of ducks mate for life. Male and female birds are equally faithful.

In killing the witch and her daughter, the husband helps the woman from the egg take her rightful place in the human community. Since society is usually dominated by masculine influences, it is not surprising that the true wife needs help in this matter from a man. In real life, many successful women in business have had male mentors, higher up in the corporation, who helped them. The joyful reunion of the man and the egg woman concludes the tale with a familiar theme— the sacred reunion, the reconciliation of wife and husband after a long separation during which they both develop.

PART IV

Sisterhood

CHAPTER 8

"The Two Sisters":

Sisters and Liberation

(an Igbo tale from Africa[1])

ong, long ago, there lived two young sisters named Omelumma and Omelukka and they loved to play outdoors, laugh, and run about like any other children. One day, their parents left for a marketplace some distance from home.

"Beware of the beasts of land and sea," their father warned, "because many people have been carried off by the monsters."

"Stay inside the house, and do not make too much noise," their mother cautioned. "When you cook, use only a small fire, so the smoke will not attract the beasts," she added. "And when you pound the grain, do it quietly, so the monsters will not hear you."

"Above all," their father admonished, "do not go outside to play with the other children. Stay inside the house."

Omelumma and Omelukka dutifully nodded their heads, and waved goodbye as their parents departed. They stayed indoors all that morning, but as the hours went by, they became hungry. So they started pounding grain to make porridge, and it soon became a game, as they laughed and raised a big noise. Then they lit a huge fire so their porridge would cook faster, forgetting their mother's warning. After they ate their fill, the two sisters saw their friends playing in the fields and ran outside to join them.

As Omelumma and Omelukka were playing, a roar came from the forest and the sea, and monsters swarmed toward the children. In the terror and confusion, the two sisters were separated, and the beasts from the sea carried off Omelumma, while the monsters from land seized Omelukka. "Alas!" the two sisters cried out to themselves, "if only we had listened to our parents! Now we will be eaten!" But the two sisters were not devoured by the beasts. They were eventually sold into slavery and taken to lands far from home.

Omelumma was fortunate, and the first man who bought her fell in love with her. He freed Omelumma, married her, and made her the mistress of his house. Omelukka, the younger sister, was not so lucky. A cruel man bought her and forced her to work night and day, young as she was, then he sold her to an even more brutal master. In this way the poor girl was sold from one wicked man to another, and many years passed.

Meanwhile, Omelumma lived comfortably with her husband, and in due time gave birth to their first child, a baby boy. Overjoyed, her husband went to the market to find a slave to help his wife. He bought a young woman who was none other than Omelukka. But the two sisters had changed so much, neither recognized the other.

Each morning, Omelumma went to the market, giving her baby to Omelukka to tend, and listing all the chores to be done. Omelukka ran herself ragged trying to finish the work. When she went outside to fetch water or firewood, leaving the baby inside the house, he would cry, so she had to rush back to comfort the child. But then she could not bring in enough water or wood and her mistress would later beat her. Yet if Omelukka let the baby cry so she could finish her chores, the neighbors told Omelumma, and she beat her slave for neglecting her child. Omelukka tried carrying the baby with her while she worked, but this slowed her down, so her mistress beat her again.

One afternoon, the baby would not stop crying until Omelukka put him on her lap and rocked him gently. A neighbor came by and asked the slave why she was not doing her chores. The poor woman leaped up, fearful that the neighbor would tell her mistress. But then the baby started crying, so Omelukka sat down again and started rocking the child. Not knowing what to do, she finally sang a lullaby:

> "Hush, hush, little baby, cry no more.
> Our mother told us not to make a big fire,
> But we made a big fire.
> Our mother told us not to make a loud noise,
> But we made a loud noise.
> Our father told us not to play outside,
> But we played outside.
> So the beasts of land and sea took us away.
> Far, far away.
> And where might my sister be?
> Far, far away.
> Hush, hush, little baby, cry no more."

An old woman heard the song and remembered the story that Omelumma had told her long ago, of being carried off by the beasts of the sea while her younger sister was seized by the monsters of land. The crone realized that the slave must be Omelumma's long-lost sister! The old woman hurried to the market to tell Omelumma.

The next day, the mistress gave her slave many jobs to do and then left for the market as usual. Only this time, Omelumma returned secretly and hid behind the house. She saw her slave rush back and forth all morning trying to keep the child from crying, while doing the chores. Finally at her wit's end, Omelukka sat down to sing her lullaby.

> "Hush, hush, little baby, cry no more.
> Our mother told us not to make a big fire,
> But we made a big fire.
> Our mother told us not to make a loud noise,
> But we made a loud noise.

Our father told us not to play outside,
But we played outside.
So the beasts of land and sea took us away.
Far, far away.
And where might my sister be?
Far, far away.
Hush, hush, little baby, cry no more."

When Omelumma heard the song, she recognized her sister, and rushed out of her hiding place, weeping with grief and remorse. Omelukka was terrified that she would be beaten. "Do not be afraid," Omelumma exclaimed, "you are my long-lost sister, Omelukka!" Omelumma knelt at her sister's feet and begged forgiveness for the cruel beatings. The two sisters embraced and wept together, out of grief and love. Then Omelumma freed her sister and vowed never again to mistreat any servant. And so the two sisters lived in happiness and love, for the rest of their lives.

THE KIDNAPPING

Although apparently simple in plot, this African tale is extraordinarily important and insightful, highlighting a vital theme in women's tales—the importance of sisterhood, and the healing vitality of women's relationships with each other. The story begins with two young sisters who are left at home while their parents go on a short trip. Mother and father warn the girls to stay indoors, and not make too much smoke or noise lest the beasts of land and sea come. This seems like a common parental trick, frightening children into obedience with lurid tales. However, there is more here; the parents' warnings—not to make noise or a big fire, or go outside— symbolize what most cultures tell women from childhood onward: keep quiet, do not argue, and stay home. Good girls should also not be fiery—passionate, aggressive, or sexual. Omelumma and Omelukka do not obey because they have not yet been turned into "good girls" and they retain their natural vitality. Unfortunately, when the two sisters go outside to play, they are captured and sold into slavery. Here a bit of historical fact is important because the tale comes from the Igbo people in what is now Nigeria. From the time of European contact, many Igbo were captured, forced into slavery, and sent to America. So the beasts of land and sea were real monsters—human beings engaged in an unspeakable trade.

Those monsters also have archetypal meanings. In being attacked and captured by slave traders, who are presumably male, Omelumma and Omelukka reiterate a prominent theme in women's tales—women are assaulted by powerful male figures, such as the villain in "The Queen and the Murderer" or Hades in the Greek myth of Persephone.

Omelumma and Omelukka played with other children, implying they lived in a village of some sort—a traditional African setting. Yet Omelumma and Omelukka's parents do not ask neighbors or relatives to look out for the two girls. This is surprising because in a traditional village, neighbors and kin help each other extensively. The parents' isolation is the plight of most families in modern, urban life, and disasters often ensue. When parents lack the help with child care that a close-knit neighborhood and an extended family provide, it is easy to become overwhelmed with stress and some mothers and fathers take out their frustrations on their children, metaphorically becoming monsters of land and sea.

FORTUNATE AND UNFORTUNATE WOMEN

When Omelumma is sold into slavery, she is bought by a kind man who falls in love with her, and frees her. Her story takes a detour through the "Cinderella" tale, where an oppressed woman is rescued by a princely man. The romantic drama is enticing to many a young girl today, but Omelumma's sister offers an antidote. Sold to a series of cruel men, who exploit her and beat her mercilessly, Omelukka brings up the dark side of the "Cinderella" story—what happens when a woman ends up with a wife-beater instead of Prince Charming, a Bluebeard rather than a blueblood.

When the fortunate sister gives birth to a baby boy, her husband buys her a servant. (Notice in the stories that the first child is usually a boy, reflecting most cultures' patriarchal preference.) The slave is none other than Omelukka, but the two sisters do not recognize each other. This is astonishing in a woman's tale. It is usually the men who cannot recognize people. But the sisters' instincts, their true selves, have been anesthetized by a brutal master-slave culture.

The contrasting roles that Omelumma and Omelukka play highlight a duality that many cultures impose on women. Either women are placed on a pedestal and treated as idealized, pampered, beautiful beings or they are degraded and exploited, forced to work without stop and expected to sacrifice everything for others. The motif emerged earlier in "The Wise Wife," where the woman alternated between being the wife of the sultan living in luxury and being a slave woman, having sex with the sultan as the prize for a gambling wager. To add insult to injury, in most societies a woman's own talents usually do not determine whether she is pampered or enslaved. What matters is whom she marries, as "The Two Sisters" dramatizes.

CRUELTY

After being given the slave, Omelumma promptly begins to mistreat her. Omelumma becomes a cruel mistress, an oppressor—cruelty and abuse are issues of power, not gender. When someone has unlimited domination, that person can become cruel. Omelumma also turns abusive after she becomes a mother, and the timing is symbolic. Taking care of young children is frustrating and infuriating at times, yet mothers are expected to be nurturing, kind, and patient with their children. So mothers often split themselves into two false selves—an unrealistically nurturing side, and a dark, frustrated, angry side. The latter often erupts in a mother's imagination, with fantasies of abandoning or killing her children. The fantasies are normal, but many mothers fear that something is wrong with them for having such feelings.

Omelukka's plight as a slave is heartrending. If she tends the child in her charge, she cannot do her chores, and so she is beaten for laziness. But if Omelukka does the chores, she must leave the baby alone, and he starts crying. So she is beaten for neglecting him. No matter what she does, she cannot win. Many working mothers will empathize with Omelukka. If they attend to sick children, they miss work and are beaten up economically, losing pay or being reprimanded by bosses. If the mothers go to work, they must leave their children alone or put them in day-care centers, and many mothers beat themselves up with feelings of guilt for "neglecting" their children.

RECOGNITION

On a particularly bad day, Omelukka can neither comfort the baby nor complete her household chores. In desperation, she sings a lullaby, telling her sad life story. Up till now, Omelukka had not mentioned her tale of being captured and sold into slavery. Like other protagonists in women's tales, Omelukka has been silenced.

Omelukka sings her song to soothe the baby in her charge. Yet through her song, she reclaims herself and her history. Indeed, as a symbol of innocence and possibility not yet shaped by social convention, the baby personifies Omelukka's own potential to develop, if she can escape her oppressive situation. The infant represents Omelukka's hidden, undeveloped self. In singing for the child, Omelukka also sings for herself. In real life, when a mother takes care of a child, she often relives in a vicarious way her own childhood, and this gives her an opportunity to reclaim who she was as a little girl, before social pressures took their toll. In fostering her child's growth, a mother can nurture her true self. The same applies to teachers and students, aunts and nieces, and to women mentoring younger women.

Omelukka expresses her story indirectly, through a song. Here we return to a theme from "The Wise Wife"—indirect communication is sometimes the only means of expression possible for women. In fact, women often use singing to express themselves when not allowed to speak up, for example in the songs of Scottish women working in old textile mills or the spirituals of African-American women in slavery.[2]

Singing is powerful because it conveys strong emotions and bypasses logic. In many ways, singing is more basic than speaking. Long before babies understand words, they respond to the melody and rhythm of speech. Late in life, a stroke may destroy a person's ability to speak, but the capacity to sing and remember songs often remains intact. Singing gives access to a deep, fundamental level of the self, so it is not surprising that Omelukka recovers herself through song.

Omelukka's singing is not enough, though, and what is crucial is that an old woman overhears her, recalls Omelumma's tale, and deduces that mistress and slave are long-lost sisters. The old woman does two extraordinary things here. First, she heeds the words of a slave, seeing through social conventions. Second, she remembers what Omelumma mentioned long ago about her tragic childhood and puts two and two together. The old woman literally remembers, joining together what had been torn apart. She is a go-between in the best sense of the term, weaving together what society has cut apart. This is exactly what the old woman does in "The Woman from the Egg," helping the egg wife change from golden duck feathers into a human being. The wise woman here does the same thing: she helps the two sisters change their form, from a beastly master-slave dyad to human sisters.

SISTERS

When the old woman tells Omelumma about the slave's song, Omelumma hides and observes Omelukka. This is another example of an indirect approach and feminine wisdom. Omelumma needs to make sure that her slave is not inventing a story about being kidnapped as a child in order to win sympathy. If her slave sings such a story by herself, it must be authentic. When Omelumma hears the lullaby, she recognizes her sister, embraces Omelukka, weeps, begs forgiveness for beating her, and frees her. The familiar fairy tale ending then occurs: the two sisters live happily ever after.

In most fairy tales about youth, cruel, aggressive characters like Omelumma would be destroyed or severely punished. (Cinderella's stepmother and stepsisters are good examples. In the original Grimms' version, they have their eyes plucked out by doves as punishment for their cruelty to Cinderella.) In stories dealing with adults, however, nasty people see the error of their ways, ask for forgiveness, and reform. This, in fact, is a major task of maturity—coming to terms with one's faults and vices.

SISTER STORIES

Sisterhood is an archetypal motif in folk stories around the world and highlights an important dimension of the feminine which is sometimes underemphasized. Goddesses, for example, are commonly described in terms of three aspects—maiden, mother, and crone, corresponding to youth, maturity, and old age. Sisterhood brings up a fourth facet, linking the other three: friendship and loyalty between women, important throughout life. In fact, mythology is full of divine sisters and especially in Native American tradition.[3] Among the Hopi, for instance, two sisters, Huruing Wuhti of the East and Huruing Wuhti of the West, created all animals and human beings. Among Australian aboriginal tribes, the two

Wauwalak sisters are credited with shaping the land and establishing the customs and rituals of the tribes, while in Mesopotamia, Istustaya and Papaya were sister goddesses who spun the threads of fate.[4] Such sacred sisters were later ignored or denigrated, becoming horrible figures, like Medusa and her two Gorgon sisters in Greek mythology.

Mythology and women's tales reflect an ancient, practical reality of most traditional societies: women help and nurture each other.[5] Within the Igbo culture, from whence "The Two Sisters" comes, for example, women depend upon mutual solidarity to cope with oppressive traditions, gathering in the *otu umuada*, an organization of sisters and aunts—women related through the motherline. The *otu umuada* mediates disputes between husbands and wives, and even punishes men who mistreat women. Other cultures have analogous organizations, like the Kinki and Bundu women's societies in West Africa. Even outside of formal women's societies, sisterhood is vital in many indigenous societies. In the Malawi region of Africa, women have a special female friend, called a *chinjira*. The two women are not related by blood, but serve as confidantes, visiting each other frequently and helping each other out financially.

In Western culture, similar women's organizations and traditions were condemned, like the society of women on the Greek island of Lesbos. The all-female community honored Aphrodite, but the women were so vilified in historical accounts that the name "Lesbos" no longer connotes authentic sisterhood, the larger spirit of the community, but simply sex between women.[6] In medieval Europe, several remarkable women's societies emerged within the Roman Catholic Church, but were eventually suppressed. The women's community at Remiremont, for instance, melded Roman Catholicism with earlier Druidic traditions, where women played prominent religious roles.[7] The Remiremont women held services at ancient menhir sites, celebrated the solstices, and on certain festival days danced through the streets—violating medieval standards of feminine behavior. The organization was finally disbanded in the seventeenth century.

Excluded from formal, public forms, sisterhood remained

vital on a personal level as friendship. Women writers such as Jane Austen and Charlotte Brontë stressed the importance of friendship among women. In Victorian England, colonial America, and nineteenth-century Germany, even though they were dominated by patriarchal values, women confided their secrets to each other, were physically demonstrative in their affection, and maintained their loyalties over long periods of time. This remains true today, as Pat O'Connor notes in her study. When a woman has at least one dependable woman friend, she enjoys life more, has greater confidence in herself, and her children are happier, more skilled socially, and do better in school.[8]

MOTHERS AND SISTERS

In "The Two Sisters," the mother is mentioned only at the beginning, and the bulk of the tale focuses on the sisters. This is typical of women's stories, in contrast to fairy tales about girls which feature mothers prominently—from fairy godmothers to evil stepmothers. Youth tales also portray sisters as jealous, vindictive, and competitive. The shift here from mothers and negative sisters to positive images of sisterhood is significant. To children, a mother is of prime importance, and siblings often vie for attention from her. Hence sisters (and brothers) are often regarded negatively, which fairy tales exaggerate for drama. In adolescence when girls adopt social conventions and forget their authentic selves, they begin to compete with each other for boys. Later, when women reclaim their true selves, they reaffirm the importance of sisterhood and women's friendships. To a grown woman, moreover, a mother is no longer the primary figure in her life, but one of many, along with her own husband and children, her colleagues at work, and women friends. Many women develop more egalitarian, sisterly relationships with their mothers in adulthood.

Christine Downing observed this evolution in her own life, noting that she first dealt with issues around her mother and father, then her own children, and finally turned to her sister. Her writing reflects her evolution, because her early books focused on ancient mother goddesses, while her later ones turned to sister goddesses. Susan Griffin eloquently sums up this mature renaissance of sisterhood: the earth, she notes, is a sister, not just a mother.[9]

Although "The Two Sisters" is short, it introduces a vital theme that other stories will develop in greater depth. The next two tales take sisterhood and interweave it with the other motifs of women's tales, presenting a more complete portrait of the deep feminine.

CHAPTER 9

"Emme":

Rescuing the True Self

(from the Efik-Ibibio people of Africa[1])

n the olden days, there lived a beautiful girl named Emme. While she was still a child, a man named Akpan wanted to marry her when she came of age. So he brought many gifts to Emme's parents, as was the custom, and the marriage was agreed to. Seven years later, when Emme reached womanhood, the wedding date was set. Emme's father gave his daughter many gifts, including a slave girl the same age as Emme, sold into bondage by her own parents. Dressed in her wedding finery, Emme set off for her husband's village, accompanied by her younger sister and her new slave.

The way was long, hot, and dusty, so when Emme arrived at a spring near Akpan's village, she stopped to rest. The slave girl knew that a spirit lived in the pool who seized anyone who entered the water. Emme and her sister did not know this, so the slave had a wicked idea. "Mistress," the slave said, "why don't you go bathing in the pool? It will cool and refresh you before you arrive at your husband's home."

Emme took off her clothes and waded into the spring.

Suddenly the slave pushed her into the depths, where the water spirit seized her. Emme's younger sister shrieked in horror, but the slave girl slapped her. "Be quiet! From now on I will be the mistress. I will marry Akpan instead of your sister, and if you tell anybody, I will kill you!" The servant put on Emme's clothes, forced the little girl to carry everything, just like a slave, and they soon arrived at Akpan's village.

He awaited them eagerly, but when he saw the ugly slave woman, he felt disappointed and puzzled. Emme had been such a beautiful girl, he wondered how she could have become so homely, but he married her as planned. The slave became the mistress of the house and made life hard for Emme's sister, sending the young girl to do the worst chores and starving, beating, and burning the child. She even forced the poor girl to use her own fingers for kindling when making a fire! Emme's sister dared not protest, fearful that the slave would kill her. When Akpan asked the false wife why she treated the little girl so cruelly, the impostor replied that the girl was only a slave.

One day, the false wife sent the little girl to fetch water from the spring where Emme had vanished. The girl went to the pool, filled her water jar, found it too heavy to lift, and began crying, fearing another beating from the cruel slave.

"Emme, dear sister, if you can hear me," the little girl cried, "please help me."

The surface of the pool parted and Emme emerged from the depths. She embraced her younger sister, who told her of being beaten by the slave. The poor girl begged to go with Emme back in the water. "Be patient," Emme said. "Justice will surely be done some day. But for now, let me help you with your load." Emme lifted the water pot, and then vanished into the pool.

The false mistress beat the little girl for taking so long at the spring, but sent her there every morning for water. Each day, Emme appeared and comforted her little sister. One morning, though, Emme did not emerge as usual. A hunter from the village was hiding nearby, stalking game, and the water spirit prevented Emme from emerging for fear the hunter would see her. The little girl cried so piteously, however, that Emme prevailed upon the water spirit to let her comfort her sister. When Emme rose from the water and embraced her sister, the hunter saw her and was astonished at her beauty. "Who could she be?" he wondered. "The little girl calls her Emme, but that is the name of Akpan's wife!" The hunter hurried away to tell Akpan.

The next day the two men hid near the pond and waited. The girl arrived, filled her pot from the spring, and then cried out, "Emme, I am here. Where are you, dear sister?" Emme rose from the water, and Akpan immediately recognized her. "She is the real Emme! The woman I married is an impostor! Emme must have been seized by the water spirit, so her slave took her place!"

Akpan went to a wise old woman, who regularly made sacrifices to the water spirit. "How can I free Emme?" he asked her. The old woman pondered a moment, and then said, "Bring me some eggs, a white chicken, a piece of white cloth, a white goat, and a white slave. I will offer them as a sacrifice to the water spirit and he will release Emme the day afterward."

Akpan and his friend obtained everything and accompanied the crone to the spring. The old woman bound the white slave, cut his throat, and pushed him into the spring. The chicken, the goat, the eggs, and the white cloth followed. Then she, Akpan, and his friend returned home.

The next morning, the crone went to the spring alone and found Emme standing beside the pool. The old woman took her home and sent a message to Akpan, telling him to come secretly to her house. When Akpan arrived, Emme asked him to bring her sister to her, and he did. The two sisters embraced and wept with relief. Then Emme told her sister to go to the false wife, taunt her, and run back to the old woman's house, where they would all be waiting.

The little girl went to the false mistress and cried out, "You are not Emme. You are only my sister's slave! You are evil and you will be punished!" The slave woman picked up a stick and chased the girl, following her into the old woman's house. When the slave woman burst inside, she saw Emme and Akpan waiting. He and his comrade seized her, took off her fine clothes, and made her into a slave once again. From then on, Emme treated the false mistress the way she had treated Emme's sister. Emme made the slave do all the hard work, beat her mercilessly, and forced her to light her fingers when kindling fires. Finally Emme tied the wicked woman to a tree until she starved to death.

As for Emme, the village celebrated her return with a great feast. She and Akpan married as planned and lived happily together as husband and wife for the rest of their days.

THE OPENING DRAMA

This African tale combines the drama of "The Woman from the Egg" and "The Two Sisters," weaving them together in a complex, creative way. The story starts off with Emme as a child, but quickly shifts to issues of marriage and mature womanhood. In embracing several stages of life, the story provides another example of the inclusive, holistic spirit of women's tales. (Men's tales usually focus on youth or midlife, but not both.) Note that Emme was betrothed to Akpan when she was only a girl, and apparently had no say in the plans. Emme also had to move to her husband's village, giving up her friends and family. Her drama tale thus begins with a familiar theme—women's oppression.

When Emme comes of age, her father gives her many wedding presents, including a slave. The slave was sold by her parents, emphasizing the theme of women's oppression. A generous man, Emme's father seems to care deeply about her. Yet calamity still befalls her. One reason may be that Emme's mother is hardly mentioned at all—the motherline is absent, which usually leads to bad results.

After a long, hot journey, Emme and her party rest by a

spring. The slave lures her into the pool, knowing that a water spirit will seize her. The episode recalls "The Woman from the Egg," where the witch attacks the true wife who then vanishes into a well. Emme's fate also resembles the Greek myth of Persephone, who was abducted by another shadowy male figure—Hades. The parallels reveal the archetypal nature of women's tales, independent of particular cultures.

After Emme is trapped in the water, the slave girl dresses in Emme's clothes, masquerades as the mistress, and marries Akpan, who does not recognize the switch. Psychologically asleep, he is unaware or unconscious of his wife's true identity. Emme, for her part, vanishes into the unconscious—her true self goes underground.

GOOD AND BAD

Beautiful, naive, sheltered, and innocent, Emme contrasts sharply with her slave, who is is ugly, ambitious, aggressive, nasty, self-seeking, streetwise, and cunning. The story reflects a stark dichotomy in most societies between "good women," who are demure, accommodating, nurturing, gentle, and chaste, and "bad women," who speak their minds, express their anger, enjoy sex, and ask for what they want. Seen in this light, it is clear that both Emme and the slave girl are false selves. They are not individual, unique persons, but stereotypes. Emme's task is to repudiate these conventions and reclaim her authentic self.

The contrast between the two women brings up another point. The slave reflects traditional notions about sin, which revolve around greed, selfishness, and unbridled ambition. As feminist theologians and writers have pointed out,[2] there is another type of sin—the evil of self-negation, of hiding one's true self, of not developing one's unique individuality. Emme, submerged in the pool, symbolizes this sin of self-submergence and self-forgetting.

The slave presumably felt jealous of Emme's privileged position. Coming from a supportive, wealthy family, Emme can look forward to a continued life of ease, while the slave girl has nothing but labor and humiliation ahead of her. Envy between women, in fact, often comes from women's limited opportunities: unable to use their talents, achieve their dreams, or speak their minds, women naturally feel angry but cannot direct their feelings at men for fear of violent retaliation. So the frustration may boil up as envy of other women.

Negative though envy might seem, it offers hidden benefit. As Luise Eichenbaum and Susie Orbach emphasize, envy and jealousy indicate a woman still has desires and ambitions. Allowed to unfold, these frustrated energies offer the potential for new life. The story hints at this point because the envious slave is active and energetic, eventually starting the chain of events that frees Emme. Symbolically, the envious part of a woman's psyche often causes trouble, and forces the woman to reclaim her true self.

THE CRUELTY OF THE FALSE WIFE

The wicked servant terrorizes the little girl into keeping quiet about Emme, providing another illustration of women being silenced. The false wife proceeds to abuse the girl, and this brutality probably comes from profound insecurity. She is really a slave, in dread of being exposed, and takes out her terror and distress on a convenient target, a defenseless child. The slave's insecurity dramatizes women's precarious place in most cultures. A woman may have great influence in her family, but should she lose her husband through death or divorce, she commonly forfeits her social status and economic well-being. Like the slave in the fairy tale, many women are in constant danger of plunging back into poverty. The slave's insecurity also has inner, psychological meanings. As Polly Young-Eisendrath and Florence Wiedermann observe, many women believe that they have a secret defect they cannot quite name, and which they fear will be exposed to the world. Some women fear they are monstrous because they sometimes become angry or ask for what they need. Other women fear that they do not deserve the good fortune they enjoy, erroneously attributing their accomplishments to luck. Fearful of being exposed as impostors, some women drive themselves to exhaustion, trying to be the perfect mother, wife, worker, and citizen. They goad themselves to work without rest, chastising themselves for not doing better, the way the slave constantly beat Emme's younger sister and made her work without rest. The challenge is to break free from this cruel inner slavemaster, and the crucial figure here is Emme's little sister.

THE LITTLE SISTER

The little girl can be interpreted on many levels. We can take her at face value, as Emme's sister, and this brings up the theme of sisterhood, which the story explores in depth. The little girl goes to fetch water one day and, unable to lift the water jar, calls on her sister, asking to join Emme in the pool—in silence and oblivion. Here the little sister expresses the despair of many young girls, beaten down by social conventions. Emme arises from the pool, helps her younger sister lift the water jug, and then offers sympathy and comfort. She tells her little sister that justice will be served some day. At this point, Emme's assurances are wishful thinking, because she has not done anything to free herself, nor has anyone else. Vital though her sympathy is to the young girl, it does not solve the underlying problems. Justice comes only when Emme leaves the pool, confronts the slave, and claims her rightful place in human society: women must take action to solve practical problems.

Notice that there is no evil old witch or wicked stepmother in the drama, as is common in youth tales. "Emme" replaces such evil mother figures with a negative sister figure—the slave woman who is about the same age as Emme. The story thus repeats the shift, first seen in "The Two Sisters," from mother to sister figures.

Emme's little sister can also be interpreted as a part of Emme, an inner figure. Then we can interpret the little girl as Emme's original self, before Emme was forced to follow feminine stereotypes. Figures like Emme's little sister often appear in women's dreams as reminders of their true selves, as Emily Hancock notes, and a woman's task is to reclaim this younger, natural self.

EMERGENCE

The slave forces the little girl to fetch water from the same pool in which Emme is imprisoned. This seems foolish. It would be safer to keep Emme's sister away from the pool, and even smarter to kill her, eliminating the only witness to the slave's crime. Yet the false wife is not stupid—we already know how cunning she is. So there must be deeper meaning to her actions. She functions as an inner enemy—an internal figure who forces a woman to develop. In engineering her abduction by the water spirit, for instance, the slave compels Emme to learn about the dark side of life and to enter the underworld. Later, by demanding that the little girl fetch water from the spring each day, the slave gives Emme a chance to return to the everyday realm. Without her underworld sojourn, Emme may have simply moved from a privileged childhood to a comfortable marriage, remaining undeveloped psychologically. The slave forces Emme to individuate, and personifies that part of a woman's psyche that pushes her, often ruthlessly, to reclaim her energy and strength.

One day a hunter sees Emme emerge from the pool and tells Akpan, who goes to the spring and recognizes Emme. He realizes that the woman he married is an impostor—he finally wakes up. He then consults an old woman, and this is noteworthy, because the hero usually just dashes off to rescue the maiden in distress. Instead, Akpan recognizes his limits and seeks the advice of a woman. He honors the deep feminine, which suggests that he is on his way to becoming a "new male," like Ivan in "Maria Morevna." Emme's story offers an important reminder here—"new men" alone cannot rescue women. The wise crone is needed, too.

We can also interpret Akpan as an inner character personifying part of Emme's psyche. He then qualifies as a positive animus figure and exemplifies the role of the animus in a woman's psyche: Akpan is a messenger, a go-between, not a rescuer or redeemer. In consulting the old woman, Akpan links Emme to the deep feminine and acts as her executive assistant—just like Ivan in "Maria Morevna."

THE CRONE

The old woman knows how to free Emme, understanding the secrets of magic and the underworld—how the unconscious works. She can be interpreted as an inner figure, representing Emme's mature self. Emme, her little sister, and the crone symbolize three aspects of the feminine—the maiden, the mature woman, and the crone, the so-called triple goddess. But the story adds an insightful twist to this traditional trinity with a fourth figure, the slave woman, who highlights the split forced on women by most cultures between a good, naive, demure woman and a bad, assertive, cunning one. The task of the crone and Emme's younger sister is to heal that split.

The wise woman tells Akpan to obtain a basket of eggs, a white cloth, a white chicken, a white goat, and a white slave as sacrifices to the water spirit. The eggs allude to the feminine domain and symbolize new life, pointing to Emme's renaissance, as she emerges from her imprisonment. Although not explicitly mentioned, the eggs would probably be white, like the other sacrificial objects. White is commonly used in women's initiations in many different African tribes,[3] and the color is symbolic of purification and sometimes death, because women initiates are said to die and then be reborn. Emme's story fits this pattern. When she disappears into the pool, she symbolically dies, and when she reappears, she is reborn. Her whole abduction, descent into the underworld, and return, in fact, form part of an initiatory experience.

The sacrifice of a slave may be horrifying to readers, but slavery and human sacrifice were common in most ancient cultures from Europe to Asia. The grim event also dramatizes an archetypal meaning: to rescue one life another must be given up, particularly in warrior traditions. In modern life, the human sacrifice women must make may involve figuratively killing off an abusive or stultifying relationship.

The story says that the slave who is sacrificed is male, rather than female: so a man is sacrificed to liberate a woman, which is surprising, since the story comes from a patrilineal culture, where men dominate. The story suggests that a woman must at some point sacrifice and subordinate masculine values to her deeper feminine self. The sacrificial slave was also white—another unexpected role reversal, since European colonialists dominated African cultures from the eighteenth century or so. During Europe's Middle Ages, however, when Arab and African cultures dominated, whites captured in wars were sometimes sold as slaves.

E M M E ' S   R E T U R N

The morning after the sacrifice, the old woman returns to the pool and finds Emme there, released by the water spirit. Significantly, Emme then goes to the old woman's home and not to Akpan's. Something similar happened in "The Woman from the Egg," where the true wife lived with the old woman for a time. Psychologically speaking, escaping from a false self can be exhilarating and inspiring, but a woman cannot simply rush back to the world with its masculine values. Women often need a brief period of solitude and reflection in a feminine realm to consolidate their insight and growth. Today, the pause may involve psychotherapy, journal writing, guided imagery, meditation, a women's shelter, or a women's group. But the time of sanctuary is vital.

When Akpan sees Emme, the first thing she does is ask him to bring her younger sister to her. Emme does not fall into his arms, thanking him for rescuing her. Instead she affirms her sister, the importance of sisterhood and the feminine. Symbolically, Emme embraces her true self, the girl within, rather than the hero or the animus.

Emme then asks her sister to lure the wicked slave to the house. Here Emme becomes active for the first time, shifting from a passive attitude, symbolized by her immersion in the pool and her stay in the old woman's house, to an active extroverted perspective, regaining her place in human society. This is another important lesson for women. The true self, dramatized by the wise crone, may be a source of profound wisdom, creativity, and healing, but the deep self is often not familiar with the ways of everyday life and the need for clever action. That is the job of the ego—attending to worldly business.

Emme uses an indirect method to confront her slave, rather than marching over with Akpan to condemn her. First Emme provokes the false wife into trying to beat the little girl, revealing just how cruel the slave is. Emme thus prompts the false wife to convict herself in front of everybody, and only then does Emme punish her by treating her the way she treated Emme's sister. Eventually, Emme ties the slave to a tree and starves her to death. As an outer event, this would be cruel, but as an inner event it reveals how Emme has reclaimed her assertive, aggressive energies—just like the queen killing the murderer in "The Queen and the Murderer." Emme is no longer naive and docile. Starving the slave is also symbolic. Emme does not feed the ambitious, cruel, demonic side of herself—her shadow. Such self-discipline is necessary in dealing with the dark side of the human heart.

WOMEN'S MYSTERIES: THE THESMOPHORIA

The basic themes of Emme's story reappear in women's rituals around the world, and the Thesmophoria, an ancient Greek rite older than the Eleusinian Mysteries, highlights the parallels.[4] The ritual began with women withdrawing from men and living in primitive huts they built themselves, preparing meals without fire. Symbolically they forsook civilization and returned to nature, the way Emme left her village and traveled in the wilderness, betwixt and between, away from society. After nine days of purification, the main ritual of the Thesmophoria would begin. The first rite was called the Kathodos or Downgoing, because the women descended into a chasm carrying suckling pigs, ritually entering the underworld, just like Emme being dragged into the pool. Before the women returned they made a blood sacrifice, killing the pigs, an offering to a male snake deity, analogous to the old woman sacrificing the goat, chicken, and slave to the male water spirit.

On the second day of the Thesmophoria, women mixed grain and rotten pig flesh and placed the substance on an altar, later planting the mixture in the fields. In this way the women celebrated the power of nature to bring life out of death. This fertility theme is not explicit in Emme's tale, but the rebirth motif is clear. Next in the Thesmophoria, the women gathered together and sat on the ground, bringing up any complaint or dispute they had with other women, and a free-for-all discussion would result, often exploding into screaming and insults. Their fighting highlights the dark side of sisterhood and friendship—the envy and jealousy between women, dramatized by the evil slave in Emme's tale. By giving a ritual space to these shadowy

energies, the Thesmophoria channels the emotion construc-
tively.

On the final day, called the Kallegeneia, or Fair Born, the
women honored Persephone and her return from the underworld. They affirmed the power of the feminine to renew
itself, to rise from the dead, the way Emme returned from the
pool. By celebrating the Thesmophoria together, women affirmed their solidarity with one another and with the deep
feminine. They created a spiritual sisterhood in their ritual,
echoing the sister theme in "Emme."

THE GOOSE SOCIETY

In Native American culture, the Goose Society among the
Arikara, Hidatsa, and Mandan tribes of the Great Plains
provides another parallel to Emme's tale. According to legend, the Goose Society was founded by a woman who
dreamed that a goose came to her and taught her two major
ceremonies. In the first, the autumn celebration, women
gathered together and set up a rack of dried meat as a gift to
the wild geese on their migration south. The south was
associated with the land of the dead, so the geese flying
there symbolized a journey into the underworld, paralleling
Emme's descent into the pool of water. In the Goose Society,
the offerings were gifts to Old-Woman-Who-Never-Dies, to
persuade her to bring new life to the earth after winter. She
personifies the life-giving power of the deep feminine. In
specifically using meat, the Goose Society recalls the sacrifice of the chicken, goat, and slave in "Emme"—life must be
sacrificed for renewal and regeneration.

In the second Goose Society rite, held in the spring, the
women put out dried meat, but this time representatives of all
the men's societies took the offerings and left gifts in return.
Each Goose Society woman then wrapped an ear of corn in
sage, and ran in a ceremonial race. The winner was the
woman to whom the Goose spirits would speak that year.

This ritual echoes Emme's story, where Emme needs Akpan's masculine help to return to the human world. Women and men, feminine and masculine, must cooperate. The race in turn provided a sacred space for envy or competition, analogous to the battle between Emme and the evil servant at the end of the fairy tale.

CHAPTER 10

"The Mother and the Demon":

Sisters of Nature

(from Japan[1])

here once was a woman who lived with her wealthy husband and their beloved daughter. When the day came for the young woman to marry, the mother was overjoyed. She accompanied her daughter in a festive bridal party as they traveled across the mountains to the husband-to-be. The bride rode in a carriage, while her mother, friends, and relatives walked alongside, singing and laughing.

Suddenly a dark cloud fell from the sky and surrounded the coach. Everyone fled, fearing an evil spirit, but the cloud lifted as quickly as it had appeared. And the bride was missing from the carriage!

"My daughter! Where is my daughter!" the mother cried.

"A demon has seized her!" all the people exclaimed. "We must run!"

"But where is my daughter? I must find her!" the mother repeated. Her relatives and friends dragged her with them as they ran from the mountains.

Safely back in her village, the mother would not rest. "I must find my daughter!" she repeated, although everyone warned her not to go back to the mountains lest the demon kill her, too. But the mother made up her mind. She packed rice to eat, donned warm clothes, tied on sturdy shoes, and set off for the mountains.

All day the mother climbed hills and followed valleys, calling out her daughter's name, but only the wind and birds answered her. By the time night fell, the mother was exhausted. She saw a light in the distance and walked toward it hoping to find shelter for the night. She found a temple in the middle of a meadow, and when she approached, a nun emerged at the door.

"Reverend Lady," the mother bowed, "I am far from home. May I stay in your temple for the night?"

The nun quickly ushered the mother in. "I have no food to offer you," the nun apologized, "but you may spend the night here."

"I thank you, Sister," the exhausted mother sighed, and lay down to sleep. The nun took off her own cloak and put it over the mother.

"You seek your daughter," the nun said gently, "and I know what happened to her and how you can find her. She was kidnapped by a demon who lives on the other side of the river that runs near here. To cross the water, you must use a magic bridge called the Abacus Bridge. It is made of beads and if you step on one, you will fall to the place of birth and perish, so be careful to step between the beads. To enter the demon's castle, you must pass his guard dogs, a big one and a little one. They are vicious, and will kill you if they catch you. But each afternoon, the beasts fall asleep for a short time, and you can enter the fortress safely."

"Thank you, Reverend Lady," the mother murmured, so worn out she could not keep her eyes open. In the morning, the mother awoke with a start. She found herself in a sunny meadow, with no nun or temple nearby—only a small, weathered stone pagoda, an old shrine from long ago. The mother had slept with her head on the pagoda, using it as a pillow. The wind blew through the grass, making a sad and lonely sound.

"Did I only dream of the temple and the nun?" the mother

wondered. Then she looked around and saw a river. Arching over it was a bridge made of beads, and on the far side of the river was a castle, with a big dog and a little dog guarding the entrance—just as the nun had described. "So it was not a dream!" the mother exclaimed. "Now I know where my daughter is! Thank you, Reverend Sister!"

The mother waited patiently until the dogs fell asleep, then climbed upon the bridge, careful to step between the beads. She crossed the river, stole past the sleeping dogs, and entered the demon's castle. "How will I find my daughter in such a big place?" she wondered. Then she heard the sound of a loom. "Perhaps that is her weaving!" the mother thought. Sure enough, she found her daughter working at a loom, and when they saw each other, mother and daughter wept with joy, ran to each other, and embraced.

"You are safe!" the mother exclaimed.

"The demon of this castle kidnapped me," the daughter explained. "He and his servants are gone for the day, so we are safe." The daughter bustled about, preparing dinner for her mother. Suddenly, there was a commotion at the castle gate, and the dogs started barking.

"The demon has returned!" the daughter cried out. "Quickly, Mother, you must hide or the demon will surely kill you!" The daughter opened a stone box next to a large wooden chest. "You will be safe in here," she told her mother, locking the stone casket shut.

The demon came into the room and started to sniff suspiciously. "I smell a human," he growled.

"Of course you do," the young woman answered. "I am human."

"No, silly woman," the demon snapped, "I smell another person."

"You must be wrong," the daughter retorted. "How could anyone pass your vicious dogs, or cross the Abacus Bridge?"

"You are hiding someone," the demon grunted, and went to a magic plant in his garden, which sprouted a blossom for each person in the castle. There were three flowers, and the demon stormed back to the young woman.

"Wife," he shouted, "you are hiding someone. My magic

plant shows that there are three people in the castle! Tell me who you are hiding, or I will kill you!"

"I am not hiding anyone!" the young woman replied, but the demon reached out to grab her. Suddenly the young woman had an idea. "Oh, I know why there are three blossoms! The third is for the baby I am carrying. I am pregnant, and it is your child!"

"What?" the demon shouted with joy. "I am to be a father? Break out the wine, bring in the drums and flutes! It is time to make merry! And let's beat the dogs! Kill them!" The demon started drinking and singing uproariously. He struck the two dogs, killed them, and danced merrily on. His servants joined in the festivities, and soon they were all drunk.

"Wife," the demon grunted, "I am falling asleep. Put me in the big wooden box." She quickly helped him into the wooden chest, shutting its seven lids and locking its seven locks. When she saw the demon's servants were all fast asleep, she ran to the stone box and let her mother out.

"Mother," she whispered, "we must escape while the demon and his servants are asleep." The two women ran out of the castle and toward the stables, thinking to flee with the demon's horses. In the livery, they found two carriages—a thousand-mile carriage and a ten-thousand-mile carriage.

"Which shall we take?" they asked each other. As they hesitated, the nun suddenly appeared beside them.

"Take neither carriage," the nun warned. "Use a boat, and escape by water." The mother and daughter ran to the river, leaped in a boat, and started rowing furiously.

In the castle, the demon woke up and started calling for his wife. "Bring me water!" he commanded, but when his wife did not respond, he started breaking out of the wooden box, smashing the seven lids and the seven locks. "Where is my wife!" he yelled. "She must have escaped!" He woke his servants and they ran to the stables. They found all the horses and carriages still there so they rushed to the river and saw the mother and daughter in the boat. "There she is, the wretch!" the demon shrieked. "And she is with somebody else. I was right, there was another human in my castle!"

The demon turned to his servants. "Drink up the river! The

two women will not escape me!" He bent down and began swallowing water. His servants did the same, and as they sucked up the river, the women's boat was swept back toward them.

"We are lost!" mother and daughter cried out, as their boat neared the demon. Suddenly the nun appeared on the vessel.

"Lift your skirts," the nun commanded. "Show your private parts to the demon! Quickly, you have no time to waste!" All three women lifted their kimonos and exposed themselves, jumping up and down. At the sight, the demon and his henchmen started laughing. "What's this!" the demon choked. "I have never seen anything so funny!" The demon and his servants spewed out the water they had swallowed, and the torrent pushed the women's boat down the river. The three women were soon far from the demon's castle.

"Reverend Sister," the mother turned to the nun, "you saved our lives. How can we thank you!"

The nun paused, then said, "There is one thing you can do for me. I am the spirit of the stone pagoda in the meadow. I often feel lonely, being by myself there. If you would bring a new stone pagoda each year to the glade, and put it next to mine, I would have company." The nun then vanished.

The mother and daughter returned home safely, and each year from then on, they brought a stone pagoda to the meadow, until there was a whole village of them, in the grassy field, deep in the mountains. And so they all lived happily ever after—mother, daughter, their families, and the nun and her new companions.

MOTHERS AND DAUGHTERS

This tale explores the relationship between a mother and her grown daughter. The drama transcends cultures—an almost identical story comes from the mountains of Kentucky[2] and both tales closely parallel the Greek myth of Demeter and Persephone.

The fairy tale begins with a mother who loves her daughter dearly, and the two apparently have a close, happy relationship, like Demeter and Persephone. So the story shifts away from the negative mother figures and mother-daughter conflicts in stories like "The Three Little Eggs" and "The Handless Woman" to focus on the positive potential of the relationship—how mothers and daughters help one another grow.

On the way to her wedding, the daughter is kidnapped by the demon—just like "The Woman from the Egg" and "Emme." The male demon here is another ominous animus. The demon also apparently traveled in a cloud or took the form of a dark cloud and this links him to gods of storm and sky, who are male in most mythologies. (In Japanese mythology, the chief troublemaker is the male god of storms.) So we can interpret the demon as a symbol of powerful males or male power in society. More generally, we can interpret him as the shadow of patrilineal cultures, the unconscious side of society. His abduction of the daughter dramatizes how women are imprisoned by confining feminine stereotypes in most cultures.

The demon appears when the daughter is leaving home, on the way to her own life. Many tensions between mother and daughter arise at this point, which is usually during adolescence and early adulthood. The daughter may resent her mother's authority and rebel. The mother, for her part, may envy her daughter's greater freedom and opportunities—chances that society did not give her. The demon may represent the resulting conflicts—and the shadow side of both mother and daughter.

INNER AND OUTER

Besides being a person in her own right, we can interpret the daughter as a part of the mother's psyche, an inner figure rather than an outer one. Here the daughter would represent the mother's young, innocent self, which was kidnapped and silenced by social convention. In searching for "the inner daughter," the mother is seeking her true self, her natural self. The daughter's dual meaning here—as the mother's young self and as a person separate from the mother—dramatizes an important aspect of the feminine psyche: as Janet Surrey put it, women normally oscillate in their sense of identity between mother and daughter roles, and a woman's identity is usually closely linked to her mother's and, if she has them, to her daughters'.[3] The mother sees her younger self in her daughter, and the daughter sees her older self in her mother. The titles of two books sum up the point: Nancy Friday's *My Mother/My Self* and Kathryn Rabuzzi's *Motherself.*

However, a very close relationship between mother and daughter can inhibit the individual development of both, as the Greek myth of Persephone underscores. At the beginning of their story, Demeter and Persephone live together in a happy, fulfilling dyad. At this stage, Persephone has no name and is simply known as Kore, or maiden, lacking any identity apart from being Demeter's daughter. Only after she is separated from her mother is she known as Persephone, becoming a separate, unique individual.

The demon in the fairy tale effects such a separation. At the beginning, mother and daughter are close and loving, and it is the demon who violently separates the two, forcing them to become unique, strong individuals. The demon represents otherness, the other, and compels mother and daughter to recognize the otherness in each other. To dramatize his otherness, the demon assumes a form completely opposite of the mother-daughter dyad—he is single, male, hostile, and violent. His violence reflects how the unconscious often experiences individuation at first—as an assault. A close mother-daughter relationship, after all, is comforting, and any change will seem like a loss or a disruption at first. So the demon can be interpreted as an inner enemy, a force deep within a woman's own psyche, pushing her toward greater individuation in her relationships.

THE SEARCH

After her daughter is abducted, the mother insists on looking for her despite the danger, just as Demeter did. Distressed as she was, though, Demeter was never in any personal danger herself, since she was an Olympian goddess. Not so with the mother here, and her friends and family warn that whatever seized her daughter may attack her. Yet she sets off anyway, demonstrating how brave she is. Her courage is all the more remarkable because the father apparently does nothing to help. The same thing occurs in Persephone's tale, where her father, Zeus, did nothing to rescue her (mainly because he had agreed to the abduction beforehand).

The mother's search for her daughter is heroic but note that her quest aims at rescue, rather than power or wealth, the traditional goals of a hero: she seeks reunion not renown, communion not conquest. Merlin Stone observed the same theme in mythology: when goddesses embark upon heroic journeys, it is to restore what has been broken or injured. Isis searched for the pieces of Osiris's body to resurrect him; the Shekina gathers up Jewish souls in exile; and Nu Kwa, a Chinese goddess, went through the world after a holocaust, repairing the cosmos.

At night, the mother meets a nun at a temple and asks for help, bringing up several recurrent themes in women's tales. First, the mother finds refuge in the wilderness, in nature, far from civilization. Second, a mysterious but knowledgeable woman aids the mother, playing a role similar to that of the wise old crone. The story, though, does not mention the nun's age, so we cannot assume she is an old woman. This highlights an important point—womanly wisdom does not require being old! Nuns are usually part of a community of religious women and this is true of Buddhist tradition, the cultural setting for the tale. Nuns are usually called sisters, and this introduces the spiritual aspect of sisterhood. Indeed, the nun resembles the Greek goddess Artemis, who lived in the wilderness and customarily remained in the company of nymphs and dryads—sisterly companions.

In the myth of Demeter and Persephone, Hecate plays a role similar to the nun's. When Demeter went searching for her daughter, nobody would help, either because they did not know what happened to Persephone or they feared angering Hades. Only Hecate, goddess of the underworld, came to Demeter's aid. (Significantly, Hecate was a descendant of the Titans, who antedated the Olympian gods and goddesses. So she represents an ancient, pre-patriarchal culture.) Artemis, Hecate, and the nun illustrate an important figure in women's stories, what might be called the sister of nature, a helpful, sisterly figure tied to the wilderness. These tales emphasize that nature and sisterhood are fundamental aspects of the deep feminine.

INNER WISDOM

When giving the mother shelter in the temple, the nun has no food to offer. But the mother needs none, having packed her own provisions. Psychologically speaking, the wise woman within a woman's soul, personified by the nun, will not provide food, money, or other material help. The inner crone is not a fairy godmother, nor does she play the role of a substitute mother, and women must take care of themselves. This means that inner psychological work or a supportive therapist is not enough. Women must also find satisfying jobs, appropriate partners, reliable day care, and safe communities. The nun does give her cloak to the mother, offering emotional warmth and comfort, a great strength of sisterhood. Even more important, the nun tells the mother about the demon who kidnapped her daughter and how to reach the young woman. This is what the mother really needs—not just support, but insight, too. The same contrast between psychological and practical help appeared prominently in "Emme," where she comforted her younger sister but did not change the little girl's awful situation. That required the wisdom of the old crone.

The next morning, the mother awakens to find herself

alone in a meadow, deep in the wilderness. Her nocturnal encounter with the nun was a dream, or a spiritual revelation. The nun is an inner figure bringing wisdom to the mother from her own inner depths. She also discovers that she used a small stone pagoda as a pillow. The pagoda would be a tiny version of the full-sized towers traditionally associated with Buddhist temples. In Japan, miniature pagodas were also used as shrines, dwelling places for various nature spirits and deities associated with many rocks, streams, plants, animals, mountains, and valleys. This suggests that the nun is a nature spirit of some sort, living in the small stone pagoda. The word "pagoda," I might add, derives from Sanskrit and means "divine female."

In making contact with a nature spirit, the mother underscores the deep link between the feminine psyche and nature. As a nature spirit, the nun is associated with a particular place, and thus with the earth. Yet she is not a mother figure, but a sister. So the nun confirms Susan Griffin's comment that the earth is also a sister, not just a mother.

THE BRIDGE

Following the nun's directions, the mother sees the demon's castle across the river, guarded by a big dog and a little dog. The river and the dogs deepen the parallel between the Japanese tale and the Greek myth of Persephone, who was dragged into the underworld—guarded by Cerberus, a three-headed dog—across the river Styx. In Hindu and Buddhist mythology, too, a dog guards the underworld, and in many other cultures the land of the dead is said to be surrounded by a river.

To reach the demon's castle, the mother must cross a magic bridge, called the Abacus Bridge, made of beads. The nun warns the mother not to step on the beads, lest she fall to the place of birth and perish. This part of the tale stumps me, so I shall offer only a few suggestions. The bridge is made of beads, and beads are an ancient form of decoration, usually associated with the feminine. The beads thus bring up the theme of feminine beauty, and in most cultures women's beauty is for men's pleasure. In warning the mother not to tread on the beads, the nun seems to tell the mother to avoid becoming caught up in that old beauty game.

To avoid the beads, the mother must step on what holds the beads together—presumably a string or wire of some kind. So her task is to focus on the thread that unites the beads, and this makes a good metaphor for her fundamental challenge—to find her deep self, her true self, the unity behind all the different roles and masks she might have adopted to survive. Indeed, many women have trouble defining who they are, partly because they play so many different roles in life and empathize so easily with others. The challenge is to find this subtle, often invisible continuity.

The hidden thread also can be interpreted as the underlying connection between mother and daughter. The beads would represent dramatic events in the relationship—the ups and downs, disagreements, and shared moments. But the thread is what connects all the times together, the enduring relationship, the continuity—the motherline.

The bridge is explicitly likened to an abacus, and the latter is used to calculate numbers, especially in business matters. Closely tied to money, the abacus is intimately connected to the notion of private property. Since the bridge leads to the demon's castle, and he personifies the unconscious side of patrilineal cultures, the story hints that a preoccupation with material wealth lies at the center of society's shadow.[4] Other women's tales repeat the motif.[5]

In warning the mother about falling to the place of birth, the nun is presumably referring to Buddhist doctrine, which says that failure to do one's tasks in this life means being reborn to complete the job in the next one. But the warning may also be literal, referring to women's role in giving birth, to being a mother. If the mother falls into this conventional role, the nun seems to warn, the mother will perish psychologically. She must move into new roles, in addition to her maternal one.

R E U N I O N

After crossing the Abacus Bridge, the mother enters the castle and hears someone weaving. She follows the sound, finds her daughter, and the two embrace joyfully. Weaving, of course, is usually a woman's task, and it is often drudgery, especially when forced upon her and when she must work alone. This seems to be the fate of the daughter, and it fits the theme of her being abducted and imprisoned in feminine stereotypes.

After their tearful embrace, the daughter prepares dinner for her mother. A role reversal takes place between them which is common in real life: mothers and adult daughters often switch back and forth, taking care of each other. Many grown daughters, for example, by pursuing careers and expressing themselves freely, inspire their mothers to move beyond conventional roles.

In feeding her mother, the daughter does something that the nun did not. Daughter and nun symbolize distinct functions, the deep feminine and the practical feminine. The nun offers wisdom, while the daughter attends to bodily needs and everyday concerns. Women need both in their lives.

The demon returns home early, and the daughter conceals her mother in a stone box, taking an active role for the first time. She is energized by her mother's arrival, possibly because her mother's courageous quest gives her a model to follow. In fact, many assertive, resourceful women credit their mothers with giving them self-confidence, as Lyn Mikel Brown and Carol Gilligan observed in their research.

The stone box in which the mother hides is reminiscent of a coffin and suggests that the mother experiences some kind of symbolic death and rebirth. What dies, I think, is the traditional maternal role, avoiding the place of birth, as the nun put it. Physically, this would involve menopause. Psychologically, it means exploring new roles, breaking free of convention, and reclaiming neglected parts of the self.

THE RUSE

When the demon returns, he suspects an interloper is present and fetches his magic plant, which reveals three people in the castle. Several points are intriguing here. First, the demon's servants apparently do not count as people. This makes sense if the demon's castle is a symbol for society's unconscious side, and the servants represent collective opinion or convention—a faceless mass of tradition, without individuality. The magic flower also sums up how most societies spy on women, giving them no privacy, no sanctuary. In Western culture, many men have a den or nook at home where they enjoy such privacy, but women have no room of their own, to use Virginia Woolf's phrase, except perhaps the kitchen, where they are subject to constant interruption. In China, with its stringent birth-control program, women even have their monthly periods monitored by local agents. Most societies try to prettify this spying and control, saying that women must be secluded for their protection. The fairy tale exposes the hypocrisy by having the demon use a flower as his spy. Something pretty is actually a means of keeping the daughter prisoner.

In returning early, the demon interrupts the happy mother-daughter reunion and replays his original role—forcing the two women to differentiate within their relationship. If he did not reappear, mother and daughter might have escaped from the castle and returned home to their unreflective, close relationship. The demon forces both women to keep on developing.

For the daughter, this means exercising her ingenuity and cunning with her pregnancy trick. The demon, completely fooled by the ruse and overjoyed to be an expectant father, forgets he was about to murder the woman. Her trick recalls the clever disguises of the woman in "The Wise Wife," and depends upon a uniquely feminine capacity: the ability to become pregnant. By invoking the power of an ancient female mystery, the young woman disarms the demon, counteracting his greater physical strength. The story hints at how women's mysteries can empower women even against the demons of social convention.

Becoming pregnant is a good symbol for creativity, for bringing new ideas to life, and for relationship, since it takes two to make a baby. So we can interpret the daughter's ruse in a more general way: she turns to creativity and relationship in dealing with the demon. The story, I think, contains a subtle message here. Instead of adopting competitive masculine values to survive in the world, women can follow a uniquely feminine path, emphasizing creativity and collaboration. Notice that while the mother had to give up "the place of birth" and the maternal role in order to cross the Abacus Bridge, the daughter must invoke the power of both. The tale suggests that birth mysteries can be empowering for younger women, but perhaps not for older ones.

THE DRUNKEN DEMON

The demon becomes drunk, kills his guard dogs, and asks his wife to put him in a large wooden box, which she gladly does. Although the daughter fooled the demon with her trick, it is his drunkenness that gives the mother and daughter the chance to escape. The theme is archetypal and appears in many myths, like that of the goddess Inanna, and her visit to the god Enki. He was, according to different sources, her father or grandfather. Delighted to see her, he arranged a feast, became totally drunk, and raised many toasts to Inanna, giving her his throne, the mastery of truth, the art of the hero, and many other powers. The next day, Enki realized what he had done and went to reclaim his powers, but Inanna refused to return them, and thus became Queen of Heaven.

The myth and fairy tale convey an important suggestion for women. Patriarchs do not willingly give up their power, but when they become drunk with their own glory, gloating in their wealth, domination, or victory, they become vulnerable, and it is often only then that they will relinquish their authority. Rather than kill patriarchs, which is what male heroes do, women may be wiser to watch for their inevitable moment of drunkenness.

The demon wanted to beat his dogs before he became drunk and not just kill them. He may simply be sadistic, but there is also deeper symbolic meaning. The two dogs function as a blood sacrifice, substituting for the mother and daughter. Here the tale recalls "Emme," where the wise old woman sacrificed a chicken, a goat, and a slave in order to free Emme.

In killing his dogs, the demon seems to be doing everything to help the mother and daughter escape. His actions make sense if he is an inner enemy—that part of a woman's psyche which pushes her, sometimes harshly, to continue developing. On the other hand, if we interpret the demon as an outer figure, representing the shadow side of society, a surprising meaning emerges. Violent and threatening as he is to the women, the demon does not really want to destroy them, but seems to hope someone will stop him. The same applies to many men today, who are often abusive toward women, but who recognize the evil that they do and secretly hope that someone will stop them.

ESCAPE BY LAND OR WATER

With the demon locked up, the mother and daughter run to the stables, planning to take the fastest mode of escape—by horse on land. Then they debate which carriage to take, the thousand-mile coach or the ten-thousand-mile one. We can interpret this as a choice between a short-term and a long-term solution. Should women focus on quotas and legal remedies for quick results, or push for educating the public, in a much slower process of cultural transformation? At this point, the nun materializes with her warning—if they go by land, the demon will catch them, so they must take a boat and flee on the river. What is the meaning of the nun's extraordinary warning?

In most cultures, the care and use of horses are typically

male occupations, and anthropologists have found that the more important horses are in a society, the less status women usually have. Where horses are used in farm work, for instance, men typically take care of the animals, control food production, and dominate society. When horses are used in warfare, of course, women have even less status because men start to treat their horses better than their wives. The animals thus allude to male power.

So in telling the mother and daughter not to take the horses, the nun warns them not to become caught up in patriarchal values. The message is apt for women today, as women move up in institutions, win public office, and take their place in society, because it is easy to become sucked into traditional power games. Margaret Thatcher, Golda Meir, and Indira Gandhi, after all, went to war, just like male leaders. Women avoid this trap, the nun suggests, by remaining true to the deep feminine, by honoring relatedness and flexibility, symbolized by water. The task is not easy, particularly in today's competitive, fast-paced culture. Taking the river implies going with the flow. This means attending to bodily rhythms, heeding inner intuitions, taking time off for reflection, and giving up the need to be in control of all situations.

When the nun materializes in the stables, she interrupts the mother and daughter and takes over a vital function from the demon—forcing the two to individuate within their relationship. While the demon separated mother and daughter in a tempestuous, violent way, personifying the conflicts which erupt between adolescent daughters and mothers, the nun symbolizes a more mature, calmer, wiser, mutual, sisterly relationship.

THE WILD DANCE

The demon eventually wakes up from his drunken stupor, breaks out of the wooden box, and searches for his missing wife. When he finds her at the river, he and his minions start drinking the water. The story graphically demonstrates the danger of trying to lock up the shadow side of society. When suppressed, the shadow breaks free and reappears with greater rage and force. Before being locked up, the demon kept the daughter imprisoned but alive. Now he threatens to kill the women. He also attacks the deep feminine itself, symbolized by the river. So the demon can be interpreted as the cultural backlash that commonly appears when women struggle to free themselves—to escape demonic social restrictions. The nun offers sage—and astounding—advice on coping with such demonic power.

The nun tells the women to lift up their skirts and expose themselves, then does so herself. The demons and his servants start laughing uproariously, and spew out the water they swallowed, sending the women downstream to safety. The sexual exposure theme appears in many other folk stories. In a Mexican tale, for instance, a girl lifts her skirt in front of a boy, and he faints dead away (notice the male loses consciousness, not the female!). In a Pueblo story, a woman leads warriors in a battle, and just before the attack, she lifts her skirt four times, exposing herself, and then defeats the enemy.[6]

Traditional Freudians might say that when the women expose their genitals, the demon and his minions thought the women were castrated, and fearing a like fate for themselves, were overwhelmed by castration anxiety, lost control of themselves, and laughed out of sheer nervousness. A more contemporary interpretation is that when the women expose their genitals, they invoke the power of female sexuality, with its connection to birth and life. Faced with this archetypal energy, what Emily Culpepper called "gynergy," the power of the male demons is neutralized.[7] (In fact, many men raised in patriarchal cultures fear women's sexuality.) The episode can also be interpreted on an inner level, reflecting women's psychology. Here the demons might represent the patriarchal view that women's bodies and feminine sexuality are evil and corrupt. When women unconsciously internalize this stereotype, they see their sexuality and bodies as a kind of demon. The nun overthrows this misogynist tradition. She celebrates women's bodies and thus drives away the demons of social convention.

WILD WOMEN

In other versions of the tale, the women do not expose their genitals, but pass wind, or pound spoons on their hips. What is common to all variants is that the women do something outrageous and unconventional with their bodies. This prompts the demons to laugh and give up their attack on the women. Today self-defense experts suggest just such a strategy when a woman is threatened by an attacker—doing something bizarre and unexpected to catch the assailant by surprise and then escape.

The liberating power of wild action and laughter also surfaces clearly in the story of Demeter and Persephone. After her daughter's abduction by Hades, Demeter despaired, withdrew into herself, and refused to eat. At the time, Demeter was disguised as a mortal and lived as a servant in a king's palace. Other women in the household noticed Demeter's despair, and tried to cheer her up, to no avail. Finally, Iambe, a daughter of the king, and Baubo, an old nursemaid, made obscene jokes. The two women put on an outrageous pantomime, in which Iambe pretended to be born from Baubo, crawling out from under her dress. The bawdy parody made Demeter laugh and roused her from her despair. Like the nun, Baubo and Iambe broke the power of a demonic male with outrageous actions.

The bawdy dance in these stories dramatizes an important feminine archetype—the wild woman. As Clarissa Pinkola Estés notes, the wild woman is a deep part of a woman's psyche which is spontaneous, free, uninhibited, close to the vitality of nature, and suppressed by social convention. Linda Leonard observes that the wild woman counteracts destructive male figures in women's dreams, exactly as the fairy tale depicts. Claire Douglas calls this feminine archetype the bawd, and links her to the wise woman. The nun in the fairy tale illustrates that link perfectly—she is outrageous and wise, a bawd and a sage. The story suggests that it is this natural woman who best neutralizes the shadow of the patriarchy. Repression, condemnation, or direct assaults on the demon often do not work. Womanly wildness does.

The primal woman is not merely the stuff of fantasy and stories. Anthropologists provide many examples in rituals from different cultures, and their accounts help enrich our understanding of this archetype.

WILD WOMEN AROUND THE WORLD

In many cultures, young women are subject to innumerable social restrictions. They cannot travel alone, often remain confined to the house, and must not talk back to men. In the same societies, though, postmenopausal women are freed from the limitations. These women may make sexual jokes with men, sometimes wear their skirts so low their pubic area shows, and are even allowed to handle the sacred objects in men's lodges. Mature women are free to become wild women—natural women.

Many secret women's rites are also wild, bawdy, and outrageous,[8] and repeat the themes of women's tales. In medieval times, for example, among the Mordvins of Russia, women would gather for an annual celebration in the home of an old woman. The women mimicked horses, wearing two little balls as testicles. (Notice the link between horses and the masculine.) When a young wife arrived at the celebrations, older women would whip her three times and say, "Lay an egg." The young wife would then produce an egg from beneath her skirt, the way Baubo "gave birth" to Iambe in the Persephone myth. In the Mordvin rite, a riotous banquet then took place, where women became drunk and sang ribald songs.

In the Baronga tribe of Africa, women performed a ritual called "the clearing of the wells," digging down to the

groundwater, jumping into the excavation, and singing obscene songs. No man was allowed to observe them doing this.
Among the Kuta, initiation into the Lisimbu women's society
involved diving naked into a body of water, while the initiate's ritual mother danced and mimicked sexual intercourse,
paralleling the nun in the fairy tale.

The traditional interpretation of the sexuality in women's
rituals focuses on fertility. In some European countries, for
example, women used to expose their genitals to growing
fields of flax and say, "Please grow as high as my genitals are
now." Among the Boro of Asia, women danced naked at
night along the banks of their sacred river, the Kanamakra, to
induce the Earth Mother and the Sky Father to make love
and cause rain to fall, so the fields would be fruitful. But
women's outrageous rites and stories have deeper meanings.
The rites and tales are frankly subversive, and I think one of
their major purposes is to shock people into reflecting on
social conventions. The primal woman is not merely an inner
archetype, she also represents a powerful force for social
change. In one incident from Australia, for example, aboriginal women gathered together to protest the wide availability
of alcohol and the problems it caused among aboriginal
males. The women marched through town, bare-breasted,
their bodies painted with traditional ritual designs, to scan-
dalize the government into taking action. Something similar
happened in colonial Africa. Women gathered together and
marched half naked through the capital, to shock the British
administrators into better treatment of native men and
women. (The response of the army was telling: native soldiers
turned away, honoring the wild women, while British troops
shot and killed the women.)

Although strongly suppressed and condemned by social
convention, wild women survive today, often as storytellers.
Older women in various cultures, including modern America, often become outrageous storytellers, who like to shock
listeners with bawdy tales, scandalous tricks, and ingenious
practical jokes. Women authors frequently follow the pattern, like Virginia Woolf, who at fifty years of age became
frank and even outrageous in her writing.

The wild woman surfaces in unexpected ways in women's crafts today. Quilting offers a charming example. A traditional theme in American quilting is Sunbonnet Sue, a demure little girl, usually shown playing with dolls or doing household chores. But several quilting circles recently amended the time-honored image, and portrayed Sunbonnet Sue burning a bra, dancing a cancan, reading pornographic books, drinking a martini, skinny-dipping, smoking, necking in a car, taking a shower with a man, and being pregnant at her wedding! Sunbonnet Sue revealed herself to be a wild woman, a natural woman.

DANCING, LAUGHING, AND WOMEN'S SPIRITUALITY

The women's bawdy dance brings up further themes. First, as Karen Signell and Claire Douglas independently note, dancing appears frequently in women's dreams, typically with a group of women. A number of therapists have also noted that dancing is deeply therapeutic for women and helps women celebrate their bodies and overthrow negative stereotypes.

Second, laughter, not force, disarms the demon and his minions, and here the story offers women a useful strategy. This certainly does not involve laughing off sexual harassment, discrimination, or rape. Nor can humor replace political action. Wit operates on a more personal, psychological basis, with men as individuals. Men will often ignore criticism, especially from women, but since most men appreciate jokes, the messages that they refuse to hear directly will often get through via humorous stories. Indeed, one of a man's tasks at midlife is to learn to laugh at himself and at patriarchal conventions, as men's tales show. So when women use humor in dealing with oppressive males, they ally themselves with that part of a man's soul that pushes him to develop.

Finally, the nun engineers the lewd dance, yet she is a religious woman. So the story suggests that women's spirituality is wild, outrageous, and sometimes obscene—involving a celebration of the female body, sexuality, and sensuality. The tale decisively rejects the traditional patriarchal split between body and spirit, where the body is corrupt and spirit is pure. The nun, in fact, is something of a witch—she lives in the wilderness, is wise in the ways of sex and other natural instincts, and ignores social conventions. She also can appear and disappear at will, materializing in the demon's stables and then later in the boat. As many women have pointed out, witches—and women's spirituality—were stamped out by most cultures. This makes women's tales all the more important: they preserve ancient images of feminine spirituality.

THE COMMUNITY

After they escape from the demon, the mother and daughter thank the nun and ask what they can do in return. The nun reveals that she is the spirit of the solitary pagoda and that she often feels lonely. She asks the mother and daughter to bring other pagodas for company, and from then on, the mother and daughter make a pilgrimage every year, adding a pagoda to the growing collection in the meadow.

Although the nun is wise and powerful, she is lonely and suffers in her isolation. Her situation captures a painful reality—the deep feminine is reviled and feared by most cultures, and this wounds it. In asking the mother and daughter for help, the nun seeks healing. Here the nun reverses the usual link between humanity and divinity. Normally humans ask gods and spirits for help, not vice versa. By asking for aid, the nun offers a new model of spirituality, shifting the traditional religious paradigm, which presents goddesses and gods as parents, to a new vision—goddesses and gods as partners. The nun is a sister more than a mother figure.

By bringing more pagodas to the meadow, the mother and daughter create a community for the nun. Symbolically, the mother and daughter create a new society, repeating a prominent theme in women's tales—women create new worlds as a result of their individual development. The community theme is also clear in the myth of Demeter and Persephone. According to legend, on her search for her daughter, Demeter established the Eleusinian Mysteries, which evolved into a major community ritual in classical Greece.

The idea of community building surfaces symbolically in many other women's rituals—it is an archetypal concern of the feminine psyche. With the Kinki, for instance, a secret women's society among the Kafu-Bullom of Sierra Leone, each initiate brings an article that is put in a sacred, secret package kept by the head of the sisterhood.[9] The collection is like the growing community of pagodas in the story. Something similar occurred in the Greek Thesmophoria, where each woman made sacred images out of dough and collectively offered them on an altar. Collaboration and communion are the focus. (By contrast, male rites emphasize individuality and separation. Among many Native American tribes, for instance, as part of his initiation, a man makes a bundle of sacred objects for himself in response to a vision. The initiate does not bring objects for a community collection.) The image of gathering a community together, I might add, elaborates on an archetypal feminine motif—weaving or spinning, which involves joining many individual threads into a larger, stronger, collective unity.

Women's art reflects this communal spirit. Margaret Hicks, for instance, constructed an extraordinary work of art in which she set up logs to form three concentric circles in the middle of a forest. In the center of the circles stood a tree trunk with a stone upon it and each visitor who came to the artwork was asked to leave a small stone as a symbol of herself or himself.[10] The collection of stones parallels the community of pagodas in the fairy tale.

A DREAM

To summarize the themes of "The Mother and the Demon," I turn to a dream reported by Polly Young-Eisendrath and

Florence Wiedermann.[11] The dream came from a woman they call "Psyche," who began therapy at thirty-five years of age. She had been sexually molested as a young child by an uncle, but after telling her parents about the incident, they confronted him. His wife divorced him, and he died of a heart attack soon afterward, leaving Psyche feeling tremendous guilt about his death, as if she were responsible for it. In therapy, Psyche had a "big" dream, which parallels "The Mother and the Demon."

In her dream Psyche stole a white alabaster statue of a nude man and woman wrapped around each other. Both of the figures were crying, holding on to each other. Carrying the statue, Psyche ran to a dock where a boat was waiting. In it sat an old woman and a younger one about Psyche's age, accompanied by a male demon. Psyche gave the women the statue and the demon then lifted Psyche into the boat. The old woman steered the boat rapidly through a waterway, and Psyche felt exhilarated by the speed of their travel.

Psyche sensed that the stolen statue was somehow linked to her childhood experience of sexual abuse. Depicting a man and a woman embracing, the statue symbolized sexuality and love, which were polluted for Psyche by her uncle. Symbolically, Psyche's sexuality—her passionate self—was abducted in childhood by the demon of incest. (Note that Persephone was kidnapped and raped by Hades, who was her uncle.) In stealing the statue, Psyche reclaims her sensuality and passion, taking back these vital energies from the demon of sexual abuse. As an adult Psyche rescues her childhood self from the early trauma, the way the mother in the fairy tale saves her daughter, a symbol of the mother's younger self.

In her dream Psyche runs to a boat, just like the mother and daughter fleeing the demon by water. Symbolically women find refuge in the deep feminine. Psyche's dream confirms the theme with the old woman in the boat. She is the archetypal wise crone, and is accompanied by a younger woman who seems to be a sisterly figure. "The Mother and the Demon" combines these two archetypal figures in the person of the nun.

The demon in Psyche's dream is surprisingly helpful rather

than harmful. I suspect the reason is that Psyche had the support of her parents in dealing with her uncle, and worked through the trauma with her efforts in therapy. Psychologically, she detoxified the demon. This is analogous to how the nun makes the demon laugh, which drains his rage against the women. The symbols and plots differ, but the basic themes in women's tales and dreams are the same, expressing the wisdom of the deep feminine.

PART V

Journey to a New World

"The Siren Wife":

Return from the Sisters

(from Italy[1])

ong ago, a woman married a sailor who was away from home most of the time, sailing the seven seas. One day while he was gone, the wife saw a king ride by and the two fell in love. The wife went to live with the king, so when the sailor returned some time later, he found his house cold and empty.

Soon enough, the king and the wife tired of each other, and she returned home. She begged her husband to forgive her, but he flew into a rage, threw her aboard his ship, set sail, and in the middle of the ocean picked her up and cast her overboard. "Faithless women!" he cried. "This is the punishment you deserve!" A moment later, the sailor came to his senses. "What have I done?" he exclaimed. "I am murdering the only woman I love!" He tried to rescue his wife, but she had vanished beneath the waves. With an empty heart, he returned home.

The wife plunged into the sea and fell among the Sirens in their gardens of coral and pearl. "What a beautiful woman!" the Sirens exclaimed. "How could anyone try to drown her?" The Sirens took the wife to their palace and revived her with their magic. "You shall be one of us," the Sirens told her, and named her "Froth." They brushed her hair, anointed her with perfume, adorned her with pearls, and put on a feast in her honor. The wife danced all night in a hall filled with women, handsome youths, and wondrous music. From then on, she lived in luxury and joy.

One day, the woman remembered her husband and was filled with sadness, for she still loved him. Deep in her heart, she knew that he loved her, too, and she yearned to see him again.

"What ails you?" the Sirens asked her.

"It is nothing," the wife said, but sorrow still lined her face, and the Sirens could not bear to see her suffer.

"Come sing with us," the Sirens suggested. "That will cheer you up!" The Sirens took her to the surface of the sea, and sang under the moonlight, teaching Froth their magic melodies. Their songs were so beautiful that they caused sailors to dive into the ocean, where the Sirens turned them into clams, coral, or crabs.

One night, as the Sirens sang, a man leaped into the water and the wife recognized him at once, for he was none other than her husband. Her heart went out to him.

"Let's turn him into a shrimp!" a Siren exclaimed over the unconscious sailor. "Or into pink coral!" another cried.

"No, no," the wife interrupted. The Sirens were surprised at her sudden interest.

"What would you want with him, Froth?" the Sirens inquired.

The wife hesitated, and then had an idea. "I want to try some magic of my own." The Sirens happily agreed. They locked the sailor in their palace, and then went off to sleep.

The wife stole up to her husband's room and sang outside. He awoke and recognized his wife's voice at once. "You are alive!" he exclaimed, overcome with joy. Then he begged forgiveness of his wife.

"I forgave you long ago," the wife whispered. "But you must be quiet. If the Sirens hear you, they will do you harm. I shall return later tonight after they leave to go singing, and I will free you then."

When night came and the Sirens went off, the wife stayed behind. She released her husband, the two embraced, and then she swam swiftly to the surface, far from the Sirens, taking him to safety. A ship soon sailed by, and the wife told her husband, "Signal them for help, so they will rescue you. As for me, I must return to the Sirens."

"Come back with me," the husband pleaded, but she shook her head sadly.

"I cannot," she explained. "I am one of the Sirens now, and I would perish if I left the sea." With that, she dived into the ocean and vanished.

The husband cried out with anguish, and the sailors on the ship heard him. "Man overboard!" they called, and pulled him from the water. The poor husband told them about his wife the Siren, but the sailors shook their heads in disbelief, thinking he had lost his mind. They set sail and took the man home.

The husband remained distraught, and all he could think about day and night was his wife. One day, lost in thought, he wandered deep in a forest, and came upon an ancient walnut tree, around which, legend said, fairies danced.

"Why such a sad face, my good man?" an old woman asked, emerging from behind the tree. The mariner nearly jumped with surprise.

"It is my wife," the husband sighed, and told the old woman about her, trapped among the Sirens.

The old woman nodded gravely. "I can help you free your wife," she said. "But I will do so on one condition."

"I will do anything!" the husband exclaimed.

The crone went on. "The task is not easy. You must bring me the flower that grows in the palace of the Sirens, which they call 'the loveliest.' Give it to me and your wife will be free and safe."

The sailor scratched his head. "How am I to obtain this flower from the bottom of the sea?"

"That is for you to solve," the old woman said softly and vanished behind the walnut tree.

The husband thought and thought, and finally set sail. In the middle of the sea, he called out for his wife. When she appeared, he quickly told her about the old woman's offer. The wife shook her head. "I cannot give you 'the loveliest.' The Sirens stole it from the fairies long ago, and if the Sirens lose it, they will perish. I will die, too, because I am a Siren now."

"No," the husband replied. "The old woman and the fairies will save you."

The wife hesitated. "I must think about this. Come back tomorrow and I will tell you my answer." Then she slipped beneath the waves.

The next day the husband set sail and met his wife again. "I will obtain this flower for you," she said. "But I need your help. You must sell everything you have, buy the most beautiful jewels in the land, hang them from your ship, and set sail. Sirens cannot resist jewels, and they will follow you. When you lure them away from their palace, I will pick the magic flower."

The husband hastened back to town. He trembled as he gathered all his belongings to sell, but he sold everything, bought the most precious jewels he could find, hung them on his ship, and set sail.

The jewels attracted the Sirens, and they followed the husband as he sailed farther and farther away from their palace. Suddenly, the ocean trembled, thunder rolled through its depths, the sea opened up, and the Sirens disappeared. The sea shook a second time, and as the mariner stared in astonishment, the old woman of the forest appeared, riding a great eagle. Behind her was his wife, safe and sound. The two women flew off into the distance, toward the sailor's home, and when he arrived home, he found his wife waiting for him. They embraced, pledged their love anew, and this time it lasted for the rest of their lives.

A DIFFICULT BEGINNING

The story begins with a woman whose husband is gone for long periods of time. Such a situation will be familiar to many women today, because men often focus on work and career rather than people and relationships. A woman is supposed to wait faithfully for the absent man's return, but the wife rejects this oppressive convention. When a king falls in love with her, she leaves home to live with him. This is the archetypal romantic fantasy of a woman meeting Prince Charming, but what is important is that the wife really leaves home to live with the king. She does not simply fantasize—she takes action. Her adventure with the king dramatizes her assertiveness and willingness to pursue her own needs and desires. Metaphorically, when the wife has an affair with him, she makes contact with her own authority, her inner king.

Eventually, the wife tires of the king, and returns home. But why should she go back to a neglectful husband? The story does not suggest that women's ultimate place is at home, because the wife goes on to even more important developments. Romance—even with a king!—is only an opening act in a much longer, more complex drama for women.

When the wife returns home, she asks her husband for forgiveness, but he flies into a rage and throws her into the sea. His murderous attack reiterates the theme of women's oppression, and the cultural backlash against women acting on their needs and desires.

THE SIRENS

When the wife falls into the sea, she does not drown, but is rescued by Sirens. She finds safety in the ocean, providing one more example that nature, especially water, offers sanctuary to women.

The Sirens are closely connected to goddess figures. In ancient China, the goddess Nu Kwa was depicted with the tail of a fish, as was Atargatis, a Mesopotamian sea goddess, and Nina, a Sumerian deity.[2] As ancient female figures, hidden in the ocean, the Sirens can be interpreted as a divine, feminine energy, normally repressed by society. The Sirens, in other words, symbolize the deep feminine, and by falling into the ocean the wife enters its mysteries.

The story repeats the motif in a subtle detail. The Sirens name the wife "Froth," which might seem whimsical or even derogatory. But the nickname points directly to the goddess Aphrodite, who was born from sea foam: the Greek word for "sea foam" or "froth" is "aphros."[3] The name Froth thus connects the Siren wife to a powerful archetype of the divine feminine. Aphrodite's attributes also help illuminate the fairy tale. The goddess personified romantic love and the importance of relationships—a fundamental theme in most women's lives. Yet Aphrodite was not bound to or dependent upon men. Some of her lovers were women, and Aphrodite delighted in spending time with nymphs—female nature spirits. Aphrodite thus stands for womanly relatedness and authenticity. She does not give up herself in relationships, but honors both love and her own integrity.

Half human and half fish, the Sirens illustrate another major theme in women's tales—communing with nature. The story, in fact, recalls "The Woman from the Egg," where the beautiful wife was attacked by the witch, jumped into the well, and turned into a fish. In both tales, a woman is assaulted by a shadowy force, plunges into a watery domain, symbolizing the deep feminine, and then takes on a fish-like form, temporarily joining the animal kingdom.

SISTERHOOD

The Sirens live together in a community, a sisterhood. As in "Emme" and "The Mother and the Demon," sister figures, not male heroes, save women in desperate straits. Several features stand out about the Sirens' sisterhood. First, they enjoy something of a paradise, residing in a beautiful palace, and apparently spending their time dancing, singing, adorning themselves, and playing games. Other stories repeat the motif:[4] not only does nature rescue women, it provides joy and delight, which contrasts sharply with women's plight in civilization.

In their dances, the Sirens had handsome youths present, presumably meaning young men. The men are not mentioned anywhere else, implying that they are secondary to the Sirens. The mermaids' domain is thus a mirror image of conventional society, reversing male preeminence. The Sirens provide Froth not just with a room of her own, to use Virginia Woolf's phrase, but with a whole realm.

BEAUTY RECONSIDERED

When the Sirens revive the wife, they adorn her with jewels, and spend much of their time beautifying themselves. In modern culture, beauty and adornment are usually considered frivolous or superficial. Here Aphrodite offers a mythological counterlesson. As the goddess of beauty and sensuality, she emphasizes that womanly beauty is divine, not frivolous. What is crucial, though, is that Aphrodite beautifies herself for her own enjoyment, not for men's sake. She celebrates the feminine body, sensuality, and what might be called women's deep beauty. Traditionally, feminine beauty is tied to youth and sex, and women are expected to look beautiful for men. By contrast, deep beauty is beauty of women, for women. Here adornment becomes a means of personal expression, where clothes and jewelry become a part of a woman's voice, reflecting her individual self, rather than being a means of silencing or burying that self. Deep beauty also involves joining in nature's splendor with the use of perfumes distilled from flowers and precious stones taken from the earth. So deep beauty is a celebration of a woman's body, of her connection to nature, and of embodied life in general—a delight in the sensual. Writers like Gertrud Koch and Jutta Bruckner trace deep beauty back to the delight that mothers and young daughters have in each other, and their pre-verbal enjoyment in adorning one another.

The Siren's magic flower, "the loveliest," elaborates on deep beauty, linking it with affection and tying love to loveliness. The connection is more than a pun, because love generates loveliness—what is loved is experienced as beautiful. In many ways, love is the root of deep beauty. (By contrast, conventional beauty usually arouses lust or greed, rather than love.)

The magic flower sustains the Sirens—love and beauty give them life. Here the flower resembles the mythic herb of life. The earliest written reference to such a plant comes from the Sumerian epic of Gilgamesh, which describes a magic plant with the power of immortality, growing at the bottom of the sea. In another Sumerian myth such magic plants specifically belonged to Ninhursag, the goddess of birth. Although seemingly a small detail, like the name "Froth," "the loveliest" points to profound feminine vitality.

"The Siren Wife" does not elaborate much on "the loveliest," and this is not surprising. Deep beauty is a feminine mystery, not to be discussed in public. The hint of secrecy brings up another aspect to the fairy tale: the Sirens resemble a woman's secret society, and the wife's encounter with them is like an initiation rite. Indeed, the story parallels the lore and rites of the Sande Society, a secret all-women's organization in West Africa.

THE SANDE AND THE SIRENS

The Sande sisterhood is one of the most prominent of West African organizations, cutting across tribal and national boundaries. According to Sande tradition, the spiritual vitality of the society comes from rivers, springs, pools, or—in territories near the coast—the sea, reiterating the water theme in women's tales. Each year, Sande women build a *kpanguima*, a ritual sanctuary, which is said to be underwater in a magic, sacred realm, a place of abundance, sharing, dancing, beauty, and rejoicing. The similarity to the Sirens' palace under the sea is striking. Men were explicitly barred from the

Sande *kpanguima*, except for one man, called the *ngegba*, who did the heavy construction and maintenance work. In the Sande realm, males and the masculine have only secondary roles—exactly like the Sirens' world.

In their initiation ceremonies, Sande novices dive into a river and then rise up again, symbolically descending into the secret, sacred, watery realm, and then returning, transformed, to the ordinary world. This is exactly what the Siren wife does—she descends into the ocean, joins the Sirens in the deep feminine, and returns to everyday life.

The Sande women are the source of all beauty, and in some tales, Tingoi, a water spirit or mermaid, is the ultimate source of beauty, paralleling "the loveliest." Moreover, in Sande tradition, the beauty of objects and animals is understood in terms of women's beauty, but every woman is considered to have beauty—not just slender women or young women. Beauty is defined by how real women look and act, not the other way around. The Sande thus honor deep beauty, and sisterhood is central to this celebration.

The Sande also play important political and cultural roles. The *sowei*, the women elders who run the Sande, mediate in marital disputes between husbands and wives and act as judges for disputes between women. Sande women often speak out on political issues affecting women's welfare, and the opinions of the *sowei* carry much weight in tribal matters. Within the Sande, women gain valuable experience in leadership, and Sande women occupy some 10 to 15 percent of the paramount chiefships, although the culture at large is patriarchal and polygynous, with one man having several wives. At home, men customarily eat before women do, and some husbands even expect their wives to kneel when serving them food! The Sande provides a vital sanctuary for women in this situation. In fact, when the *kpanguima* is built, and the Sande is in session, no man can prevent a woman from going to the *kpanguima*. Every woman, even from outside the village or tribe, is welcome in the ritual compound. Though the men complain vociferously that the women only loaf in the *kpanguima*, the men dare not interfere.

Within the enclave, the women feast, relax, and joke, treating one another as equals. Gone is the usual hierarchy imposed by the polygynous culture, where senior wives command junior wives. Solidarity among women is the Sande ideal, and the women's society has a saying that wherever several women are gathered, there is Sande. The equality and mutuality reinforce the shift in women's tales from a vertical mother-daughter model to a more sisterly spirit. The women's movement today, of course, knows the importance of sisterhood in psychological, spiritual, economic, and political domains. What the Sande rite and the Siren story add is the role of deep beauty in sisterhood—beauty for women and among women, a sacrament of the feminine.

WOMEN'S RITES

Similar themes emerge in women's rituals from other cultures. Australian aboriginal women, for instance, have numerous secret rites including those for childbirth, ceremonies to bring pubescent girls to puberty, and love rituals, intended to keep husbands faithful or to attract lovers to a woman. The love rituals have clear parallels to "The Siren Wife" and the Sande. Led by a middle-aged or older woman, the rite is held in the daytime, usually a mile or so away from camp. Men avoid the site, for fear of falling ill from the women's power. Like the Sirens and the Sande, the Australian women create a feminine realm, separate from men. In their ceremony, the women paint symbolic signs on their bodies and oil their skin until they shine. The spirit is festive, with much joking, laughing, and teasing of one another. The women enjoy each other's company, as they adorn themselves for their sake, not for men. In painting magical symbols on their bodies, the women also make their bodies sacred—adornment is a sacrament, not a diversion. As part of the rite, women also adorn their fighting sticks, or *miliri*, to imbue them with power, in case they must defend themselves if an argument with a husband or lover turns violent. So if they celebrate deep beauty, the women also call up their aggressive power, to protect themselves against men. Neither the Sirens nor the aboriginal women split beauty from power, as patriarchal cultures typically do. Women's rites and tales emphasize that feminine beauty is robust and fierce.

YEARNING

After the wife lives with the Sirens for a while, she begins to miss her husband. Yet why would she do so, since her husband tried to kill her? She is not a victim of the abused wife syndrome where wives remain in horrible situations because they have no means of escape: the Sirens provide the wife with a perfect women's shelter. Other tales also show women leaving abusive or neglectful husbands, reclaiming their strength and wisdom, and then returning by choice to their husbands. What is the meaning of this return?

The wife returns home out of love, recognizing that she loves her husband and believing he still loves her. In fact, the husband deeply regretted his attempt to murder his wife, so she is accurate in her judgment of him. Her desire to reconcile with him reflects the power of her love, faith in her own judgments, courage to take a risk, and an affirmation of the importance of relationship in her life.

As the wife thinks of her husband, she becomes sad, and the mermaids try to cheer her up, teaching her their magic songs and taking her with them on their moonlight adventures, where they lure sailors into drowning themselves. The Sirens' antipathy toward men has many meanings. On one level, it reflects a conventional male view of Sirens—that they are deadly, deceptive, wicked creatures, whose only delight is to destroy men. The fairy tale reverses this stereotype by presenting the Sirens as helpful figures, who rescue Froth and give her a new life. The story also inverts convention in another way. While most cultures make women into sex objects for men, the Sirens turn this role against men, using their sex appeal to lure sailors to their deaths. The Sirens' hostility to men, in fact, only reciprocates men's attacks on women in most societies, and the mermaids can be interpreted as a symbol of feminine energy, demanding to be heard, and using the only language that patriarchy heeds— violence and force.

On yet a deeper level, the Sirens' attacks on men reflect the traditional secrecy involved in women's rites. In the Greek Thesmophoria, men and even male animals were excluded; Australian aboriginal women threaten men with dire consequences if they approach the secret ceremonies; and no men are allowed into the sacred Sande compound (except the *ngegba*, the groundskeeper).

RESCUE

One evening, the husband leaps into the sea, bewitched by the Sirens, and the wife rescues him. Later he awakens, recognizes his wife, and begs her forgiveness. Here the wife reverses the usual gender roles in fairy tales and rescues her hapless husband. In awakening him, she also provides another example of an unconscious man being roused by a resourceful woman. In asking for forgiveness from his wife, the husband confirms the wife's judgment of him: she accurately saw past his rage to the good hidden within his heart. In forgiving and rescuing her husband, the wife begins writing a peace treaty in the proverbial war between the sexes. Note that it is she, not her husband, who makes the first move. Men raised according to heroic traditions usually see relationships in terms of competition or battle, so they easily treat their wives as servants or enemies.

When the Sirens go to sleep, the wife takes her husband to the ocean surface, where he is rescued by a passing ship. Although he begs her to return with him, she explains that she cannot, because she has become a Siren and must remain in the ocean. This introduces an enormously important theme. The wife is stuck in the ocean, just as Emme was imprisoned in the pool of water and the wife in "The Woman from the Egg" was trapped in the well. The Siren wife seems to recognize her situation, too: when the mermaids asked Froth why she was depressed, she did not tell them that she longed for her husband. She probably realized that the Sirens would oppose her desire to return to him. So she is caught in a dilemma. Although they rescued her at the beginning of the story, the Sirens have now become a problem for her, an obstacle to her continued development. The story thus introduces the shadow side of deep sisterhood—its possible negative effects—and how women's close relationships with each other can complicate a woman's individuation. Luise Eichenbaum and Susie Orbach commented on the problem, noting that women often remain loyal to other women even when the friendships become constricting or destructive. Many women, for example, imagine that if they were to become successful in their work, or develop psychologically as individuals, they might somehow hurt their women friends. So women sometimes tend to deemphasize their competence and uniqueness with female friends and stress conformity and community instead.

TROUBLE RETURNING

The Siren predicament holds deeper meaning. In folklore, people who enter the fairy world often become stuck there, unable to return to the human world. In psychological terms, an individual may become trapped in the realm of archetypes—for example, by becoming fascinated with numinous images, and using these archetypes to escape from everyday problems. As Marion Woodman observed, a woman may identify herself with ancient goddess figures and unconsciously feel she is as bountiful, inexhaustible, and powerful as a goddess. She may then run herself into the ground trying to be superhuman, or she may become as demanding, capricious, and devouring as goddesses. The numinous, archetypal world must be balanced with the every-day realm of ordinary human society. Thinking about god-desses and sacred sisters is much easier than working out problems with a mother or a husband, or learning to speak up at work!

Annis Pratt and Irene Neher studied how women's litera-ture portrays this process of returning to society. A dramatic example comes from Kate Chopin's novel *The Awakening*, which resembles "The Siren Wife" in many ways. In the book, Edna, the protagonist, awakens to her own uniqueness when she swims, one evening, naked and alone in the sea. After-ward, Edna gradually realizes the tremendous obstacles fac-ing women trying to become authentic individuals in society. Rather than return to a conventional, submissive role, or battle social oppression, Edna one night swims out to sea and drowns. She rejects human society, dives into the deep femi-nine, and does not return.

THE WISE OLD WOMAN

After the wife rescues her husband, he vows to do everything to free her. One day he meets an old woman deep in the forest—the archetypal wise crone, symbolizing a woman's true self. The story links the crone to the fairies and this reference to fairies is important, because in European folk-lore, fairies are ruled by queens rather than kings: fairies seem to be matrilineal. The walnut tree, associated with the crone, reiterates the feminine emphasis. In Greek and Roman tradition, walnuts were served at weddings as a symbol of fertility and fruitfulness, two functions associated with mother goddesses. In many European fairy tales, the heroine is given magic walnuts which contain beautiful dresses or jewels. So the walnut tree represents a many-layered symbol of the feminine self.

When the husband tells the old woman about his wife, she knows exactly how to free her. A remarkable drama unfolds here. The wife is trapped with the Sirens, who represent one part of the deep feminine. So another part of the deep feminine, symbolized by the crone, sends help. Psychologically speaking, the wife represents the ego, which has become stuck in an archetype, in a numinous world of sisterhood. So from even deeper in the psyche, the true self stirs, and sends the old woman to help the ego to escape and continue its development.

The old woman tells the husband she can free his wife if he obtains the Sirens' magic flower. Notice that the crone does not give the husband a free gift. She proposes a trade, which contrasts with the fairy godmothers in youth tales, who offer help with no strings attached. The difference between youth tales and midlife stories reflects the realism of maturity—there are no free lunches!

Since the crone is wise, we can assume that she knows what will happen to the Sirens if she regains "the loveliest"—all the mermaids will die. So she is willing to kill and thus parallels the crone in "Emme," who sacrificed a chicken, a goat, and a slave to free Emme. Again we see how a symbolic sacrifice is sometimes necessary in women's development.

THE GO-BETWEEN

After talking with the crone, the husband goes to his wife and asks her to steal the magic flower. Notice that the husband does not rescue the wife directly. Although his role is crucial, the story does not return to the usual drama of youth tales, where the hero rescues the heroine. The husband plays the role of go-between, rather than hero. An assistant to the wife, he mediates between her, trapped with the Sirens, and the wise woman, representing the wife's true self. Exactly this theme appeared in "Emme," where Akpan acts as a go-between, and in "Maria Morevna," where Ivan plays that role. Both men help their wives make contact with the wisdom of the deep feminine.

As a go-between, the husband can help the Siren wife only so much. She must decide whether or not to steal the flower, risking her life. She must also figure out how to take "the loveliest" and actually do so. Although the initiative and responsibility lie upon her shoulders, husband and wife cooperate and complement each other. The tale began with mutual antagonism between them—she left him for a lover, and he tried to murder her. Their hostility, however, has now become interdependence. The wife cannot leave the Sirens on her own, yet the husband cannot rescue her, even with the old woman's advice. For her part, the crone seems unable to obtain "the loveliest" on her own, and she needs the help of the wife and husband. Mutuality becomes the key.

The husband is a merchant seaman and this adds further insight to his role as go-between. As a trader, working at various ports, his function is to connect distant parties. That is precisely what he does in linking his wife to the wise woman. Moreover, he sails upon the surface of the sea, while his wife lives below. Symbolically, she has direct contact with the unconscious, while he does not.

The tale specifically notes that the Sirens stole "the loveliest" from the fairies, and that the crone and the fairies want the flower back. So there is an opposition between the Sirens, living in the ocean, and the wise woman, living in the forest with the fairies. In dreams and fairy tales, sea and forest usually represent the unconscious. The story thus implies that the feminine unconscious is split into two camps. What is the meaning of this schism?

THE SIRENS AND THE FAIRIES

As half-fish, half-human creatures, the Sirens symbolize a close connection with instinct and animals. The old woman, by contrast, is allied with the fairies, who are magical, immortal, and able to fly. These three qualities link the fairies to a spiritual realm. (Fairies, in many ways, are pagan versions of angels; or, rather, angels are Christian versions of fairies.) By contrast, the Sirens are mortal, since they will die without "the loveliest," emphasizing their link to the animal realm. I suggest that the fairies and the Sirens symbolize spirit and instinct, soul and body, mind and matter. This is a traditional dualism in patriarchal cultures, and the tale repeats the duality in two details. The Sirens possess "the loveliest," which gives them life and power. As a source of life, this flower recalls the biblical Tree of Life in the Garden of Eden. By contrast, the crone appears next to a magic tree in the forest. As a wise woman who knows about the Sirens and how to free the wife from them, the crone represents knowledge. So her tree recalls the Tree of Knowledge. The opposition between the flower, as a source of life, and the crone's tree, as a symbol of knowledge, reiterates a split between life and knowledge, instinct and spirit, body and mind. This duality probably arose with patriarchal states, as Susan Griffin, Naomi Goldenberg, Mary Lou Randour, Carrin Dunne, and others have argued. The split is not present in many indigenous tribal cultures, where no distinction is made between spirit and body. So the schism between the Sirens and the fairies reflects a later cultural model imposed on an original, integrated whole. The story goes on to show how the wife and the old woman restore this wholeness, healing an ancient wound in the feminine psyche.

After thinking about the matter, the wife decides to steal the Sirens' flower, trusting that her husband is correct about the crone rescuing her. Knowing that the Sirens covet jewels, the wife tells her husband to sell everything he owns, buy precious gems, hang them from his ship, and sail near the Sirens to lure them away from the magic plant. The wife knows that she cannot match the Sirens' magic or their numbers, so she outwits them. But her plan is wise in another way—it enforces poetic justice. To save his wife, the husband must sell everything he earned from his lifetime of sailing the seas, the profit from many years of neglecting his wife. In sacrificing his wealth, the husband demonstrates that he truly loves his wife, finally putting their relationship above his work, a normal developmental task for men at midlife. The husband also reverses the usual plot of youth tales, which show women sacrificing everything for husband and family. Now it is the husband who makes the sacrifice. Luring the Sirens away from their palace, the husband also turns the tables on them. Just as the Sirens enticed him and other men into drowning, the husband draws the Sirens to their doom with jewels. The Sirens, too, can be greedy, preoccupied with possessions.

When the wife steals the flower, the sea trembles and swallows up the Sirens. Again, a symbolic "killing" is often necessary for a woman to free herself. The story makes the action even more dramatic, since the wife must kill the very women who rescued her in the first place.

TRANSFORMATION

Although the story implies that the Sirens perish, there is another possible interpretation. When the Sirens vanish, the old woman appears, flying on the back of a great eagle, with the wife behind her. The story does not fill in details, so we are left to wonder where the eagle came from.[5] Here a comment from Marie-Louise von Franz, the Jungian analyst who wrote extensively on fairy tales, is crucial. She noted that in most fairy tales, symbolic characters do not vanish or die, but rather change into other, equally symbolic forms. These transformations mirror real life, she observed, because an individual's burning psychological issues usually do not vanish or die off, but rather change into new forms. The psychic energy is not lost, but is transformed. So the disappearance of the Sirens and the sudden appearance of the eagle suggests that the Sirens are transformed into the bird. As an animal, the eagle continues to symbolize the instinctual realm. But as a bird, the eagle also symbolizes spirit. So as a symbol, the eagle integrates spirit and instinct. The eagle also retains a connection to the Sirens, because mythology presents Sirens in two forms: one is the well-known mermaid, and the other is a half-bird, half-human creature. The latter is an ancient symbol, because sculptures from early prehistoric agricultural settlements portray women with bird masks, who appear to be half human and half bird, sitting on thrones. The feminine symbolism behind the eagle may sound surprising, since it has been a masculine, patriarchal emblem, at least since imperial Rome. In the far older shamanic tradition, however, an eagle is often depicted as the mother of shamans.

The combination of the old woman and the eagle suggests that the schism between the mermaids and the fairies, between spirit and body, has been healed. In obtaining "the loveliest" the Siren wife symbolically reconciles two realms, split by patriarchal tradition. The same theme appeared in "The Woman from the Egg," where the protagonist came from an egg, high in a tree, linking her to sky and spirit, and later turned into a fish, hidden in a well, tying her to water and instinct. But she later became duck feathers, and a duck crosses between the realms of sky and earth, spirit and instinct.

Although the old woman is wise and powerful, she cannot obtain "the loveliest" by herself. She needs the help of the wife and husband. Symbolically, the crone cannot integrate spirit and instinct, heaven and earth. The wife's courage and resolute action are crucial to the process. This repeats an important motif from "The Mother and the Demon," where the nun was wise and magical but needed help from the mother and the daughter in finding companionship and community. The tales emphasize that women's spirituality involves a mutually beneficial partnership between the divine and the human.

INITIATION AND RETURN

When the husband sees his wife riding on the eagle with the old woman, he sails home and finds his wife there. She reenters the human world and this return to ordinary life and relationships completes her initiatory experience. As Clarissa Pinkola Estés notes in *Women Who Run with the Wolves,* women at some point in their lives must make a pilgrimage to their soul home, to the wildness deep within, and this often takes the image of diving into water, as "The Siren Wife" dramatizes. Just as important, Estés emphasizes, is returning to the world.

The struggle to return to everyday life emerges vividly in a woman's dream, reported by Polly Young-Eisendrath and Florence Wiedermann. A forty-six-year-old, professional woman, well respected in her field, Linda dreamed she was in a sorority house, not feeling well. (In reality, she had a cold at the time of the dream.) Around Linda were six beautiful vases of flowers, arranged in a circle. A blond woman came in and talked about a wonderful energy she had found in herself, spreading her legs apart to reveal the source of the vitality. The scene then shifted, and Linda was with her parents in their home. Linda lay on the floor, wrapped in a fur coat and feeling ill. Her mother was furious at her and accused Linda of having a nervous breakdown. Linda hotly denied the accusation, and said her mother was the one having a breakdown. Linda then went upstairs, too angry to talk to her mother. Later Linda and her parents sat down to dinner, and her mother asked if she and Linda were going to talk. When Linda did not answer, one of her friends entered the room, and Linda greeted the woman by raising her eyebrows.

In the dream, Linda finds herself in a sorority house—literally in a sisterhood, just like the wife among the Sirens. Linda does not feel well, and in real life had a mild, temporary illness. This brings up an important motif—an encounter with the deep feminine often is precipitated by a crisis, like the Siren wife being attacked by her husband, or an illness, like depression or chronic fatigue syndrome.

In Linda's dream, she finds herself surrounded by beautiful vases filled with flowers. The blossoms recall "the loveliest" of the Sirens and reiterate the theme of deep beauty. In Linda's dream, a blond woman tells her about a mysterious power she has discovered, referring to her genitals as its source. She points to "gynergy," purely feminine energy, and symbolically introduces Linda to the mysteries of the deep feminine, the way the Sirens taught Froth their lore. Linda's dream shifts scenes and she finds herself at her parents' house, that is, returning to ordinary, everyday life. But the return is problematic: Linda lies on the floor, feeling sick. She also wears a fur coat, which brings up images of half-human, half-animal hybrids, like the Sirens, pointing to the link between nature and the deep feminine. However, Linda is now in an ordinary house, so lying on the floor in a fur coat is inappropriate. Linda's mother is also furious at her, indicating that Linda still has a mother complex to deal with—a common problem of everyday life! Immersion in the deep feminine does not solve the emotional trials of being human.

Linda's mother accuses her of having a nervous breakdown. Psychologically, Linda's mother cannot see that what Linda is going through is an initiation, not a breakdown. Indeed, for people raised in a patriarchal culture, the deep feminine is likely to seem crazy, sick, or threatening at first. Apparently unable to explain the importance of what she has been through, Linda accuses her mother of having the nervous breakdown. In a sense, this may be true—her mother may have lost contact with the deep feminine and her true self, so that she can no longer recognize their manifestations. On the other hand, Linda is responding to her mother in a juvenile way: "It's not me with the problem, it's you!" Linda stalks off, leaving the mother-daughter problem unresolved, so Linda's initiation is not yet complete.

Later in the dream, Linda sits down to dinner with her parents, her mother wants to talk, Linda refuses, and a woman friend appears. The dream is enigmatic here, but to my reading, the friend offers some hope of helping Linda reconcile with her mother, just like the nun in "The Mother and the Demon." The friend represents a sister figure and thus offers a symbolic link between the deep feminine and everyday life and a reminder of the remaining task: balancing the two realms.

THE JOURNEY THROUGH ART

A parallel to "The Siren Wife" also appears in the paintings of Leonor Fini, a twentieth-century artist. Several commentators, such as Estella Lauter,[6] have divided Fini's career into distinct stages which parallel the fairy tale. When Fini was in her twenties and thirties, her paintings centered on women who resembled ancient goddesses, like Isis, Demeter, or Ceres, with men appearing only as secondary figures. (The men are also usually sleeping!) Fini thus begins with clear images of feminine power and energy, the way "The Siren Wife" begins with the wife leaving home and having an affair with a king, demonstrating her assertiveness.

After Fini turned forty, she focused on animal and plant images, which often merged with human faces and figures. Her paintings recall the Sirens and the theme of communing with nature. Significantly, mermaids are an explicit theme in Fini's painting *The Veil*, which marks the shift from her goddess figures to her human-nature hybrids.

From the age of forty-seven, Fini returned to painting female figures, but the women are now in groups, often in threes, suggesting the theme of sisterhood. In this phase, Fini painted women in beautiful colors, sometimes nude, sometimes elegantly dressed, and they illustrate deep beauty. Not surprisingly, men are relatively insignificant in this group of Fini's paintings.

Despite her emphasis on beauty, Fini does not ignore the dark side of life. In *The Strangers*, for instance, Fini paints several beautiful women who handle human body parts. The severed hands, feet, and heads are gruesome and seem out of place with the beauty and elegance of the painting as a whole. But the body parts allude to some kind of violence and are thus analogous to the Siren wife destroying the mermaids in the fairy tale.

In her next phase, Fini began portraying male figures in a more prominent and positive light. The reappearance of the male figures suggests a return from the deep feminine to mundane life, the way the Siren wife reconciles with her husband and returns home. Fini's final works seem less dramatic, distinctive, and numinous, compared to her earlier paintings, but this is exactly what would be expected as an individual returns from an archetypal journey back to everyday reality. Women who make this journey return in wisdom, having gained access to the deep feminine and the true beauty of their deep self.

CHAPTER 12

"Princess Marya and the Burbot":

Rescuing the Prince

(from the Nenets of Siberia[1])

nce, far away, there lived a Princess so beautiful that many, many princes came seeking her hand. But her father the Tsar refused them all, thinking none of them good enough for her. One day, an old man asked if his son might marry the Princess.

"Who is your son?" the Tsar inquired.

"Your Majesty," the old man replied, "my son is a burbot."

"But that is a fish that lives on the bottom of the river!" the Tsar exclaimed. "What you say is ridiculous!"

"Yet it is true," the old man persisted. "For many years my wife and I grieved because we had no children. Then one day, while fishing, I found the Burbot on the riverbank. The fish asked me to spare his life and promised to be a son to me and my wife, so I took him home. Now he has grown up, and asked me to arrange a marriage with your daughter."

"Why would I let the Princess marry a fish?" the Tsar demanded.

At that moment, she spoke up from behind a screen near

the Tsar's throne. "Father, why don't you give the Burbot a task. If he succeeds, I will marry him, but if he fails, then put him to death. That is how the Russians do it."

The Tsar thought a moment. "Well, old man, your son can marry my daughter if he builds a new palace for her, more magnificent than mine. And he must do this by tomorrow morning! Otherwise I will have his head cut off—and yours, for good measure!"

The old man nearly fainted with horror, but when he returned home and told his son about the Tsar's demand, the Burbot said, "Do not fear, Father. Go to sleep tonight, and tomorrow we will see what we will see."

That night, the Burbot slithered to the door of the house, leaped over the threshold, turned into a handsome young man, lifted an iron staff, and stuck its point into the ground. Instantly, thirty men with weapons appeared and asked, "What is your wish?"

"Build me a palace next to the Tsar's," the Burbot commanded, "and make it more beautiful than his."

"As you command," the men replied. The Burbot returned home, stepped over the threshold, turned back into a fish, and went to bed. The next morning, he woke the old man. "Father," he said, "take an axe and go to the Tsar's palace, then come back and tell me what you see."

The old man went to the palace and could not believe his eyes. Next to it was a palace even more beautiful than the Tsar's. The old man went up to the new palace and struck it with his axe, but not a chip of stone flew off. He hurried home to tell his son what he had seen.

"Now," the son said, "go to the Tsar and ask him to let me marry his daughter." Meanwhile, the Tsar had seen the new palace and was dumbfounded. "The old man's son is no ordinary man!" the ruler thought to himself. But he hated to have his daughter marry a fish, so when the old man approached him, the Tsar said, "I have another task for your son. He must build a new church, as beautiful as my cathedral. And he must build three bridges—one going from the old cathedral to the new one, another from the new church to the new palace, and a third bridge from my home to their palace. If your son does not build all this by tomorrow, both you and he will die."

The old man trembled with terror, and thought, "I should have killed the Burbot at the river!" But when he told his son about the Tsar's demand, the Burbot only smiled. "Do not fear, Father. Go to sleep and tomorrow we will see what we will see."

That night, after the old man and his wife went to sleep, the Burbot crawled over the threshold, changed into a handsome young man, and struck the tip of his iron staff into the ground. Thirty warriors appeared and the Burbot commanded them to build him a church and three bridges, as the Tsar had demanded.

"As you desire," the thirty men said, and marched off. The Burbot went back to his house, stepped over the threshold, turned back into a fish, and went to bed.

The next morning, the Burbot woke the old man. "Father," he said, "take an axe and go to the Tsar's palace. Then come back and tell me what you see." The old man set off, and when he arrived at the palace, he rubbed his eyes in disbelief. Beside it stood a new church, more beautiful than the Tsar's cathedral, and three bridges, one leading from the old church to the new, another going from the new church to the new palace, and the third linking the Tsar's palace and the Burbot's. The old man swung his axe at the church and the three bridges, but not a splinter of stone flew off. He hurried back to his son with the good news.

"And now," the Burbot asked his father, "go to the Tsar and see what he has to say."

The old man found the Tsar staring with wonder at the new church and the three bridges. But the Tsar said, "Tell your son that I have one last task for him. I want him to bring me a sled and three horses, more splendid than anything I have. If he succeeds, he will marry the Princess, no matter what people say. But if he fails, you and your son will have your heads cut off."

"I should never have listened to the Burbot!" the old man thought to himself. But when he returned home and told his son what had happened, the Burbot smiled. "Rest easy tonight, Father, and tomorrow we shall see what we shall see."

Later that night, the Burbot crawled over the threshold, turned into a handsome young man, and stuck his iron staff into the ground. Thirty men appeared and he commanded them, "Find me a sleigh with three horses, more marvelous than anything the Tsar has."

"As you command," the thirty men replied and departed. The young man crossed the threshold, turned back into a fish, and went to sleep. The next morning, he woke the old man. "Father, go to the Tsar, then come back and tell me what you see."

The old man hurried to the palace, and stared in amazement at a sled with three horses, all more beautiful than anything the Tsar had. When the old man returned home with the news, the Burbot said, "And now, Father, go to the Tsar and ask for his daughter's hand!"

The Tsar in the meantime had seen the sleigh and three horses, so when the old man arrived, the monarch declared, "Your son fulfilled my three tasks, so I will keep my promise. Bring him here and the Princess will marry him this very day, no matter what people say."

The old man rushed home and told his son the good news. "Well then, Father," the Burbot said, "put me in a sack, and carry me to the palace for the wedding feast!" Along the way, the townspeople gathered and laughed because the Princess was marrying a fish. When the old man arrived at the palace, he placed the Burbot on a stool, and the feasting began. At last everyone rode to the new church, and the Princess and the Burbot were married. The feasting began all over again, and lasted a week longer. Finally, the Princess and the Burbot retired to their new home.

The couple lived together for three years, and each night, the Burbot took off his fish skin, turning into a handsome man. But each morning, he donned his fish skin again, and so no one but the Princess knew his secret. Everyone continued to mock her for marrying a fish.

One morning, Princess Marya arose earlier than usual. She sat alone, feeling sad and ashamed. "Everyone laughs at me for marrying a fish," she told herself, "and I am sorely tired of it." Suddenly she had an idea. "If I burn my husband's fish skin before he awakens, he must remain a man!" She seized the fishy suit, threw it into the fire, and went into the bedroom, but her husband had vanished. At that moment, a little bird flew in the window.

"Alas, Princess Marya," the bird said. "Had you waited three days longer, your husband would have been freed from an evil spell. He would have remained human the rest of his life, but now you have lost him." With those words, the bird flew out the window.

"What have I done?" Marya exclaimed. "If only I had known! Why did my husband not tell me! What am I to do?" For a week the Princess sorrowed, then she rose up and vowed, "I will seek my husband and rescue him, no matter what happens." That day, she left her palace, setting off for where she knew not. Her only clue was the direction in which the little bird had flown. At the edge of town, the Princess came upon an old woman, leaning out of the window of a small hut.

"Why such a sad look, Princess Marya?" the crone asked.

"Alas!" Marya answered. "I burned my husband's fish skin, and lost him to an evil spell. So I am searching for him."

"You will never find him traveling the way you are," the old woman shook her head. "Go back home, and have the blacksmiths make you three pairs of iron boots, three iron hats, and three loaves of iron bread. Then come back here and I will tell you where to search for your husband, but if you find him, you will be a lucky woman, indeed."

Princess Marya thanked the crone for her advice and returned home. She asked the smiths to forge her three pairs of iron boots, three iron hats, and three loaves of iron bread. Then she returned to the old woman at the edge of the wilderness.

"It is too late in the day to travel further," the crone said. "Have dinner with me and rest here for the night. Then you can leave in the morning, fresh and strong." Princess Marya thanked the old woman and stayed with her. Early the next day, the crone offered her a bit of advice.

"After you leave here, look for a great hole in the earth," the old woman instructed. "When you come to the abyss, put on a pair of your iron boots, one of the iron hats, and eat a loaf of iron bread. Then climb down. You will meet many people there, shouting, singing, and weeping, and they will beg you to stay with them, but you must press on without pause. If you stop, you will never leave the cave. When you have worn out the three pairs of iron boots and the three hats, and eaten all the loaves of iron bread, you will come to the end of the passage. Outside lives my sister, and she will tell you what to do next."

Princess Marya trembled to hear what lay before her, but she thanked the old woman and set off. How long Marya traveled, no one knows, but her path stopped suddenly at the edge of a chasm. She peered down and saw no bottom. Undaunted, she put on a pair of iron boots and an iron hat, ate a loaf of iron bread, and began climbing into the void. Down, down, down she went, until she came to a gloomy tunnel. There she heard people shouting, singing, and weeping, asking her to stay with them, but she ignored them and pressed onward. The floor of the cave was strewn with iron blades, and even though she wore iron shoes, her feet were wounded. With every step, she bled. Hanging from the roof of the cave were iron spikes, and try as she might to avoid them, she hit her head constantly, so that blood trickled down her face like tears.

As Princess Marya went deeper into the darkness, the shouting, singing, and weeping around her grew louder. People clamored for her to stop, but she kept to her path. For how long she struggled, she could not say, but when she ate the last iron loaf, wore out the last pair of iron boots, and frayed her last iron hat, she saw a light glimmering in the distance. She reached the end of the terrible cave, pulled herself out into sunlight, and collapsed upon a grassy bank. For a week she lay still, too weak to move, then she stood up, faint with hunger, and limped onward. She came to a house and knocked on the door. Baba Yaga, the great witch, appeared at the entrance.

"Princess Marya!" Baba Yaga exclaimed. "Where are you going in such a state? My sister must have sent you here!"

"Alas," Marya replied, "I burned my husband's fish skin and lost him. But I love him dearly, so I search the earth for him."

Baba Yaga sighed. "It is ten years now since your husband passed my house. He is human now, but in those years, he married the daughter of the Fire King, and he now lives with her in her palace. I will tell you how you can find him and win him back, but first come inside, rest, and eat."

For a week, the Princess stayed with Baba Yaga, regaining her strength. Then the old woman turned to Marya. "The time has come for you to see your husband. He lives yonder with the daughter of the Fire King," and Baba Yaga pointed to a distant palace. "This is what you must do," Baba Yaga went on. "In the garden around their palace is a small hill. Sit on the grassy mound and brush your hair with this comb." Baba Yaga handed Marya a beautiful golden comb. "The daughter of the Fire King will see you and come out, asking to buy the comb from you. She will be with two other women, and they will look exactly alike. So you must be careful to pick out the right woman, who will be the one in the middle. Tell her you will trade the comb for a night alone with the Burbot, but do not give her the comb until you are with your husband."

Princess Marya thanked Baba Yaga for her help and left the house. She came to a great palace, stopped in the garden, and sat upon a little grassy mound. She began combing her hair with the golden comb, and three women soon came up to her. The middle one exclaimed, "I have never seen such a beautiful comb. Will you sell it to me? I can pay you whatever you like."

"I will not sell it for money," Marya replied. "But I will trade it for something else."

"What do you wish?" the daughter of the Fire King inquired eagerly.

"Just to spend a night alone with your husband," Marya answered.

"Oh, that is nothing," the Fire King's daughter said. "You can do that this very night. Now give me the comb."

"No," Marya said, "it is yours only when I step into your husband's room."

"Very well," the daughter of the Fire King frowned. "It will be evening soon enough, so come with me." At the palace door she went inside, leaving Marya to wait, reappearing a few moments later. "You can come in now," she motioned to Marya, leading Marya to the bedroom. She took the golden comb from Marya, and left her alone with the Burbot. Marya rushed to her husband and called out his name. But he slept and did not move at all. She wept, and told him of her long journey to find him, but still he did not stir. When morning arrived, the daughter of the Fire King rushed in and threw Marya out.

Marya returned to Baba Yaga, heartbroken and discouraged, and sorrowed for a week. Then Baba Yaga gave Marya a beautiful gold ring. "Wear this ring," Baba Yaga advised. "Go to the palace again and sit in the garden. The three women will come to you once more, and the middle one will ask to buy the ring. Tell her that you will exchange it for a night alone with the Burbot but do not give her the ring until you are in your husband's room."

Filled with new hope, Marya went to the palace and sat in the garden, wearing the golden ring. The three women appeared, and the middle one asked to buy it.

"I will not sell it," Princess Marya explained, speaking to the woman in the middle. "But I will trade it for a night alone with your husband!"

"That is easily done!" the woman agreed. "But first give me the ring."

"No," Marya insisted. "It is yours only when I am in your husband's room."

"Very well, follow me," the Fire King's daughter said. She went into the palace a moment, while Marya waited outside, then returned and led Marya to the Burbot.

Marya rushed to her husband's side and called out his

name, but he slept and did not stir. She pleaded and cried, describing her long journey through the abyss, but still he slept. When dawn came, the Fire King's daughter flung open the door, and sent Marya on her way. The Princess returned to Baba Yaga in despair.

"I could not wake my husband!" Marya exclaimed, telling Baba Yaga everything that had happened.

"The daughter of the Fire King gave him a sleeping potion!" Baba Yaga murmured thoughtfully. "She is a tricky one." Princess Marya wept for a week, yearning for her husband, then Baba Yaga fetched a beautiful kerchief from a cabinet. "You must go to your husband once more, Marya," the old woman said, "but this is your last chance to regain him. Use this kerchief as you did with the comb and ring. There is no scarf more beautiful than this, and the Fire King's daughter will covet it. Trade the kerchief for a night with your husband, but if you do not wake him this time, you will never see him again. This is the last time I will help you."

Marya thanked Baba Yaga, left for the palace, and sat upon the grassy mound as before, wearing the beautiful kerchief. The three women approached her and the middle one asked for the scarf. "I have never seen anything so marvelous!" she exclaimed. "I will buy the kerchief from you."

"I will not sell it," Marya replied, "but I will trade it for a night with your husband, the Burbot."

"That is nothing," the Fire King's daughter exclaimed. "Now let me have the kerchief."

"It is yours when I stand beside your husband!" Marya insisted.

"Oh, very well," the Burbot's new wife grumbled. "Follow me." She led Marya to the palace door, went in alone a moment, reappeared, and then ushered the Princess into the Burbot's room. "Now give me the kerchief!" she demanded and Marya handed it over.

Marya rushed to her husband's side and called his name. But though she pleaded and cried out all night, he did not stir. Dawn finally came, and Marya became desperate. Overcome with grief, she wept. Suddenly the door to the room opened, and the Fire King's daughter entered triumphantly. "Your time is up! You must leave at once!" she crowed.

At that moment, one of Marya's tears fell upon the Burbot's face. He awoke with a start. "Is it raining?" he cried.

"Leave now!" the Fire King's daughter yelled at Princess Marya.

The Burbot saw Marya standing beside him and recognized her at once. "Marya! It is you! You have come at last!"

"Get out!" the Fire King's daughter told Marya, trying to pull her out of the room.

"Let her be!" the Burbot told his second wife. "She is Marya, my first and true wife." He embraced Marya, and she told him everything that had happened since he vanished. Then the Burbot summoned all the elders of the land, put on a great feast for them and then asked, "Which of these women is my true wife? The one who risked her life to find me, wearing out three pairs of iron boots, three iron hats, and eating three iron loaves? Or the one who sold me for a comb, a ring, and a kerchief?"

The elders replied in one voice, "Your true wife is Marya, and it is she you must live with."

The Burbot nodded, turned to Marya and said, "It is time we returned home." Then he told the daughter of the Fire King, "You must find someone else to marry. I am going back home, with my true wife."

The Burbot picked up a rusty old box. "Marya, close your eyes," he said gently. Without hesitation, she shut her eyes, and in the next moment, she felt a soft wind upon her face. "Now Marya, open your eyes," her husband whispered.

When Marya looked around her, she was amazed. Gone was the palace of the Fire King's daughter. Instead, she and the Burbot stood in an open field next to a river. Ahead of them was a bustling town.

"Do you recognize the place?" the Burbot asked.

"Yes," Marya said, "I think I do."

"It is your father's kingdom," the Burbot said, as he opened his box again.

Marya swooned and when she awoke, she found herself in a beautiful palace, her very own home, built by the Burbot.

Lying on a couch next to her was her husband, fast asleep. A few moments later, he awoke.

"You gave me three tasks before we were married," the Burbot explained to Marya. "And that is why you had to suffer so much later. But now we are together once more." As the two embraced, the Burbot's old father and mother came in, followed by Marya's parents, the Tsar and Tsarina. They all sat down together for a great feast, and from that day onward, Marya and her husband lived happily together. In due time, when the old Tsar and Tsarina died, Marya and the Burbot became the new rulers of the land, and they lived in joy and love for the rest of their days.

MARYA AND MEN

This story features two protagonists, Princess Marya and the Burbot, but Marya is the main character: she is the only one with a proper name while everyone else has a generic title. Marya's father is simply called "the Tsar," the Burbot's father is "an old man," the Fire King's daughter is described as such or as "the Burbot's new wife," while the Burbot is named after a kind of fish.

Many readers will recognize the similarity between Marya's tale and the Greek myth of Psyche and Amor. Indeed, the two stories are different versions of the same drama with many variants from around the world.[2] I chose Marya's version because the story is unusually comprehensive and comes from a culture relatively far from Western influence— the Nenets, a Siberian tribe.

Marya's tale starts with many men coming to win her hand in marriage, but her father, the Tsar, refuses them all. Her situation summarizes women's position in most cultures. Although she is a Princess enjoying a privileged life, she has no say in whom she will marry, because her father, a patri-arch, will decide. Her privilege is pseudo-privilege. Marya must also sit behind a screen near her father's throne, and cannot be seen publicly—she is barred from public life. So the story brings up the theme of women's oppression, even for a Princess.

THE TASK

However, Marya is not passive or helpless in this situation. When the old man asks the Tsar to let the Burbot marry Marya, the monarch scoffs at the offer, but before he can refuse, Marya intervenes. She suggests that the Burbot be given a task. If he succeeds in it, she will marry him; if he fails, he will die. In speaking up, Marya reveals that she has not given up her voice: she has not been completely silenced by social pressures. It also seems that Marya senses the importance of the Burbot's request, perhaps intuitively knowing that he is no ordinary man and that he might be a suitable mate for her. She can see behind outward appearances.

In suggesting that the Burbot fulfill a task on pain of death, Marya equalizes the rules of the marriage game. Marriage would fix Marya's situation for life, so she wagers her whole life in marrying. When she makes death the result of a man's unsuccessful proposal, Marya forces suitors like the Burbot to take the same risk as she does.

The Tsar follows his daughter's advice, and this is noteworthy. He heeds her advice, validates her opinion, and thus encourages her development as an individual. This may help explain her courage and resourcefulness later in the story.

In suggesting that her father give the Burbot a task, Marya explains that the Russians customarily did that. Some cultural context explains her comment. The Nenets were an independent, nomadic people, who hunted, fished, and herded reindeer in the Arctic regions, until the Russians began expanding their empire during the eighteenth and nineteenth centuries. Like Native Americans in America, the Nenets were no match for modern rifles or the many diseases that the Russians brought, such as tuberculosis, influenza, and syphilis.[3] The Nenets and other Siberian tribes were quickly defeated, "pacified," and forced to adopt Russian ways. The very notion of a tsar and a princess, in fact, reflects Russian influences, since the Nenets traditionally had chiefs and shamans, not absolute monarchs.

THE BURBOT

Marya's husband is a burbot, a type of fish. In other versions of the tale, the type of animal differs, but the husband is always some kind of beast—a bear in the Norwegian tale "East of the Sun, West of the Moon," a lion in the Grimms' version, "The Singing Soaring Lark," and a camel in the Palestinian variant, "The Camel Husband." What is the symbolism behind these animal-husbands?

We can interpret the Burbot as an inner character, a part of Marya herself, namely, her masculine side. He would then be an animus figure and his subhuman, animal nature suggests that Marya is not conscious of her masculine strengths. This interpretation does not fit the story because Marya is outspoken from the beginning, and later goes bravely in search of her husband. Courageous, assertive, and resourceful, she is not unconscious of her masculine energies. The Burbot is better interpreted as an outer figure, as a man in his own right.

The Burbot's animal nature can then be interpreted rather literally: Marya sees him as a beast—as a crude, uncivilized creature. This is certainly a view many women have of men. Freudians usually interpret this opinion in terms of women's fear of sex with men, and most cultures teach women to fear sexuality in general, and their own in particular, condemning female bodies and desires as sinful, corrupt, and dangerous. But historically, women had their own reasons to fear sexuality: before modern birth control, sex often led to pregnancy, and thus to the risk of death in childbirth. In competitive cultures, of course, men often do act like beasts—violent, ruthless, and callous. So the bestial theme comments on the social order.

Marya's tale specifically makes her husband a fish, rather than a lion or other more traditionally "masculine," predatory animal. The Burbot is in a sense a male version of a mermaid, and this link to water suggests he has an affinity for the feminine, an openness to honoring women, and the potential to develop beyond conventional male roles, to become a "new male." Indeed, in fairy tales, half-animal men like the Burbot often turn into caring partners. Women writers repeat the theme, portraying what Annis Pratt calls "the green world lover." Gentle and nurturing, yet passionate and fierce, these male figures cherish and support women. As Linda Leonard and Karen Signell observe, women often dream of such men.

The Burbot was a fish because of some kind of spell, but who cast it is not clear. In the Norwegian version, the curse comes from the man's stepmother, while in the Greek myth of Psyche and Amor, it is Amor's mother, Aphrodite, who is the source of the problem. In fact, many young men live under the psychological spell of their mothers, which makes them unavailable for a deep, authentic relationship. The Burbot's enchantment also means that he is not free and whole. As an incomplete or stunted male, he contrasts sharply with the ominous animus in stories like "The Queen and the Murderer." The shift from a dangerous male to a disabled one reflects women's development: as women reclaim their strength and wisdom, they see more clearly behind men's heroic facades and glimpse the psychic incompleteness that lies behind macho posturing.

BUILDING A NEW WORLD

The Burbot must succeed in three tasks to marry Marya, and the theme is common in fairy tales. But usually the young man must do something heroic, such as kill a dragon, find the water of life, or win a great treasure. Gaining glory and booty are the usual tests. The Burbot's tasks break from this heroic convention, and they each involve affirming women and the feminine. The tests determine whether he has the potential to become a worthy mate. This parallels how the woman from the egg in Chapter 7 demanded water from the young man, to see if he could deal with the feminine and with feelings.

The Burbot's first challenge is to build a palace where he and the Princess will live, near the Tsar. This means that the Princess will not leave her family to live among the Burbot's kin, uprooting herself to enter her husband's world, the usual custom in most societies. The reverse is true: the Burbot is to leave his home and live near the Princess's family, a practice typical of matrilineal cultures, where women have much more honor and influence. Symbolically, Marya challenges the Burbot to build a new home, a new world, which honors the feminine, inspired by matrilineal rather than patriarchal convention.

The Burbot's second task is to build a new church, so the wedding will not take place in the old royal chapel. Symbolically, the relationship between Marya and the Burbot as wife and husband will not follow traditional patriarchal rituals or roles. More broadly, the new church symbolizes a fresh spiritual perspective. Marya realizes that it is not enough for her and the Burbot to create a new home, a new secular order, freed from patriarchal tradition. They must also build a new spiritual outlook, a task men and women face today, too, as Mary Daly, Susan Griffin, Mary Giles, Merlin Stone, and Mary Lou Randour emphasize.

As part of his second task, the Burbot must also build three bridges, connecting the new church to the old one, the new church to the new palace, and the new palace to the Tsar's residence. Metaphorically, the new world must be consciously linked to the old one. Leaving the old patriarchal world and building new realms for women is only the first step on a longer journey. The next challenge is to link these new woman-affirming institutions to the rest of society.

The three bridges have further symbolic meanings. Bridges emphasize the horizontal, in contrast to towers, obelisks, pyramids, and skyscrapers, which accentuate the vertical.

Towering structures are favorites of kings, and the image of being higher than somebody else and looking down on them lies at the core of hierarchical societies. Bridges provide a more "feminine" alternative focusing on horizontal interaction—mutuality and equality.

The Burbot's final task is to obtain a beautiful sleigh with three magnificent horses. This might seem like a small request after building a palace, a church, and three bridges. It is also an odd task, but the challenge is symbolic. As noted before, the Nenets were originally a nomadic, reindeer-herding culture living in the Arctic regions. With the land ice-bound much of the year, the Nenets traveled by sleigh, pulled by reindeer. In asking for a sleigh rather than a carriage, Marya honors the old Nenets tradition. By having horses rather than reindeer, though, Marya also acknowledges the profound changes that occurred in Nenets society with Russian colonization. She recognizes that a simple return to the old ways is no longer possible. Instead, the old must be integrated with the new. The challenge is to weave a future from the best strands of the past and present.

BREAKING THE SILENCE

After their marriage, Marya and the Burbot live together for three years. By day he is a fish, but every night he turns into a handsome young man. Marya finally burns the Burbot's fish skin to keep him human. Notice that she apparently cannot tell anybody that her husband is human at night. (If she told people, they would not laugh at her for marrying a fish, as the tale says they do.) Like other protagonists in women's tales, Marya is silenced. However, she is a remarkable woman and does not tolerate the situation. She burns the Burbot's fish skin instead, symbolically defying oppressive restrictions. Marya also burns the Burbot's fish skin early one morning, while he is still sleeping. Here we return to a familiar theme in women's tales: the women are awake and changing things, but the men are asleep or unconscious.

A small detail in the story highlights the importance of Marya's defiance. Marya is called merely "the Princess" until the day she burns her husband's fish skin. Only then does the original version of the story begin to use her proper name, "Marya." So she has no unique identity until she defies her oppressive situation, following her own counsel. The story is profoundly insightful: women can express their unique individuality only if they defy the taboos and silence imposed upon them. By burning up fishy patriarchal limitations, women reclaim their true names.

The reason Marya burned the Burbot's fish skin, the story says, is that she was tired of people laughing at her, and the same theme appears in the other versions of the story. So she might seem weak, giving in to public pressure and social convention. But she is actually quite strong, as the rest of the story demonstrates. A better interpretation is that Marya responds to what other people think because she affirms the importance of relationships, and human life is a web of such connections. Yielding to social influences seems like a weakness only in competitive cultures, which idealize the solitary hero. In fact, if Marya ignored public opinion, she would never have gone on her quest, or discovered the depth of her strength and the power of her love. Nor would she have freed her husband from his enforced marriage to the Fire King's daughter and, by extension, liberated society from oppressive traditions.

The public pressure to which Marya submits is actually a demand from society that she participate in the world. The same demand was clear in "The Queen and the Murderer" where the Queen wanted to keep her marriage to the King secret, but was eventually forced to appear in public and confront the murderer.

FIRE AND BURNING

Marya destroys the fish skin by burning it, and the fire imagery reappears in most other versions of the story. In mythol-

ogy humanity usually obtains fire by breaking a taboo. In
Greek myth, for instance, Prometheus stole fire from the gods
to give to humanity, and Spider Woman does the same in
Native American lore. So the fire theme reemphasizes the
defiance behind the destruction of the fish skin.

In mythology, fire is also closely linked to ancient goddesses. The folklore of many Siberian tribes, for instance,
describes a feminine fire spirit who governs the hearth fire,[4]
like Hestia, the Greek goddess. And the hearth, allowing
cooking and warm shelters, is the foundation of all human
cultures. Fire also symbolizes fierceness, of which Pele, the
Polynesian fire spirit, goddess of volcanoes, is a good example. An archetypal wild woman, she was spontaneous, fierce,
tempestuous, yet also tender. So fire points to women's passionate caring and love, the fierceness of a woman protecting
her child or community. Indeed, when Marya burns the Burbot's fish skin, she parallels what the feminists of the 1960s
did, burning bras in a passionate protest against misogynist
traditions.

Fire and passion include sexuality, and reclaiming feminine sexuality is vital to women. It is no accident that the
women's movement is so deep, widespread, and powerful
today, after the invention of reliable birth control. Less fearful
of unexpected pregnancies, women can begin to celebrate
their bodies and passions. The result has been dramatic, as
women have explored long-repressed feminine energies.

THE BURBOT VANISHES

After Marya burns her husband's fish skin, he vanishes and
a little bird reveals that he was under a spell. She discovers
the truth about him and so gains consciousness. At the same
time, she loses him, and the theme occurs in all other variants of the tale. Her action, however, ultimately leads to her
individuation, the liberation of her husband, and an authentic egalitarian union between them.[5] Her new consciousness
transforms the world. Here Marya reverses the story of Eve.

In the Bible, Eve ate from the Tree of Knowledge, and thus gained consciousness. But she was also exiled from Paradise and condemned as the source of humanity's sinfulness. Marya's story rejects this patriarchal condemnation.

The little bird tells Marya that if she had waited three more days, the spell on her husband would have been broken forever. Marya wonders why he did not tell her earlier, and most women can empathize with her situation because men often do not explain what is going on. Yet behind men's silence may lie great need or vulnerability.

Many women will also find the fact that the Burbot vanishes just before Marya learns his secret all too familiar: when women become close and emotionally intimate, men often flee. The fish skin is a defense—like the bravado of the macho hero—and only at night, when no one else can see, do men take off their costumes and reveal their vulnerable side. Marya's story insists that women do not have to put up with such constricted intimacy. A full, egalitarian relationship is possible with a man—but only after much work by both parties.

THE SEARCH

After losing the Burbot, Marya sorrowed for a week and then set off to find her husband. But why does she want him back? As she later tells Baba Yaga, she loves her husband dearly, and that is why she searches for him. She undertakes her arduous journey out of love. She does not seek glory or power on her quest, but reunion and rescue. The message is profoundly relevant today, when women and men look at each other warily, separated into different camps. Between women's anger and male backlash there seems little hope for reconciliation. Marya's tale reassures us that authentic love based on equality and mutuality makes reunion possible.

In searching for her husband, Marya does not know where to go, and other versions repeat the theme. In a Norwegian variant, the wife must go "east of the sun, west of the moon"—to the ends of the world. In the Grimms' version, the wife vows to go "wherever the wind blows and as long as the cock crows." These protagonists journey into the unknown because they have broken with social convention and have no traditional guidelines. Indeed, on her journey Marya writes a new script for women, an example of a resourceful, strong woman pursuing what she values and loves, using wisdom and negotiation, rather than battle or victory.

Marya decides to follow the little bird, and it can be interpreted as the "gut feelings," intuitive images that emerge from the unconscious. These underlie what Mary Belenky and her colleagues called women's "passionate knowing." The challenge is to pay attention to these messages: if Marya had not noticed in which direction the bird flew, she might have wandered fruitlessly forever.

THE CRONE AND THE DESCENT

After Marya embarks upon her journey, she meets an old woman who gives her essential advice. This archetypal crone lives at the end of town. In women's stories, the wise woman usually appears in the middle of the wilderness, not at its edge. She is nearer and more accessible to Marya, I think, because the Princess has not been completely silenced and retains contact with her natural self.

The crone warns Marya about being unprepared for the journey. Marya has naively set out on her quest presumably believing that love and courage are enough to sustain her. This is important advice today as women throw off ancient fetters, feeling excited and optimistic about venturing into government, business, and educational institutions. But ever more subtle and powerful opponents remain, from conservative backlash to the glass ceiling. The crone advises women what preparations are needed.

She tells Marya to obtain hats, boots, and bread made from iron, and the iron theme reappears in the English version,

"The Black Bull of Norroway," and the Italian one, "King Crin." The mythological meaning of iron is surprisingly uniform across cultures. Durable, strong, and firm, iron usually symbolizes strength of character. In wearing an iron hat and iron boots and eating the iron bread, the story suggests that Marya deepens her natural courage and strength. In Greek and Roman folklore, iron was also associated with Ares and Mars, the gods of war, probably because iron is essential in weaponry. Significantly, Marya uses the iron for protection, not for offense, and even makes something nurturing— bread—from the cold metal. Symbolically she adopts the iron strength of a warrior, but remains true to her feminine self. Her whole quest, after all, is motivated by her love for the Burbot, not thirst for power or wealth.

After obtaining the iron implements, Marya descends into a tunnel, where iron spikes wound her. This brings up another mythological meaning of iron—its link to evil. Many cultures, for example, call the present time the "Iron Age," because it is torn by war and ruled by evil people, compared to a long-gone "Golden Age," where men and women were noble and peaceful. In going into the cave, Marya enters an evil place, a shadowy domain. She descends into the underworld. The iron motif, with its link to warfare, suggests that this underworld is the shadow side of warrior culture, of heroic and patriarchal traditions. That is, Marya confronts not only her own personal shadow, but the unconscious side of society. This is exactly what the mother did in "The Mother and the Demon" when she entered the demon's castle.

Despite her iron boots and iron hats, Marya is wounded by the spikes in the ceiling and the blades on the floor. So all the preparation in the world, and her great strength and courage, cannot protect her. Many successful women experience something similar when they fall into depression at midlife, despite their accomplishments and secure relationships. Although such women may chastise themselves for not pulling themselves out of their gloom, accustomed as they are to mastering difficult situations, their plight is not a personal failure, but a basic task in human development—coming to terms with the underworld, the dark side of life, with tragedy and vulnerability.

G H O S T S

While struggling through the abyss, Marya hears many people singing, shouting, and weeping, asking her to stay with them. Warned by the crone, Marya ignores the pleas and continues on her way. Psyche has almost exactly the same task in the Greek version of the story: as she enters the underworld, spirits of the dead beg her for help, and her task is to ignore their piteous pleas, heartwrenching though they are. Both tales highlight an important challenge for women—placing limits on their altruistic impulses to help other people. The pleading may come from an aging mother, endlessly needy children, a dependent husband, or a demanding boss. But a woman must remain loyal to her own quest and reject conventional stereotypes, which expect women to sacrifice themselves for others. Failure here leads to becoming trapped in the underworld, in depression and despair.

Yet Marya is self-sacrificing in a sense—she risks her life for the Burbot. What is crucial is that she acts from her own heart, following a decision she freely made. She is not under a spell, or desperate for a man, or following cultural imperatives. She obeys her own feelings and follows the instructions of the crone, the deep feminine. So Marya is both self-sacrificing and self-actualizing, and breaks the traditional dichotomy between the two.

The pleading people in the underworld seem to be ghosts and introduce another dimension to Marya's ordeal. Ghosts and dead people make a good symbol for issues that women inherit from their parents, and their parents' parents. Separating these ancestral problems from personal ones can be profoundly liberating. As teenagers, for example, most women recognize their parents' flaws, and rebel against parental authority. By midlife, most women realize where their parents' faults came from—from the previous generation, the parents' parents. The insight helps women accept their mothers and fathers as human beings. Metaphorically, grown daughters learn to recognize the ghosts that haunt their parents and not become entangled with them.

The ghosts may also be regrets, second thoughts, "oughts" and "should haves." "I should have taken that job, even though I was scared to." "If only I had known about his drinking . . ." "I ought to lose more weight and eat less." Marya's tale warns that dwelling on ghostly "oughts" and "should haves" can trap a woman in the underworld. But how is a woman to distinguish between ghostly pleas from the past and the voice of her true self? Between the chattering of social convention and the authority of her inner desires? Notice that the underworld people speak all at once, like a crowd or mob, saying many different things simultaneously. By contrast, the crone, personifying Marya's deep self, speaks in a single voice and stands behind what she says. This suggests that when a woman's deep self speaks, it will not be in a mumble or a whisper. "The Three Little Eggs" illustrates the point, because the magic eggs speak clearly and unequivocally. The voice of the true self also appears in dreams as a mysterious, but authoritative utterance. Or it surfaces in an intuition where a woman simply *knows* something. The ghostly voices, in contrast, are nagging and pestering, like gnats, and they convey convention, not conviction, causing worry, not insight.

BABA YAGA

After a long, painful journey through the abyss, Marya climbs out, collapses on a grassy bank, stays there for a week, and recovers from her wounds. The story says nothing about her eating or drinking, so she apparently regains her strength purely from nature and the deep feminine, recalling how the handless maiden in Chapter 6 was healed by the wilderness.

Marya's situation here corresponds to a difficult phase in psychotherapy. When women make the descent into the unconscious, they come face to face with the psychological issues that underlie their depression or anxiety—personal ghosts, societal demons, and ancestral problems. Armed with insight, many women reemerge from their descent only to find that their everyday problems and suffering remain. So it may seem as if the whole effort in therapy, the painful descent and return, was for naught. Yet in this difficult period, new life and healing emerge, paradoxically through inactivity. Indeed, in lying on the grass for a week, Marya becomes passive for the first time. Until now, she has taken the lead in most things, suggesting that her father give the Burbot a task, burning the fish skin, and struggling through the abyss. Now Marya starts to balance her highly energetic, active life, learning to wait and to be open to unexpected elements—like the healing power of the earth. This is particularly important for women like Marya, who have resisted giving up their native power and voice. The challenge for them is to trust that when all their conscious efforts fail, unknown powers will emerge from deep within. No hero is needed—just patience for the deep self to do its work.

When Marya resumes her journey, she meets Baba Yaga. The archetypal witch in Russian fairy tales, Baba Yaga is usually evil and eats children, yet here she is completely helpful. She knows exactly what happened to the Burbot and gives Marya three priceless gifts to help her rescue him. Why is Baba Yaga helpful here and yet destructive in other tales? She personifies the power of the deep feminine, and to girls or young women this numinous power can be overwhelming. Metaphorically, Baba Yaga eats fragile egos. But Marya is ready for her. She has the strength to benefit from the witch's primordial power and knowledge. In portraying Baba Yaga as a positive figure, Marya's tale also breaks with misogynist convention, which equates powerful women with evil witches. The fairy story is thus surprisingly modern, since many feminists today celebrate witches as wise women, working to reverse centuries of patriarchal condemnation.

Significantly, Baba Yaga and the first crone are sisters, bringing up the sisterhood theme.

THE DAUGHTER OF
THE FIRE KING

Baba Yaga explains that the Burbot passed by ten years ago
and is now married to the daughter of the Fire King. The
latter represents a false wife and a false self, like the ones in
"Emme" and "The Woman from the Egg." The Fire King's
daughter trades a night with her husband for golden objects,
putting material posessions above relationship. But this only
mirrors market societies, like Western culture, where everything has a price and where relationships are commodities
that can be bought and sold.

The Fire King's daughter appears in the company of two
other women who look identical to her. This suggests that she
is not a unique individual but rather a clone. She represents a
cultural stereotype, rather than a real person. The three
women clones also highlight another feature of hierarchical
cultures: individuals are interchangeable with each other,
and what counts is their role, the function they carry out in
the system. The story accentuates this point by giving the
second wife no name. She is identified only by her relationship to two men—as the daughter of the Fire King and as the
Burbot's second wife.

As the former, the false wife is linked to fire and thus to
passion. But her passion focuses on beautiful objects: she is,
so to speak, a consummate consumer. Significantly, Marya is
also the daughter of a king—the Tsar. Yet she has not become
a clone or stereotype because she has always listened to her
heart and not to convention.

Besides representing a false self, the Burbot's second wife
can be interpreted in another way: she may represent the
anima of the Burbot, his feminine side. As is true with many
men raised in heroic traditions, the Burbot has not developed
his ability to relate to others on a deep level, to honor emo-

tions and intuitions. So his anima takes the form of cultural stereotype.

THE GOLDEN GIFTS

Baba Yaga gives Marya a golden comb, a gold ring, and a beautiful kerchief to help her reclaim her husband. The objects involved vary in different versions of the story, but they are always linked to the feminine domain, are usually used by women to beautify themselves, and thus allude to deep beauty. Indeed, Marya's tale parallels "The Siren Wife" in striking ways. The magic of the Sirens came from "the loveliest," hidden deep in the ocean and symbolizing deep beauty. Marya's golden comb, ring, and kerchief are surpassingly lovely, and come from Baba Yaga, the primordial feminine who lives deep in the unconscious. The Siren wife encounters the mermaids and deep beauty only after being thrown into the sea and almost drowning. Symbolically, she dies and is reborn into the deep feminine. Similarly, Marya must pass through the underworld, among the ghosts of the dead, before she meets Baba Yaga and receives the golden gifts.

GOLD AND FIRE

Marya's comb and ring are gold, and in other versions most of the gifts are also gold. In most traditions, gold is considered a symbol of nobility and purity, since it never tarnishes. This is surely a virtue of Marya, since she has remained true to herself, never wavering from her quest even in the underworld. Her purity, though, is not that of the innocent virgin, but of a woman who is one with herself. Because of its color, gold is often associated with the sun, and thus with illumination and insight. And greater awareness is Marya's goal—she burned the fish skin to break through his secrecy.

Because of gold's link to the sun, the metal is often considered masculine. (This is especially true in heroic cultures,
because heroes habitually hoard gold.) Yet gold is malleable,
soft and ductile. It is flexible, where iron is rigid, and can be
easily combined with many different compounds, unlike
other metals. So gold represents an integration of masculine
and feminine, of individuality and relationships. Marya
achieves that integration—she affirms relationship and love
in her quest for her husband, but she exercises her strength,
courage, and assertiveness along the way.

Gold also has negative connotations, of course, and as a
measure of wealth symbolizes greed and corruption. Marya
shows none of this, unlike the Fire King's daughter. Significantly, gold is the second metal to appear in Marya's tale, the
first being iron. In shifting from iron to gold, the story hints at
ancient alchemy which sought to transform iron (or lead)
into gold. Carl Jung pointed out that alchemy can be interpreted in psychological terms. For example, in alchemy both
iron and gold are associated with fire, but iron is a "baser"
metal than gold, and so points to a "lower" type of fire, unlike
gold's "nobler" form. Psychologically speaking, iron symbolizes basic instincts, like anger and lust, while gold points to
more evolved states, like insight and love. Moving from iron
to gold thus symbolizes a process of emotional and instinctual
maturation, which Marya illustrates.

Many women experience this alchemical transformation
from fire and iron to gold through feminism. Inspired by the
feminist movement, women protest oppressive, misogynist
traditions, symbolically burning fishy stereotypes. But this
inspiration often becomes despair, as women experience a
backlash from society. Women then make the arduous journey through the underworld, struggling with society's
shadow, learning about iron on the way. The result is Baba
Yaga's gold—the wisdom, courage, creativity, cleverness,
power, and splendor of the deep feminine.

THE AWAKENING

In her advice Baba Yaga warns Marya that when she meets the three women, she must negotiate with the one in the middle, who will be the daughter of the Fire King. Marya must identify what people and issues are truly important to her, ignoring the rest as distraction. For women today the distraction might take the form of a promotion into a position of apparent authority and leadership, yet the office may be only a token one, with little authority but many responsibilities. Women need discriminating judgment here, to keep to their true path. Baba Yaga's second warning is that Marya must not give the comb, ring, or kerchief to the false wife until she is physically in the Burbot's bedroom. The lesson is clear. Women—and men—who operate from a false self are not to be trusted.

Marya follows Baba Yaga's advice, but the false wife foils Marya's attempts to talk to the Burbot by drugging him. He sleeps through the night, oblivious to Marya's pleas. The story reiterates the familiar theme of the sleeping man. There are no sleeping beauties in women's tales—rather unconscious men.

When Baba Yaga gives Marya the third gift, the kerchief, she warns that this is Marya's last chance. Baba Yaga cannot help Marya indefinitely. While she also tells Marya about the sleeping potion, she offers no suggestions on what to do. Marya must come up with something on her own. This is very much like psychotherapy. A woman's therapist can offer invaluable advice and support, but she must act on her own at some point on the journey, exercising her own courage, cunning, and wisdom.

Marya goes to her husband a third time, but is still unable to wake him. At the last moment, one of her tears falls on him and he awakens, recognizing his true wife. Here the story may seem to revert to stereotypes of weak, weepy women, but Marya is anything but that, so we must seek deeper meanings. Tears symbolize grief, of course, which usually comes from love and relationship. Water in general also makes a good symbol for love and relationship, because water can dissolve most materials, joining separate substances. Water also fills up empty places, the way love fills the human soul. Water is flexible and life-giving, too—just like love—and is also closely linked to the deep feminine. So it is the power of relationship and the deep feminine which wake the Burbot.

In focusing on Marya's tears and the water theme, the story balances Marya's fiery energies from earlier on. Symbolically, Marya integrates fire and water, the power of anger and sexuality, on the one hand, and love and relatedness on the other. It is this integration—Marya's full individuation—that awakens the Burbot from his drugged sleep. In weeping, Marya also sorrows for herself, and not just for the Burbot. It is specifically her feeling for herself, I think, that awakens her husband. This reverses the convention that women are supposed to feel for men, expressing men's feelings for men's benefit, while ignoring their own.

When the Burbot wakes up, he thinks rain fell on him, and it takes him a moment to recognize that Marya's tears woke him. A man's first reflex is often to look at objective issues, rather than interpersonal ones—to focus on facts rather than feelings, weather rather than relationships. The habit is vexing to most women, but the tale suggests how women can help move men beyond this stage—by focusing on grief rather than anger, through water rather than fire: at midlife when men struggle to grow beyond traditional heroic patterns, they resonate more to sorrow and water than to anger and fire.

CHANGING SOCIETY

When the Burbot recognizes Marya, he summons the elders and asks them who they think is his true wife. Marya, he points out, risked everything to save him, whereas the Fire King's daughter sold him out of greed. The elders declare that

Marya is the true wife. Their judgment may seem obvious from the story, but it is profoundly significant.

In most cultures, elders—especially male ones—are guardians of tradition and often constitute the most conservative element in a society. In declaring Marya to be the true wife, the elders validate her journey and individual development. This is astonishing, since Marya has broken so many social restrictions. In fact, she is everything that a woman should not be in patriarchal cultures—outspoken, determined, passionate, assertive, persistent, resourceful, courageous, insightful, and wise. Yet the elders declare her to be the true wife, rejecting the daughter of the Fire King, who follows traditional feminine stereotypes. This implies that society now accepts strong, individuated women like Marya. She has awakened not only her husband, but the world, too.

THE RUSTY BOX

Her husband next uses an old rusty box to magically transport Marya and him back to her homeland. The story does not explain what the box is or where it came from, as a man's tale would. In men's stories, after the protagonist abandons the heroic and patriarchal paradigm at midlife, a male teacher appears who typically gives the man a magic box, containing primordial masculine energies.[6] The box is often connected with wind spirits, a theme hinted at when Marya feels a breeze on her face as she is transported back to her land. The story says that the box is rusty, implying it is made of iron but is old. If iron connotes heroic energy, focused on battle, the box is post-heroic.

Before using his magic box, the Burbot asks Marya to close her eyes and she does so without hesitation. Throughout the tale, Marya has worked toward greater consciousness but now the Burbot asks her to forgo consciousness for a moment. In essence, he asks her to trust him. In turn, he trusts

her by returning to her homeland where she is a royal
princess and he is a commoner. The point is crucial for
women and men today. Women have begun expressing their
anger over social oppression and exercising their native
power and energy. The next step involves women reconciling
with those men who have moved beyond heroism and patriarchal privilege. Trust is essential in this reconciliation. And
society will change only as women and men develop this
deeper, sacred reunion.

There is another meaning to Marya closing her eyes. The
Burbot's magic box involves the deep masculine, which must
be kept secret from women, just as the deep feminine must be
protected from men's eyes.[7]

WAKING TOGETHER

After Marya and the Burbot return home, he opens his
magic box and Marya faints, but so does the Burbot. In fact,
Marya wakes up first. If the magic makes the Burbot sleep,
too, we must be dealing with something besides male mysteries. What might that be? A crude answer is sex: Marya
wakes up with the Burbot sleeping next to her, implying
they slept together. But there is more meaning here. I suggest what is involved is the sacred union between woman
and man, not a conventional marriage relationship, but a
deeper, authentic communion, where each individual treats
the other as a mystery, something beyond consciousness
and rationality.

After he awakens, the Burbot explains to Marya that she
had to go through her ordeals because she gave him three
tasks to accomplish before they married. They are now equal,
because both suffered for each other. Neither can say, "Look
at what I did for you! Do you appreciate all my sacrifices?" Yet
the Burbot's comment seems somewhat petty, reflecting a tit-
for-tat attitude. It is a reminder, though, that in any relationship, even one based on an authentic sacred reunion, human
faults will appear. The sacred reunion exists on a deep, nu-

minous level, and individuals cannot remain long in that archetypal realm. In returning to everyday living, the shadow reappears, and women and men naturally start quibbling with each other. Deep love—the reunion of the deep feminine and the deep masculine—does not guarantee domestic tranquility! In fact, the story shows that deep communion is possible only with much fire and tears.

EPILOGUE

— 🜨 —

Handed down over many generations, from mother to daughter and woman to woman, the twelve stories in this collection are filled with astonishing insights, as useful today as they were centuries ago. The wisdom of women's tales, like the voice of a woman's deep self, is timeless yet timely, utopian yet useful. The dramas show ideal paths a woman may take through life, at the same time offering practical advice on troublesome husbands or bosses, difficult mothers, and oppressive societies. Most valuable of all, the stories reveal the resources within each woman's soul, often obscured by social pressures—the wise crone, the vibrant little girl, the wild sister, and nature itself.

Women's tales are far too rich to summarize in any simple fashion, but if I were charged with doing so by a fairy-tale tsar, on pain of death, I would say the stories revolve around four distinct tasks: *defying the demon, reclaiming the true self, dancing with wild sisters,* and *waking the world.*

DEFYING THE DEMON

"The Queen and the Murderer" dramatizes the task of defying the demon, when the harried Queen finally confronts and kills the murderer. The felon personifies all the oppression and scorn that misogynist cultures heap upon women, and women's journey of individuation begins when they identify, confront, battle, outwit, and overthrow these cultural demons. By now, the women's movement has made this task seem self-evident, but it still takes courage for each individual to start. Nor is the demon always male, because mothers sometimes play a demonic role, as "The Three Little Eggs" makes clear. The brave woman had to slay an ogress, who dramatizes negative maternal influences. The demon is not always external, either, and as an inner figure, he often personifies a woman's own shadowy aspect, her anger and frustration, the way Koschey the Deathless brought out the Tsarina's dark side in "Maria Morevna."

In defying demons, emotional violence is sometimes necessary, not only for a woman's self-defense, but also for her growth. The crone in "Emme" had to kill a chicken, a goat, and a slave to free Emme, and the Siren wife had to sacrifice all the mermaids in order to return home. Individuation, like birth, is often a painful process, and destructive or obstructive relationships must sometimes be killed off before a woman can move ahead with life.

RECLAIMING THE TRUE SELF

Closely tied to defying the demon is the task of reclaiming the true self. That inner spirit, a woman's true being, is often hidden during adolescence, when young women encounter crushing social pressures to be "nice girls." Women are forced into silence, stifling their dreams, and a false self—demure, accommodating, and acceptable to convention—displaces the true self. As "The Woman from the Egg" and "Emme" graphically illustrate, the impostor self takes over, throwing the true self into the unconscious, which fairy tales portray as a fall into a well or being dragged into a pond. A woman's task is to reclaim her true self and take her rightful place in the world. In the process, a woman learns to heed her inner voice, gaining access to the wisdom of the deep self, just like the desperate mother in "The Three Little Eggs." Along the way, women exercise their heroic energies, like the protagonist of "The Warrior Wife," who went from abandoned wife to triumphant warrior. Those heroic virtues are essential for women to survive in competitive cultures.

For women who have not given up their voice and power

in adolescence—usually those who grew up with supportive fathers or unconventional mothers—reclaiming the self takes a different form. Accustomed to mastery and competence, at midlife these women come to terms with suffering, vulnerability, and helplessness. "Maria Morevna" illustrates this process when the Tsarina is brought down by Koschey the Deathless, just as Inanna, the great Sumerian goddess, was, on her descent into the underworld. The painful experience of vulnerability helps women balance power and powerlessness, and that integration leads to a new form of leadership or influence, distinct from heroic and patriarchal tradition. The new paradigm involves empowerment, where a woman does not command or dominate, but collaborates, inspires, and teaches, the way the protagonist of "The Wise Wife" transformed the callous, bellicose Sultan into a devoted husband and father. "Maria Morevna" provides another perspective on women's leadership with the image of herding wild animals. Herding offers a new model of resolving conflicting inner impulses, settling disputes among unruly children, or mediating between competing co-workers. This approach avoids the suppression of dissent or forcing obedience, as is the traditional patriarchal model.

Perhaps the most astonishing aspect of a woman reclaiming her deep self is the discovery that her soul embraces all of nature. The link unfolds gradually, starting when a woman finds comfort, refuge, healing, and inspiration in the wilderness, as the maimed woman did in "The Handless Woman," or the harried mother did in "The Three Little Eggs." In gardening, taking a walk in the woods, or simply enjoying a flower's beauty, women discover that they can empathize with and relate to animals, plants, and the stars—not just people. The protagonist of "The Woman from the Egg" dramatized this extraordinary depth and breadth of empathy by turning into a fish and then into a duck, symbolically merging with nature. In doing so, she heals the old theological split between animals and humans, body and mind, instinct and spirit.

D A N C I N G   W I T H   W I L D   S I S T E R S

Communion with nature can be terrifying because of its numinous power. This leads to the third task in women's tales—dancing with wild sisters. In the company of other women, in spiritual sisterhood, women celebrate the deep feminine without being overcome by its immense vitality. Sisterly solidarity also helps neutralize some of the oppression and pain women suffer in most cultures. In "The Two Sisters," when the mistress discovers that her slave is really her long-lost sister, both women break free of the master-slave mentality typical of hierarchical cultures. Similarly, in "The Siren Wife," the Sirens rescue Froth from her murderous husband and introduce her to a deep sisterhood. The wife learns the sacrament of deep beauty, where women celebrate beauty for their sake, not men's. The sisterhood in women's tales offers glimpses of ancient, egalitarian, matrilineal societies that antedate heroes and kings.

The sister figures in women's tales are wild—linked to the wilderness, far from civilization, like the nun in "The Mother and the Demon." She leads the mother and daughter in their outrageous dance, exposing themselves to the demon and his accomplices and overcoming their power. These wild sisters also transform the mother-daughter relationship into one of sisterly equality and mutuality. Significantly, the sister theme transmutes humanity's connection to the divine. Women discover that nature and goddesses need women's care and attention, the way the nun asked the mother and daughter to bring companions for her in the wilderness. The relationship between women and the earth, women and goddesses, becomes mutual, not maternal, a matter of interaction and not supplication, working together rather than worship. As women reclaim their inner and outer authority, they discover that the earth is a sister as well as a mother.

WAKING THE WORLD

The final challenge for women is waking the world. This means waking up men who have fallen asleep, drugged by male privilege. In contrast to youth tales where the woman sleeps, waiting for a man to awaken her, it is now the woman who must wake up the man. Women often begin the process dramatically, the way the queen shot the murderer in "The Queen and the Murderer"—the gunshot woke up the whole palace. Waking the world also means breaking through the secrecy and illusions that society maintains, as "Princess Marya and the Burbot" demonstrates: women must burn away constricting customs. The result is illumination, an increase in consciousness, and not just of women, but of men, too. To succeed here, women's tales insist, women need their fiery passions—anger and sexuality. But women also need golden fire, too, the wisdom, cunning, and insight of Baba Yaga, the deep feminine.

Ultimately, waking the world means transforming it, creating a place where women are honored for their strength, independence, and wisdom. Women's tales make amply clear that feminine development ultimately aims at changing society. A woman's journey goes beyond the private and psychological, to public and cultural issues. The stories emphasize the point by making insightful—and subversive—comments on prevailing culture. The tales are about psyche and society, the personal and the collective. The tales also insist that social change goes hand-in-hand with the transformation of intimate relationships—between wives and husbands, individual women and individual men. Waking the world ultimately aims at a sacred reunion—transforming the most private of bonds. Individual work, interpersonal transformation, and cultural evolution journey together. The stories do not separate inner and outer worlds, but insist that development must occur in both realms.

WOMEN'S AND MEN'S TALES

As I reflected on what to write for this epilogue, I began to recognize more clearly how women's and men's tales complement each other. Although they portray different tasks, all the challenges lead in the same direction. Women and men alike, though we may forget it, walk the same road in maturity—toward emancipation and sacred communion.

Men's tales show that men's first task in maturity is leaving the hero, that is, giving up traditional heroic roles and patriarchal prerogatives. This is equivalent to women defying the demon, except that men start from a privileged position. For both women and men, however, the direction is the same—toward a new, post-patriarchal realm, inner and outer, psychological and societal. Men's next task is honoring the feminine, reversing society's denigration of women, emotion, intuition, and relationship. This parallels women's task of reclaiming the true self, and requires overthrowing oppressive social convention. For both sexes, the goal is balance and integration, raising up what was laid low by cultural traditions, and bringing down what was too high.

The third task for men is traveling with the spirit brother. He is a shaman-Trickster, whose function is to break with convention, to mock sacred dogmas, to force people to think, and ultimately to liberate society from outdated institutions. When men travel with him, they follow the lead of women in dancing with wild sisters. The aims of the spirit brother and the wild sisters are one and the same: the renaissance of creativity, spontaneity, and authenticity. Men's tales end with the sacred reunion, where husband and wife are reconciled as equals on a deeper, more intimate level. Women's stories also present the reunion motif, but emphasize a different aspect of it—waking the world. Women's tales insist that the new relationship between women and men requires and produces a new world order. Men's tales thus focus on the private dimension of emancipation, while women's stories focus on the public. This reverses traditional gender roles, where women are supposed to take care of family and house, while men run the world. So men's tales follow the lead of women's stories: both genres reverse gender roles.

Women's tales are an inspiration and a challenge, a goad and a reassurance, a promise and a warning. The dramas warn what happens when women do not heed their inner voice or reclaim their talents—they become false selves, like the Fire King's daughter in "Princess Marya and the Burbot" or the slave-impostor in "Emme." If women persevere on their journeys, despite the fear, heartache, and cultural backlash, the stories promise an immeasurable reward—women awaken to the true self and the deep feminine within, and in the process they wake up the whole world. The journey of women is long, difficult, and often confusing, but its ultimate result is the redemption of all worlds, inner and outer.

NOTES

PROLOGUE

1. Cf. Young-Eisendrath and Widermann (1987); Lippard (1976); Nelson (1991).

1. "THE QUEEN AND THE MURDERER": OPPRESSION AND SELF-LIBERATION

1. Calvino (1980).
2. These stories are Type 956 in the Aarne-Thompson Index of Folktale Motifs (Aarne and Thompson, 1961). Examples include the Gypsy tale "The Maid of the Mill" (Sampson, 1984), the French story "Anne-Marie" (Zipes, 1988), the Hungarian tale "Pretty Maid Inbronka" (Degh, 1965), and the Russian drama "The Robbers" (Afanas'ev, 1973).
3. Leonard (1982); Lauter and Rupprecht (1985); von Franz (1980); Mankowitz (1984).
4. Lauter (1984, 1985); Pratt (1981, 1985); Waelti-Walters (1982); Pearson and Pope (1981).
5. The most extreme case of such an attack would be incest. The present tale does not portray this calamity, but other fairy tales do, such as "Wooden Maria" from Italy (Calvino, 1980), "All-Fur" from the Grimms, "The Princess in the Suit of Leather" from Egypt (Bushnaq, 1986), and many versions of "The Handless Woman" (Chapter 6).
6. E.g., the French story "Bluebeard," the Greek myth of Persephone, the South African tale "Kenkebe" (Radin, 1983), and "The Thousand and One Nights" from Arabia.
7. Pratt (1981, 1985); Pearson and Pope (1981); Waelti-Walters (1982).
8. Sherman (1987); Johnson (1977); Chiriboga and Gigy (1975); Chiriboga and Lowenthal (1975).

9. Brown and Gilligan (1992); Eichorn et al. (1981); Belenky, Clinchy, Goldberger, and Tarule (1986); Hancock (1989).
10. E.g., "The Little Wise Woman" from Africa (Radin, 1983) or "Three Eyes" from Cyprus (Kawai, 1988).
11. E.g., "The Girl Who Banished Seven Youths" from Morocco and "A Lost Shoe of Gold" from Saudi Arabia (Bushnaq, 1986), "The Seven Swans" and "Mrizala and Her Bridegroom Death" from Germany (Grimm and Grimm, 1944; Ranke, 1966), and "Wormwood" and "Silent for Seven Years" from Italy (Calvino, 1980).
12. I review the research in *Once Upon a Midlife*.
13. Horner (1987); Gilligan (1982); Birkhauser-Oeri (1988).

2. "THE WARRIOR WIFE": RECLAIMING POWER

1. Erdoes and Ortiz (1984).
2. E.g., the German tale "The Innkeeper of Moscow" (Ranke, 1966), the Chinese story "A Woman's Love" (Liyi, 1985), the Italian tale "Beauty-with-the-Seven-Dresses" (Calvino, 1980), and the Pueblo Indian tale "Pohana, the Warrior-Woman" (Stone, 1979).
3. Sanday (1981); Trocolli (1992); Gewertz (1988).
4. E.g., "The Innkeeper of Moscow" from Germany (Ranke, 1966), "A Woman's Love" from China (Liyi, 1985), "Fanta-Ghiro the Beautiful" from Italy (Calvino, 1980), and "The Lute Player" from Russia (Afanas'ev, 1973).
5. Lippard (1976); Keyes (1993).
6. Gottner-Abendroth (1991).

3. "MARIA MOREVNA": THE LIMITS OF POWER

1. Afanas'ev (1973); Phelps (1981).
2. I am indebted to my colleague Vassily Barlak for his comments on the Russian names in the story.
3. Young-Eisendrath and Widermann (1987); Kraisonswasdi (1989); Stiver (1991c); Astin and Leland (1991); Northcutt (1991); Leonard (1982); Helgesen (1990).
4. Robbins (1990); Lowinsky (1992); Young-Eisendrath and Widermann (1987).

5. E.g., Shakespeare's *The Taming of the Shrew*. These are story types 900 and 905A* in the Aarne-Thompson Index of Folktale Motifs.
6. Hoch-Smith (1978).
7. Northcutt (1991); Young-Eisendrath and Widermann (1987); Woolger and Woolger (1989); Surrey (1991a,b,c), Lowinsky (1992).
8. Woolger and Woolger (1989); Robbins (1990).
9. Douglas (1990); Jordan (1991).
10. Kraisonswasdi (1989).

4. ''THE THREE LITTLE EGGS'': THE POWER OF INTUITION

1. Berger (1969).
2. Eliade (1975).
3. Helgesen (1990); Stiver (1991); Northcutt (1991).
4. Belenky, Clinchy, Goldberger, and Tarule (1986).
5. Gilligan (1982); Woodman (1987); Birkhauser-Oeri (1988); Caplan (1987); Stiver (1991b); Kaplan (1991).
6. Horner (1987); Weigle (1982).
7. Surrey (1991c); Stiver (1991c); Miller (1991); Young-Eisendrath and Widermann (1987); Eichenbaum and Orbach (1987); Jordan, Kaplan, Miller, Stiver, and Surrey (1991).
8. Douglas (1990); Young-Eisendrath and Widermann (1987).

5. ''THE WISE WIFE'': CLEVERNESS AND COURAGE

1. Adapted from "The Sultan's Camp Follower" in Bushnaq (1986).
2. E.g., "Catarina the Wise" from Italy (Calvino, 1980), "Three Measures of Salt" from Greece (Carter, 1990), "Kamala and the Seven Thieves" from the Punjab (Phelps, 1978), and "Killed for a Horse" from the Hausa in Africa (Abrahams, 1983).
3. E.g., the tale "The Peasant's Wise Daughter" (Grimm and Grimm, 1944) or "The Legend of Knockmany" from Ireland (Phelps, 1978).
4. Bateson (1990); Heilbrun (1988); Weigel (1985); Radner and Lanser (1993); Stewart (1993); Langlois (1993).
5. Stewart (1993).
6. Helgesen (1990).
7. Bateson (1990), p. 239.

8. The number three appears frequently in fairy tales and has various meanings, as many have discussed. Perhaps most relevant here is the association of the number with struggle, for example, two people vying for the affections of a third, and the implication of a reconciliation, as in thesis versus antithesis ending in a synthesis.

9. I discuss this in *Once Upon a Midlife* and *Beyond the Hero*.

6. "THE HANDLESS WOMAN": HEALING AND WILDERNESS

1. Kawai (1988).
2. Douglas (1990).
3. Pratt (1981, 1985); Neher (1989).
4. Wheelwright (1989).
5. Craighead (1982), p. 75.

7. "THE WOMAN FROM THE EGG": RESURRECTION AND NATURE

1. Ranke (1966).
2. E.g., "The Goose Girl" and "The Black Bride and the White Bride" from the Grimm brothers (Grimm and Grimm, 1944); "The Merchant's Daughter and the Maidservant" from Russia (Afanas'ev, 1973); "The Girl Who Spoke Jasmines and Lilies" from Iraq and "Jubeinah and the Slave" from Palestine (Bushnaq, 1986); "The Dead Man's Palace" from Italy (Calvino, 1980); "The Divided Daughter" from China (Roberts, 1979); and "Mulha" from South Africa (Phelps, 1981).
3. Gottner-Abendroth (1991).
4. I discuss the research in *Once Upon a Midlife*.
5. Ferrara (1983).
6. I discuss the evidence in *Beyond the Hero*.
7. E.g., "The Lute Player" and "The Golden Tree" in my book *Once Upon a Midlife*.

8. "THE TWO SISTERS": SISTERS AND LIBERATION

1. Abrahams (1983).
2. Bourke (1993).
3. Stone (1979); Weigle (1982); Wissler (1916).
4. Stone (1979); Weigle (1982).
5. Moore (1988).
6. Stone (1979); Woolger and Woolger (1989).
7. Monestier (1963).
8. O'Connor (1992).
9. Lauter (1984); Downing (1990).

9. "EMME": RESCUING THE TRUE SELF

1. Radin (1983).
2. Wright (1982); Weigel (1985); Randour (1987).
3. Boone (1986); Eliade (1975).
4. Meador (1986); Johansen (1975); Skov (1975).

10. "THE MOTHER AND THE DEMON": THE SISTERS OF NATURE

1. Kawai (1988).
2. "The Little Girl and the Giant" (Roberts, 1955). See also "Mother Come Back" and "The Girl Who Stayed in the Fork of a Tree," both from the Bena Mukuni of Africa, as well as "The City Where Men Are Mended" and "The Town Where None Might Go to Sleep" from the Hausa of Africa (Abrahams, 1983; Radin, 1983).
3. Surrey (1991b, 1991c).
4. E.g., Ehrenberg (1989); Lerner (1986).
5. In the Grimms' version of "The Handless Maiden," for example, the father makes a bargain with the devil to become rich, in exchange for whatever is standing in his backyard. The father later discovers that his daughter was there, and the devil comes to take her. She manages to escape the devil, but only by having her hands cut off. So the wealth of

the father comes from his daughter's maiming. Symbolically, patriarchal property derives from women's oppression. The Grimms' story repeats the theme a little later in the story, after the handless maiden leaves home. On her wanderings she comes to a garden with a beautiful pear tree and eats a fruit. The tree belongs to a young king who has a peculiar practice—he numbers every pear on the tree and counts them daily. So the king quickly discovers that one fruit is missing and soon meets the handless maiden. The king's habit of counting the pears dramatizes the patriarchal focus on private property, and accounting. The numbered pears are symbolically equivalent to the Abacus Bridge in the Japanese story.

6. Jordan (1985); Stone (1979).
7. Daly (1992).
8. Eliade (1960); La Fontaine (1985); Wissler (1916); Kraemer (1988); Monestier (1963).
9. Butt-Thompson (1969).
10. Gottner-Abendroth (1991).
11. Young-Eisendrath and Widermann (1987).

11. ''THE SIREN WIFE'': RETURN FROM THE SISTERS

1. Calvino (1980).
2. Stone (1979).
3. Downing (1990). Something similar occurs in Hebrew tradition, where Adam was made from dust, while Lilith, who preceded Eve, was made from slime—closely linked to froth. See Dunne (1989).
4. E.g., "The Three Little Eggs" in Chapter 4 and "The Golden Tree" in my book *Once Upon a Midlife*.
5. Italo Calvino notes in his anthology of Italian folktales that the original version of the story had the old woman and wife riding a broom. Calvino changed the broom to an eagle, because he could find no other example in Italian folklore of broom riding. Symbolically, riding an eagle and riding a broomstick are closely related, as I shall discuss later. I find the eagle image, however, to be consistent with other women's tales, so I have kept Calvino's ending.
6. Lauter (1984, 1985); Ferrara (1983).

12. ''PRINCESS MARYA AND THE BURBOT'': RESCUING THE PRINCE

1. Zheleznova (1980).
2. E.g., "East of the Sun, West of the Moon" (Avenel, 1984); "White Bear King Valemon" (Asbjornsen and Moe, 1982); "The Nixie of the Mill Pond" and "The Singing Soaring Lark" (Grimm and Grimm, 1944); "The Black Bull of Norroway" (Phelps, 1978); "The Canary Prince," "Filo d'Oro," "Filomena," "The Handmade King," "The King's Son in the Henhouse," and "The Foppish King" (Calvino, 1980); "The Camel Husband" (Bushnaq, 1986); "Luisa" (Weigle, 1982); and "Elijah's Violin" (Schwartz, 1985). The basic story is Type 425 in Aarne and Thompson (1961).
3. Riordan (1989).
4. Zheleznova (1980).
5. All versions of Marya's tale explain that an evil spell forces the husband to leave his wife and the magic, responsible for the wife's suffering, comes from a witch, a troll, or some other kind of villain. If we apply this fairy tale explanation to the biblical story of Eve, an astonishing new perspective emerges: Eve suffers for eating the fruit of knowledge because of an evil spell. But here the source of the magic would be God, not a troll or a witch! The suggestion, naturally, is heresy, but women's tales are full of such outrageous messages.
6. See my book *Beyond the Hero*.
7. The same theme appears in "The Singing Soaring Lark" (Grimm and Grimm, 1944).

BIBLIOGRAPHY

Aarne, A., and S. Thompson. 1961. *The Types of the Folktale: A Classification and Bibliography.* Helsinki: Academia Scientarium Finnica.

Abrahams, Roger. 1985. *Afro-American Folktales.* New York: Pantheon.

Afanas'ev, Aleksandr. 1973. *Russian Fairy Tales.* Trans. Norbert Guterman. New York: Pantheon.

Aman, Dra. S. D. B. 1991. *Folk Tales from Indonesia.* Jakarta, Indonesia: Djambatan.

Asbjornsen, Peter Christen, and Jorgen Moe. 1982. Trans. Pat Shaw and Carl Norman. *Norwegian Folktales.* New York: Pantheon.

Astin, Helen, and Carole Leland. 1991. *Women of Influence, Women of Vision: A Cross-Generational Study of Leaders and Social Change.* San Francisco: Jossey-Bass.

Auerbach, Nina, and U. C. Knoepflmacher (eds.). 1992. *Forbidden Journeys: Fairy Tales and Fantasies by Victorian Women Writers.* Chicago: University of Chicago Press.

Baldwin, Karen. 1985. " 'Woof!' A Word on Women's Role in Family Storytelling." In Jordan and Kalcik (eds.), pp. 149–62.

Bateson, Mary Catherine. 1990. *Composing a Life.* New York: Penguin.

Belenky, Mary Field, B. M. Clinchy, N. R. Goldberger, and J. M. Tarule. 1986. *Women's Ways of Knowing: The Development of Self, Voice and Mind.* New York: Basic Books.

Berger, Terry. 1969. *Black Fairy Tales.* New York: Atheneum.

Birkhauser-Oeri, Sibylle. 1988. *The Mother: Archetypal Image in Fairy Tales.* Toronto: Inner City Books.

Bly, Robert. 1990. *Iron John: A Book About Men.* Reading, Mass.: Addison-Wesley.

Boone, Sylvia Ardyn. 1986. *Radiance from the Waters: Ideals of Feminine Beauty in Mende Art.* New Haven, Conn.: Yale University Press.

Boos, Claire (ed.). 1984. *Scandinavian Folk and Fairy Tales.* New York: Crown/Avenel.

Bourke, Angela. 1993. "More in Anger than in Sorrow: Irish Women's Lament Poetry." In Radner (ed.), pp. 160–82.

Brown, J. K., and V. Kerns (eds.). 1985. *In Her Prime: A New View of Middle-Aged Women.* South Hadley, Mass.: Bergin & Garvey.

Brown, Lyn Mikel, and Carol Gilligan. 1992. *Meeting at the Crossroads:*

Women's Psychology and Girls' Development. Cambridge, Mass.: Harvard University Press.

Bruckner, Jutta. 1985. "Women Behind the Camera." In Ecker (ed.), pp. 120–24.

Bushnaq, Iner. 1986. *Arab Folktales.* New York: Pantheon.

Butt-Thompson, F. W. 1969. *West African Secret Societies: Their Organizations, Officials and Teaching.* New York: Argosy-Antiquarian.

Calvino, Italo. 1980. *Italian Folktales.* New York: Pantheon.

Caplan, Paula. 1987. "The Myth of Women's Masochism." In Walsh (ed.), pp. 78–96.

Cardozo-Freeman, Inez. 1975. "Maria Blanca." In Farrer (ed.), pp. 12–24.

Carter, Angela (ed.). 1990. *The Old Wives' Fairy Tale Book.* New York: Pantheon.

Cherazi, Shahla. 1987. "Female Psychology: A Review." In Walsh (ed.), pp. 22–38.

Chinen, Allan. 1989. *In the Ever After: Fairy Tales and the Second Half of Life.* Chicago: Chiron.

———. 1992. *Once Upon a Midlife: Classic Stories and Mythic Tales to Illuminate the Middle Years.* Los Angeles: Tarcher.

———. 1993. *Beyond the Hero: Classic Stories of Men in Search of Soul.* Los Angeles: Tarcher.

Chiriboga, D., and L. Gigy. 1975. "Perspectives on the Life Course." In M. Fiske Lowenthal, M. Thurnher, and D. Chiriboga (eds.), *Four Stages of Life.* San Francisco: Jossey-Bass, pp. 122–45.

Chiriboga, D., and M. Fiske Lowenthal. 1975. "Complexities of Adaptation." In M. Fiske Lowenthal, M. Thurnher, and D. Chiriboga (eds.), *Four Stages of Life.* San Francisco: Jossey-Bass, pp. 99–121.

Claassen, Cheryl. 1991. "Gender, Shellfishing and the Shell Mound Archaic." In Gero and Conkey (eds.), pp. 276–300.

Courlander, Harold, and George Herzog. 1978. *The Cow-Tail Switch and Other West African Stories.* New York: Henry Holt.

Craighead, Meinrad. 1982. "Immanent Mother." In Giles (ed.), pp. 71–83.

Daly, Mary. 1992. *Outercourse: The Be-Dazzling Voyage.* San Francisco: Harper San Francisco.

Degh, Linda. 1965. *Folktales of Hungary.* Chicago: University of Chicago Press.

———. 1985. "Dial a Story, Dial an Audience: Two Rural Women Narrators in an Urban Setting." In Jordan and Kalcik (eds.), pp. 3–25.

Donnelly, Dorothy. 1982. "The Sexual Mystic: Embodied Spirituality." In Giles (ed.), pp. 120–41.

Douglas, Claire. 1990. *The Woman in the Mirror: Analytical Psychology and the Feminine.* Boston: Sigo Press.

———. 1993. *Translate This Darkness: The Life of Christiana Morgan.* New York: Simon & Schuster.

Downing, Christine. 1990. *Psyche's Sisters: Re-Imagining the Meaning of Sisterhood*. New York: Continuum.

Dundes, Alan. 1987. "The Psychoanalytic Study of the Grimms' Tales with Special Reference to 'The Maiden Without Hands' (AT 706)." *Germanic Review*, 62: 50–65.

Dunne, Carrin. 1989. *Behold Woman: A Jungian Approach to Feminist Theology*. Wilmette, Ill.: Chiron.

Eccles, Jacquelynne. 1987. "Gender Roles and Achievement Patterns: An Expectancy Value Perspective." In June Machover Reinisch, Leonard A. Rosenblum, and Stephanie A. Sanders (eds.), *Masculinity/Femininity: Basic Perspectives*. Oxford: Oxford University Press, pp. 240–80.

Ecker, Gisela (ed.). 1985. *Feminist Aesthetics*. London: The Women's Press.

Eckert, Penelope. 1990. "Cooperative Competition in Adolescent 'Girl Talk.' " *Discourse Processes*, 13: 91–122.

Eder, Donna. 1988. "Building Cohesion Through Collaborative Narration." *Social Psychology Quarterly*, 51: 225–35.

Ehrenberg, Margaret. 1989. *Women in Prehistory*. Norman: University of Oklahoma Press.

Eichenbaum, Luise, and Susie Orbach. 1987. *Between Women: Love, Envy and Competition in Women's Friendships*. New York: Penguin.

Eichorn, Dorothy, John Clausen, Norma Haan, Marjorie Honzik, and Paul Mussen (eds.). 1981. *Present and Past in Middle Life*. New York: Academic Press.

Eliade, Mircea. 1960. *Myths, Dreams, and Mysteries: The Encounter Between Contemporary Faiths and Archaic Realities*. New York: Harper & Brothers.

———. 1975. *Rites and Symbols of Initiation: The Mysteries of Birth and Rebirth*. San Francisco: Harper.

Erdoes, Richard, and Alfonso Ortiz. 1984. *American Indian Myths and Legends*. New York: Pantheon.

Estés, Clarissa Pinkola. 1992. *Women Who Run with the Wolves: Myths and Stories of the Wild Woman Archetype*. New York: Ballantine.

Farrer, Claire (ed.). 1975a. *Women and Folklore: Images and Genres*. Prospect Heights, Ill.: Waveland.

———. 1975b. "Introduction." In Farrer (ed., 1975a), pp. xi–xxi.

Ferrara, Comune di, Galleria Civica d'Arte Moderna. 1983. *Leonor Fini*. Ferrara: Edizioni d'Arte Casalecchio di Reno.

Fierz-David, Linda. 1988. *Women's Dionysian Initiation: The Villa of Mysteries in Pompeii*. Dallas: Spring.

Fleming, Patricia. 1984. "Persephone's Search for Her Mother." *Psychological Perspectives*, 15: 127–47.

Fraser, Antonia. 1989. *The Warrior Queens*. New York: Knopf.

Friday, Nancy. 1977. *My Mother / My Self: The Daughter's Search for Identity*. New York: Delacorte.

Fuerstein, Laura Arens. 1992. "Females in Bondage: The Early Role of

Mother and Father in the Woman's Tie to Abusive Men." In Siegel (ed.), pp. 9–24.

Gero, Joan, and Margaret Conkey (eds.). 1991. *Engendering Archaeology: Women and Prehistory.* Oxford: Basil Blackwell.

Gewertz, Deborah (ed.). 1988. *Myths of Matriarchy Reconsidered.* Sydney: University of Sydney.

Giles, Mary E. (ed.). 1982. *The Feminist Mystic and Other Essays on Women and Spirituality.* New York: Crossroad.

Gilligan, Carol. 1982. *In a Different Voice: Psychological Theory and Women's Development.* Cambridge, Mass.: Harvard University Press.

Gimbutas, Marija. 1982. *The Goddesses and Gods of Old Europe: Myths and Cult Images.* London: Thames & Hudson.

Goldenberg, Naomi R. 1993. *Resurrecting the Body: Feminism, Religion, and Psychotherapy.* New York: Crossroad.

Gordon, Susan. 1993. "The Powers of the Handless Maiden." In Radner (ed.), pp. 252–88.

Gottner-Abendroth, Heide. 1991. *The Dancing Goddess: Principles of a Matriarchal Aesthetic.* Trans. Maureen T. Krause. Boston: Beacon.

Grimm, J., and W. Grimm. 1944. *The Complete Grimms' Fairy Tales.* Trans. Margaret Hunt. New York: Pantheon.

Hamilton, Annette. 1988. "Knowledge and Misrecognition: Mythology and Gender in Aboriginal Australia." In Gewertz (ed.), pp. 57–73.

Hancock, Emily. 1989. *The Girl Within.* New York: Ballantine.

Harding, M. Esther. 1934. *The Way of All Women: A Psychological Interpretation.* New York: Longmans, Green.

Heilbrun, Carolyn. 1988. *Writing a Woman's Life.* New York: Ballantine.

Helgesen, Sally. 1990. *The Female Advantage: Women's Ways of Leadership.* New York: Doubleday.

Hoch-Smith, Judith. 1978. "Radical Yoruba Female Sexuality: The Witch and the Prostitute." In Hoch-Smith and Spring (eds., 1978a), pp. 245–67.

Hoch-Smith, Judith, and Anita Spring (eds.). 1978a. *Women in Ritual and Symbolic Roles.* New York: Plenum.

———. 1978b. "Introduction." In Hoch-Smith and Spring (eds., 1978a), pp. 1–23.

Hodgetts, E. 1890. *From the Land of the Tsar.* London: Gilbert & Rivington.

Horner, Matina. 1987. "Toward an Understanding of Achievement-Related Conflicts in Women." In Walsh (ed.), pp. 169–84.

Huang, Mei. 1990. *Transforming the Cinderella Dream: From Frances Burney to Charlotte Brontë.* New Brunswick, N.J.: Rutgers University Press.

Jackson, Thomas. 1991. "Pounding Acorn: Women's Production as Social and Economic Focus." In Gero and Conkey (eds.), pp. 301–25.

Jacobsen, Thorkild. 1984. "Mesopotamian Religious Literature and Mythology." In *Encyclopaedia Britannica.* Chicago: Britannica.

Jahner, Elaine. 1985. "Woman Remembering: Life History as Exemplary Pattern." In Jordan and Kalcik (eds.), pp. 214–33.

Johansen, J. Pr. 1975. "The Thesmophoria as a Women's Festival." *Temenos*, 11: 78–87.

Johnson, Robert A. 1977. *She: Understanding Feminine Psychology*. San Francisco: Harper & Row.

Jordan, Judith. 1991. "Empathy and Self Boundaries." In Jordan et al. (eds.), pp. 67–80.

Jordan, Judith V., Alexandra Kaplan, Jean Baker Miller, Irene Stiver, and Janet Surrey (eds.). 1991. *Women's Growth in Connection: Writings from the Stone Center*. New York: Guilford.

Jordan, Rosan. 1985. "The Vaginal Serpent and Other Themes from Mexican-American Women's Lore." In Jordan and Kalcik (eds.), pp. 26–44.

Jordan, Rosan, and Susan Kalcik (eds.). 1985. *Women's Folklore, Women's Culture*. Philadelphia: University of Pennsylvania Press.

Jung, C. G. 1976. *The Visions Seminars*, Books 1 and 2. Zurich: Spring.

Kaberry, Phyllis. 1950. *Aboriginal Woman: Sacred and Profane*. New York: The Humanities Press.

Kalcik, Susan. 1975. " '. . . Like Ann's Gynecologist or the Time I Was Almost Raped': Personal Narratives in Women's Rap Groups." *Journal of American Folklore*, 88: 3–11.

Kaplan, Alexandra. 1991. "The 'Self-in-Relation': Implications for Depression in Women." In Jordan et al. (eds.), pp. 206–22.

Kaplan, Janet. 1988. *Unexpected Journeys: The Art and Life of Remedios Varo*. New York: Abbeville.

Kawai, Hayao. 1988. *The Japanese Psyche: Major Motifs in the Fairy Tales of Japan*. Trans. H. Kawaii and Sachiko Reece. Dallas: Spring.

Keyes, Cheryl. 1993. " 'We're More than a Novelty, Boys': Strategies of Female Rappers in the Rap Music Tradition." In Radner (ed.), pp. 203–20.

Knedler, John Warren. 1942. "The Girl Without Hands: Latin-American Versions." *Hispanic Review*, 10: 314–24.

Koch, Gertrud. 1985. "Why Women Go to Men's Films." In Ecker (ed.), pp. 108–19.

Kolbenschlag, Madonna. 1988a. *Kiss Sleeping Beauty Good-Bye*. San Francisco: Harper & Row.

———. 1988b. *Lost in the Land of Oz*. San Francisco: Harper & Row.

Kraemer, Ross. 1988. *Maenads, Martyrs, Matrons, Monastics: A Sourcebook on Women's Religions in the Greco-Roman World*. Philadelphia: Fortress.

Kraisonswasdi, Napasri. 1989. *Women Executives: A Sociological Study in Role Effectiveness*. Jaipur: Rawat.

La Fontaine, Jean. 1985. *Initiation: Ritual Drama and Secret Knowledge Across the World*. New York: Penguin.

Langellier, Kristin, and Eric Peterson. 1992. "Spinstorying: An Analysis of Women Storytelling." In Elizabeth Fine and Jean Haskell Spear (eds.), *Performance, Culture and Identity*. Westport, Conn.: Prager, pp. 157–80.

Langlois, Janet. 1993. "Mothers' Double Talk." In Radner (ed.), pp. 80–97.

Lauter, Estella. 1984. *Women as Mythmakers: Poetry and Visual Art by Twentieth Century Women*. Bloomington: Indiana University Press.

———. 1985. "Visual Images by Women: A Test Case for the Theory of Archetypes." In Lauter and Rupprecht (eds.), pp. 46–83.

Lauter, Estella, and Carol Schreier Rupprecht (eds.). 1985. *Feminist Archetypal Theory: Interdisciplinary Re-visions of Jungian Thought*. Knoxville: University of Tennessee Press.

Leonard, Linda. 1982. *The Wounded Woman: Healing the Father-Daughter Relationship*. Athens, Ohio: Swallow.

———. 1993. *Meeting the Madwoman: An Inner Challenge for the Feminine Spirit*. New York: Bantam.

Lerner, Gerda. 1986. *The Creation of Patriarchy*. New York: Oxford University Press.

Lincoln, J. N. 1936. "The Legend of the Handless Maiden." *Hispanic Review*, 4: 277–80.

Lippard, Lucy R. 1976. *From the Center: Feminist Essays on Women's Art*. New York: Dutton.

Liyi, H. 1985. *The Spring of Butterflies and Other Folktales of China's Minority Peoples*. New York: Lothrop, Lee & Shepard.

Lowinsky, Naomi Ruth. 1992. *Stories from the Motherline: Reclaiming the Mother-Daughter Bond, Finding Our Feminine Souls*. Los Angeles: Tarcher.

Mahdi, Louise, Steven Foster, and Meredith Little (eds.). 1987. *Betwixt and Between: Patterns of Masculine and Feminine Initiation*. Lasalle, Ill.: Open Court.

Mails, Thomas. 1973. *Dog Soldiers, Bear Men and Buffalo Women: A Study of the Societies and Cults of the Plains Indians*. Englewood Cliffs, N.J.: Prentice-Hall.

Mankowitz, Ann. 1984. *Change of Life: A Psychological Study of Dreams and the Menopause*. Toronto: Inner City Books.

Meador, Betty. 1986. "The Thesmophoria." *Psychological Perspectives*, 17: 25–45.

Middleton-Keirn, Susan. 1978. "Convivial Sisterhood: Spirit Mediumship and Client-Core Network Among Black South African Women." In Hoch-Smith and Spring (eds.), pp. 191–205.

Miller, Jean Baker. 1991. "Women and Power." In Jordan et al. (eds.), pp. 197–205.

Mitchell, Carol. 1985. "Some Differences in Male and Female Joke-Telling." In Jordan and Kalcik (eds.), pp. 163–86.

Mohrmann, Renate. 1985. "Occupation: Woman Artist—On the Changing Relations Between Being a Woman and Artistic Production." In Ecker (ed.), pp. 150–61.

Monestier, Marianne. 1963. *Les Sociétés Secrètes Féminines*. Paris: Les Productions de Paris.

Moon, Sheila. 1983. *Dreams of a Woman: An Analyst's Inner Journey*. Boston: Sigo.

Moore, Henrietta. 1988. *Feminism and Anthropology*. Minneapolis: University of Minnesota Press.

Mulcahy, Joanne. 1993. " 'How They Knew': Women's Talk About Healing on Kodiak Island, Alaska." In Radner (ed.), pp. 183–202.

Murdock, Maureen. 1990. *The Heroine's Journey*. Boston: Shambhala.

Nadelson, Carol C., and Malkah T. Notman (eds.). 1982. *The Woman Patient*, vol. 2: *Concepts of Femininity and the Life Cycle*. New York: Plenum.

Neher, Irene. 1989. *The Female Hero's Quest for Identity in Novels by Modern American Women Writers: The Function of Nature Imagery, Moments of Vision and Dreams in the Hero's Development*. Frankfurt-am-Main: Peter Lang.

Nelson, Gertrud Mueller. 1991. *Here All Dwell Free: Stories to Heal the Wounded Feminine*. New York: Doubleday.

Neumann, Erich. 1959. *The Psychological Stages of Feminine Development*. Dallas: Spring.

Northcutt, Cecilia Ann. 1991. *Successful Career Women: Their Professional and Personal Characteristics*. New York: Greenwood.

Notman, Malkah. 1982a. "Feminine Development: Changes in Psychoanalytic Theory." In Nadelson and Notman (eds.), pp. 3–30.

———. 1982b. "Midlife Concerns of Women: Menopause." In Nadelson and Notman (eds.), pp. 135–44.

———. 1982c. "The Midlife Years and After: Opportunities and Limitations: Clinical Issues." *Journal of Geriatric Psychiatry*, 15: 173–86.

O'Connor, Pat. 1992. *Friendships Between Women*. New York: Guilford.

Paul, Lois. 1978. "Careers of Midwives in a Mayan Community." In Hoch-Smith and Spring (eds.), pp. 129–49.

Pearson, Carol, and Katherine Pope. 1981. *The Female Hero in American and British Literature*. New York: Bowker.

Perera, Sylvia Brinton. 1985. "The Descent of Inanna: Myth and Therapy." In Lauter and Rupprecht (eds.), pp. 137–86.

Pershing, Linda. 1993. " 'She Really Wanted to Be Her Own Woman': Scandalous Sunbonnet Sue." In Radner (ed.), pp. 98–125.

Phelps, Ethel Johnston. 1978. *Tatterhood and Other Tales*. New York: The Feminist Press.

———. 1981. *The Maid of the North: Feminist Folk Tales from around the World*. New York: Henry Holt.

Pollock, Susan. 1991. "Women in a Men's World: Images of Sumerian Women." In Gero, and Conkey (eds.), pp. 366–87.

Pratt, Annis. 1981. *Archetypal Patterns in Women's Fiction*. Sussex, England: Harvester.

———. 1985. "Spinning Among Fields: Jung, Frye, Lévi-Strauss and Feminist Archetypal Theory." In Lauter and Rupprecht (eds.), pp. 93–136.

Rabuzzi, Kathryn Allen. 1988. *Motherself: A Mythic Analysis of Motherhood* Bloomington: Indiana University Press.

Radin, Paul. 1983. *African Folktales*. New York: Schocken.

Radner, Joan Newlon (ed.). 1993. *Feminist Messages: Coding in Women's Folk Culture*. Urbana: University of Illinois Press.

Radner, Joan Newlon, and Susan Lanser. 1993. "Strategies of Coding in Women's Cultures." In Radner (ed.), pp. 1–29.

Ralph, Phyllis C. 1989. *Victorian Transformations: Fairy Tales, Adolescence and the Novel of Female Development*. New York: Peter Verlag.

Randour, Mary Lou. 1987. *Women's Psyche, Women's Spirit*. New York: Columbia University Press.

Ranke, Kurt. 1966. *Folktales of Germany*. Chicago: University of Chicago Press.

Riordan, James. 1985. *The Woman in the Moon and Other Tales of Forgotten Heroines*. New York: Dial.

———. 1989. *The Sun Maiden and the Crescent Moon: Siberian Folk Tales*. New York: Interlink.

Robbins, Joan Hamerman. 1990. *Knowing Herself: Women Tell Their Stories in Psychotherapy*. New York: Plenum.

Roberts, Leonard. 1955. *South from Hell-fer-Sartin: Kentucky Mountain Folk Tales*. Lexington: University of Kentucky Press.

Roberts, Moss. 1979. *Chinese Fairy Tales and Fantasies*. New York: Pantheon.

Robinson, Forrest G. 1992. *Love's Story Told: A Life of Henry A. Murray*. Cambridge, Mass.: Harvard University Press.

Rogers, Annie. 1993. "Voice, Play and a Practice of Ordinary Courage in Girls' and Women's Lives." *Harvard Educational Review*, 63: 265–95.

Rosenblatt, Sidney. 1992. "Thumbelina and the Development of Female Sexuality." In Siegel (ed.), pp. 121–30.

Rubin, Lillian B. 1979. *Women of a Certain Age: The Midlife Search for Self*. San Francisco: Harper & Row.

Sampson, John. 1984. *Gypsy Folk Tales*. Salem, N.H.: Salem House.

Sanday, Peggy Reeves. 1981. *Female Power and Male Dominance: On the Origins of Sexual Inequality*. Cambridge, England: Cambridge University Press.

Schwartz, Howard. 1985. *Elijah's Violin and Other Jewish Fairy Tales*. New York: Harper Colophon.

Sexton, James. 1992. *Mayan Folktales: Folklore from Lake Atitlán, Guatemala*. New York: Doubleday.

Shainess, Natalie. 1987. "Vulnerability to Violence: Masochism as Process." In Walsh (ed.), pp. 62–77.

Sharp, H. 1981. "Old Age Among the Chipewyan." In Amoss and Harrell (eds.), *Other Ways of Growing Old,* Stanford: Stanford University Press, pp. 99–110.

Sherman, Edmund. 1987. *Meaning in Mid-Life Transitions.* Albany: State University of New York.

Siegel, Elaine (ed.). 1992. *Psychoanalytic Perspectives on Women.* New York: Brunner/Mazel.

Signell, Karen. 1990. *Wisdom of the Heart: Working with Women's Dreams.* New York: Bantam.

Sinclair, K. P. 1985. "A Study in Pride and Prejudice: Maori Women at Midlife." In Brown and Kerns (eds.), pp. 117–34.

Singham, Lorna Rhodes Amara. 1978. "The Misery of the Embodied: Representations of Women in Sinhalese Myth." In Hoch-Smith and Spring (eds.), pp. 101–26.

Sinnott, Jan D. 1986. *Sex Roles and Aging: Theory and Research from a Systems Perspective.* Basel: Karger.

Skov, G. E. 1975. "The Priestess of Demeter and Kore and Her Role in the Initiation of Women at the Festival of the Haloa at Eleusis." *Temenos,* 11: 136–47.

Spector, Janet. 1991. "What This Awl Means: Toward a Feminist Archaeology." In Gero and Conkey (eds.), pp. 388–406.

Spring, Anita. 1978. "Epidemiology of Spirit Possession Among the Luvale of Zambia." In Hoch-Smith and Spring (eds.), pp. 165–90.

Steinem, Gloria. 1993. *Revolution from Within: A Book of Self-Esteem.* Boston: Little, Brown.

Stewart, Polly. 1993. "Wishful Willful Wily Women: Lessons for Female Success in the Child Ballads." In Radner (ed.), pp. 54–80.

Stiver, Irene. 1991a. "The Meaning of Care: Reframing Treatment Models." In Jordan et al. (eds.), pp. 250–67.

———. 1991b. "The Meanings of 'Dependency' in Female-Male Relationships." In Jordan et al. (eds.), pp. 141–61.

———. 1991c. "Work Inhibitions in Women." In Jordan et al. (eds.), pp. 223–36.

Stone, Kay. 1975. "Things Walt Disney Never Told Us." In Farrer (ed.), pp. 42–50.

———. 1985. "The Misuses of Enchantment: Controversies on the Significance of Fairy Tales." In Jordan and Kalcik (eds.), pp. 125–45.

———. 1993. "Burning Brightly: New Light from an Old Tale." In Radner (ed.), pp. 289–305.

Stone, Merlin. 1979. *Ancient Mirrors of Womanhood: Our Goddess and Heroine Heritage.* Virginia Station, N.Y.: New Sibylline Books.

Surrey, Janet. 1991a. "Eating Patterns as a Reflection of Women's Development." In Jordan et al. (eds.), pp. 237–49.

———. 1991b. "Relationship and Empowerment." In Jordan et al. (eds.), pp. 162–80.

———. 1991c. "The 'Self-in-Relation': A Theory of Women's Development." In Jordan et al. (eds.), pp. 51–66.

Tatar, M. 1987. *The Hard Facts of the Grimms' Fairy Tales*. Princeton, N.J.: Princeton University Press.

Tayler, Royall. 1987. *Japanese Tales*. New York: Pantheon.

Trocolli, Ruth. 1992. "Colonization and Women's Production: The Timucua of Florida." In Claassen (ed.), pp. 95–102.

von Franz, Marie-Louise. 1980. *A Psychological Interpretation of The Golden Ass of Apuleius*. Dallas: Spring.

Waelti-Walters, Jennifer. 1982. *Fairy Tales and the Female Imagination*. Montreal: Eden.

Walsh, Mary (ed.). 1987. *The Psychology of Women: Ongoing Debates*. New Haven, Conn.: Yale University Press.

Weigel, Sigrid. 1985. "Double Focus." In Ecker (ed.), pp. 59–80.

Weigle, Marta. 1982. *Spiders and Spinsters: Women and Mythology*. Albuquerque: University of New Mexico Press.

Wheelwright, Jane, 1989. "In Old Age: The Process of Becoming an Individual." Paper presented at the C. G. Jung Institute of San Francisco, March 11–12, 1989.

Wissler, Clark (ed.). 1916. *Societies of the Plains Indians*. Anthropological Papers of the American Museum of Natural History, XI. New York: American Museum of Natural History.

Wolf, Christa. 1985. "A Letter, About Unequivocal and Ambiguous Meaning, Definiteness and Indefiniteness; About Ancient Conditions and New Viewscopes; About Objectivity." In Ecker (ed.), pp. 95–107.

Wolkstein, Diane. 1991. *Dream Songs: Abulafia, Part of My Heart*. New York: Cloudstone.

Wolkstein, Diane, and Samuel Kramer. 1983. *Inanna: Queen of Heaven and Earth*. New York: Harper & Row.

Woodman, Marion. 1987. "From Concrete to Consciousness: The Emergence of the Feminine." In Mahdi, Foster, and Little (eds.), pp. 201–22.

Woolger, Jennifer Barker, and Roger Woolger. 1989. *The Goddess Within: A Guide to the Eternal Myths that Shape Women's Lives*. New York: Fawcett Columbine.

Wright, Wendy. 1982. "The Feminine Dimension of Contemplation." In Giles (ed., 1982a), pp. 103–19.

Yocom, Margaret. 1985. "Woman to Woman: Fieldwork and the Private Sphere." In Jordan and Kalcik (eds.), pp. 45–53.

Young-Eisendrath, Polly, and Florence Wiedermann. 1987. *Female Authority: Empowering Women through Psychotherapy*. New York: Guilford.

Zheleznova, Irina. 1980. *Northern Lights: Fairy Tales of the Peoples of the North*. Moscow: Progress Publishers.

Zipes, Jack. 1988. *The Brothers Grimm: From Enchanted Forests to the Modern World*. New York: Routledge.

INDEX

ABOUT THE AUTHOR

ALLAN B. CHINEN, M.D., is a psychiatrist in private practice in San Francisco and is on the clinical faculty of the University of California, San Francisco. He is also the author of *In the Ever After: Fairy Tales and the Second Half of Life, Once Upon a Midlife: Classic Stories and Mythic Tales to Illuminate the Middle Years,* and *Beyond the Hero: Classic Stories of Men in Search of Soul.*